THE PURIFYING FIRE

AGENTS OF ARTIFICE
by Ari Marmell

THE PURIFYING FIRE
by Laura Resnick

ALARA UNBROKEN
by Doug Beyer

ARTIFACTS CYCLE I
THE THRAN
by J. Robert King

THE BROTHERS' WAR
by Jeff Grub

ARTIFACTS CYCLE II
PLANESWALKER
by Lynn Abbey

TIME STREAMS
by J. Robert King

BLOODLINES
by Loren L. Coleman
September 2009

MAGIC
The Gathering

A PLANESWALKER NOVEL

THE PURIFYING FIRE
laura resnick

Magic: The Gathering
The Purifying Fire

©2009 Wizards of the Coast LLC

Published by Wizards of the Coast LLC

MAGIC: THE GATHERING, WIZARDS OF THE COAST, their respective logos and PLANESWALKER are trademarks of Wizards of the Coast LLC in the U.S.A. and other countries.

Printed in the U.S.A.

Cover art by Michael Komarck

First Printing: July 2009

9 8 7 6 5 4 3 2 1

ISBN: 978-0-7869-5298-4
620-25065000-001-EN

Library of Congress Cataloging-in-Publication Data

Resnick, Laura, 1962-
  The purifying fire : a planeswalker novel / Laura Resnick.
    p. cm. -- (Magic, the gathering.) (Planeswalker)
  ISBN 978-0-7869-5298-4 (alk. paper)
  I. Title.
  PS3568.E689P87 2009
  813'.54--dc22

                                                           2009016153

U.S., CANADA,
ASIA, PACIFIC, & LATIN AMERICA
Wizards of the Coast LLC
P.O. Box 707
Renton, WA 98057-0707
+1-800-324-6496

EUROPEAN HEADQUARTERS
Hasbro UK Ltd
Caswell Way
Newport, Gwent NP9 0YH
GREAT BRITAIN
Save this address for your records.

Visit our web site at www.wizards.com

THE PURIFYING FIRE

CHAPTER ONE

Is that the scroll the monks are talking about?" Brannon asked.

"Yes, it is." Chandra Nalaar smiled at the ginger-headed boy as she held out the scroll, neatly rolled up and encased in an ancient leather sheath. "The brothers are done with their work, so I thought I'd take a look at it, see what all the excitement is about."

"I heard it has strange writing that only a few of the monks can read," the boy said.

"That's right," Chandra said, sitting next to Brannon. "I can't read it, but the monks will tell me what is says."

The two of them were in a common room at Keral Keep, a place of learning and study for the fire mages of Regatha.

Brannon asked, "Where did you get the scroll?"

"Far away." Chandra was used to dodging questions about her travels throughout the Multiverse. It was easier for most people to accept lies than to understand what it meant to move back and forth among the infinite planes of reality. "Do you want to look at it with me?"

She had looked at the scroll before, but that was on a plane called Kephalai where she had "liberated" it from the Sanctum of the Stars. Once back on Regatha, she had handed the scroll over to the monks at Keral Keep.

The scroll was said to be unique, the only record of a fire spell more powerful than any known. Its origin was utterly mysterious, and it had been fiercely protected on Kephalai. Chandra might not be able to interpret its meaning on her own, but she was curious enough to want another look.

The monks in the monastery's scriptorium were very interested in the scroll, enough that young Brannon was curious about it too.

"Yes," he said eagerly, "let's look at it. Unroll it!"

"All right. But remember," she cautioned. "It's very old and fragile, so—"

"Uh, Chandra?"

"—we have to be careful not to—"

"*Chandra.*" Brannon was looking past her, his eyes wide with alarm.

She turned to look at whatever had captured his attention and shot to her feet when she saw a tall, menacing stranger standing at one end of the room.

"Chandra Nalaar, give me that scroll!" he said, his tone as much a demand as the words.

How does he know my name?

"Brannon, get out of here!" she said. "*Now.*"

"But—"

"*Go!*"

Recognizing her tone, the boy turned and ran, seeking the safety of the stone halls of the monastery and the presence of others.

"Give me the scroll," said the stranger, "and no one gets hurt."

Chandra's attention was immediately drawn to the cold, cerulean intensity of his eyes, glowing in the shadow of his cowled cloak. She could sense his intrusion into her thoughts. *A telepath.*

Chandra had only just returned to this plane, and her comings and goings at the monastery passed without fanfare. No one on Regatha knew about the scroll unless one of the monks had renounced his vows and become loose-lipped. This stranger, she realized with a hot flood of surprise, must have come from Kephalai.

"You're a planeswalker," she breathed.

"I'm not going to ask again," he warned her. "And you won't live long enough to be sorry you resisted."

If he had followed her æther trail through the Blind Eternities, he must be very skilled. A trick like that wasn't for beginners.

But he had picked the wrong person to follow.

"I see there's only one of you," she said, feeling her blood heat for combat.

"One is all it will take," he replied.

With hair-trigger speed, Chandra's fists lit up like torches as she thrust them toward the stranger, hurling a pair of fireballs like meteors.

But the mage was ready. As if he knew what she would do even before she did it, he met the fireballs with an ice-blue liquid mass that issued from his outstretched arms.

The counter attack was followed by a surge of power that flowed forth and encircled Chandra, glowing with the same cerulean intensity of his eyes. With Chandra momentarily paralyzed, the mind mage started mapping her consciousness, looking for the lynchpin he could use to disable her.

Chandra loathed mind mages. What could be more despicable than poking around in another person's private thoughts and feelings? The violation, along with the strangle-hold of the spell, kindled her rage like phosphorous.

By now, conscious thought was no longer an option for Chandra. The world around her slowed to a geological pace, and she could feel the power of the mountain inside her. Immovable, dominating, volcanic in its fury, it grew from that darkest part of herself, that diamond of rage deep in her core until . . .

Boom.

An incomparable concussive blast left Chandra at ground zero, leveling everything around her and blasting a hole in the wall where the mind mage had been.

An eerie quiet pervaded the room. Sparks flickered and died in the dead air. "Didn't mean to blow my top like that," she muttered to no one in particular, as she surveyed the damage.

Chandra was sure he wasn't dead, though. She knew it wouldn't be that easy to kill an experienced planeswalker.

"Chandra!" Brannon cried from beyond the hole in the outer wall.

"Brannon! What are you doing out there?" she shouted. "Get inside the monastery. *Now!*"

Instead of listening to her, the boy turned and ran again. What is the matter with him, she wondered.

Not daring to leave it behind, Chandra took the scroll and went after him. She couldn't leave it unprotected with a mind mage running around.

As she stepped through the hole, she saw the stranger standing on a rocky ledge that overlooked her position, holding the small ginger-haired boy by the throat. Just like a kid to get in middle of things, she thought.

Brannon struggled to breathe, his feet dangling just above the ground.

"No!" Chandra's stomach knotted with fear at the sight of her young friend in the planeswalker's powerful grip.

"Don't make me kill the child," the stranger said.

Brannon kicked and gasped in pain even as he tried to speak. "Let me g . . . *aaagh* . . ." The phrase trailed off in a choked gurgle. Tears of pain and fear rolled down his reddened cheeks.

Chandra hated to lose. She absolutely *hated* it!

But she knew the scroll in her hand, however unique, wasn't worth Brannon's life. She held it up as an offering and called, "Don't hurt him! You can have the scroll."

Chandra heard how hoarse with dread her voice sounded. She watched the mind mage give Brannon a sharp shake, to make him stop squirming.

"That's all I came for," the planeswalker said. "As long as I get it right now, he's fine."

He looked cold, but not cruel. She believed that capturing Brannon was business, not pleasure.

So she tossed the scroll up to him.

It landed a few feet in front of him. "A wise decision. My impression is that you don't make many."

But before he could turn the boy over, Chandra heard her name called from the monastery. She turned to see Brannon looking out from the hole she had blasted in the wall.

"Chandra! What's happening?" he shouted from a distance.

An illusion!

"All right, mindbender . . . You want to play?"

With a quickness to match her temper, Chandra leaped into the air, an aura of flame surrounding her as she recited a spell. Spreading her arms and expanding her chest like a bellows, all the air in a thirty foot radius went dead as she sapped the oxygen she needed as fuel for her fire. She paused at the top of her breath until it felt like she would explode with the effort, and when she let go, explode she nearly did. With all her might she exhaled, eyes wide, tongue extended like some primal totem. Her breath had the force of a cannon and burned with chemical intensity.

The stranger balled up, shielding his body with his cloak. The force of the blast unsteadied him, but he obviously had been able to conjure some protection. He emerged merely singed when everything around him had been reduced to charcoal. The scroll had fallen from his grasp, but lay out of both their reaches.

"Nice trick," he mocked. "I bet you're a big hit with the boys."

Jokes? This guy has to go down, Chandra thought.

But he was just getting started. The mage's eyes glowed brightly, and his skin changed, newly streaked blue-grey. Chandra knew something was coming but she didn't know what. Still, she should have known this guy wouldn't fight his own fights. He summoned an massive cloud elemental that swooped down to knock Chandra off her feet before veering to where the scroll lay on the ground.

Two can play at that game, thought Chandra as she summoned her own fire elemental to meet the cloud. The two titans collided with a sharp hiss, flame and vapor locked in a mercurial embrace.

With the elementals occupied, the mind mage made a move to recover the scroll himself, but Chandra was on point as she raised a wall of fire between him and his quarry.

"You're going to have to work for it, mindbender." Chandra was just starting to have fun.

Still, the stranger was undeterred. He ran down the wall to where he had last seen the scroll and stepped through the flame, an icy corona surrounding him. Chandra was waiting, though, her fist cocked, blazing hot. She hit him with a left cross that had the weight of the world behind it, and sent the mage flying backward, his body like a rag doll's as he tumbled over the rocks.

As the flames died down, Chandra surveyed the scene. She had done well. The elementals had died fighting and there was plenty of scorched earth, but she had done well.

"Chandra, that was amazing!"

She turned to see Brannon. "You shouldn't be out here, kiddo."

"What happened to him?"

"He took a nasty spill. He won't be back again."

"Are you sure?" he asked pointing in the direction of the mage. There were several cloaked figures, all exactly alike, moving in different directions.

"He's just trying to trick me. He doesn't want me to know which one is actually him," said Chandra pointing to the illusions. "Look, he's running away."

"I don't think so," said the boy in a strange voice. "I think he's going to get that scroll."

When she turned back, Chandra saw the familiar eerie blue glow in Brannon's eyes and she knew . . . But right in that moment of realization, the mage hit her with a mental attack that caught her completely off-guard. She crumpled as her vision faded to black.

⚹ ⚹ ⚹ ⚹ ⚹

"Chandra, are you all right?" The real Brannon reached her side and started helping her rise from the ground. "What happened? I saw your fire elemental. Wow, I've never seen anything that big! Not even Mother Luti can make 'em that big." The boy was nearly ecstatic. "And then there was a sort of . . . a blue wave of light or something. What *was* that?"

"That was the stranger," Chandra said grumpily. "Being . . . *clever*."

ϕ

"The scroll!" Brannon said, seeing that her hands were empty. "Where's the scroll?"

"What are you talking about, Brannon?"

"He got it. He must have taken it!"

"The scroll?"

"I know you said the monks finished their work. But don't we need it any more?" he asked.

"What do you mean?"

"Did they copy it in their workshop? Is that what you said?"

"Kiddo, this is crazy talk. Everything is all right. He's not coming back," she assured him.

"Well I hope so, 'cause he was creepy." Brannon asked, eyeing their surroundings a little anxiously.

"Yes," she said. "But he's gone."

Chandra tried to clear her head. Something was missing. Why did that fight just happen? Who was that guy?

But the more she tried to think about it, the more it hurt. What is that kid talking about with the scroll?

CHAPTER TWO

Chandra was mad. And when she got mad, she liked to set things on fire.

Call it her little weakness.

She felt heat racing through her, turning her blood into curling flames of power that sparked out through her fingertips, her eyes, and the auburn tendrils of her long hair.

"You're saying you copied down the scroll *wrong*?" she demanded of Brother Sergil. "After all the trouble I went through to steal it? After how important I told you it was? You're saying that you and the other brothers made a mess of *your* part of the job? After I nearly got killed doing *my* part right?"

Brother Sergil, who evidently didn't feel deeply attached to his mortal existence, snapped, "Perhaps if you hadn't let someone steal the scroll *back* so soon after you brought it here, we wouldn't have a problem now!"

"Oh, *really*?" Chandra could feel her skin glowing with the power that her anger unleashed. True, she had lost the scroll, but that mage had been good. "And if anyone had bothered to *help* me fight off that mage, maybe the scroll would still be at the monastery, instead of who-knows-where?" Her memory of the scroll had not come back. The mind mage had been thorough in cleansing it from her mind. She remembered everything she had done retrieving it, everything about the fight . . . But he had cut the scroll out with artisanal precision.

"All right, that's enough," said Luti, the mother mage of Keral Keep. "From *both* of you."

Chandra said, "What's the point of my bringing you something so valuable if you can't even—"

"*Stop*," said Luti.

"We've done our part as well as anyone could expect!" Brother Sergil said. "All I'm saying is—"

"Not as well as *I* expected! How did you—" Chandra stepped back with a sharp intake of breath as a small fireball exploded between her and Brother Sergil. The monk staggered backward, too, stumbling on the rough red stones that paved the monastery courtyard.

They both looked at Mother Luti in surprised silence.

"That's better," Luti said, her fingers glowing with the lingering effect of forming and throwing that fiery projectile between them. Her glance flickered over Chandra. "Quench your hair, young woman."

"What? Oh." Chandra became aware of the haze of fiery heat and pulsating flames surrounding her head. It wasn't a roaring blaze, but it was certainly a loss of control. She took a calming breath and brushed her palms over her hair, smoothing the dancing flames back into her auburn mane until Luti's nod indicated they had disappeared altogether.

"Until you can master your power better," Luti said, "it would be a good idea to learn to manage your temper."

Chandra let the comment pass without protest. She didn't like orders or reprimands, but she had come to the Keralian Monastery to *learn* to master her power, after all.

And she had once again just demonstrated how little control over it she had.

"You have an extraordinary gift," Luti said. "Tremendous power. But as it is with our passions, it is with the fire you wield; they are good servants, but bad masters."

"It would help," Chandra said, glaring at Brother Sergil, "if people wouldn't—"

"Nothing will help," Luti said. "Certainly not other people. Only *you* can change the way your power manifests. Only within yourself can you find a way to master it in a reality which will, after all, always contain annoyances, distractions, fears, and sorrows."

"Right." Hoping to avoid another of Luti's lectures on the nature of life, Chandra hastened to change the subject. "Now what about the scroll?"

≈ ≈ ≈ ≈ ≈

The pyromancers, scholars, and initiates at Keral Keep had no idea where the scroll had come from. And neither did Mother Luti, for that matter, but she alone did know where Chandra got it. Luti ran the haven for pyromancers and firemages, who came to study and practice in the monastery on Mount Kerlia, a potent source of power. She knew a lot.

There was wisdom to be learned from her, to be sure, but the great stone walls of the fortress that crowned the summit of Mount Keralia pulsed with mana as red as the rock it was built upon. This was why mages came from all over Regatha.

The most skilled fire mages on the entire plane dwelled within the stony halls of the monastery, but none of them, including Luti, were as powerful as Chandra.

Perhaps Luti would have suspected the truth about Chandra even if she hadn't been told: Chandra was a planeswalker.

Luti was well-versed in the legend of Jaya Ballard, the bombastic fire mage whose long-ago sojourn on Regatha had inspired the founding of this monastery. Jaya was a planeswalker, too. And planeswalkers were . . . different.

When she witnessed, first-hand, the magnitude of Chandra's power, Luti could only think of the celebrated pyromancy of Jaya Ballard, stories she assumed had grown like mushroom clouds with the passage of time. In any case, Chandra chose to privately reveal her nature to Luti soon after coming to Regatha, after deciding it wouldn't make sense to seek instruction in controlling her power while concealing what she could do.

It was a choice, Luti later told her, that demonstrated Chandra was capable of reasoned decisions when she applied herself.

Luti kept Chandra's secret mostly out of a desire that fire remain the most tangible of the visible mysteries on Regatha. She feared the acolytes at Keral Keep would look for answers in Chandra, rather than find their own path. To everyone else at the monastery, Chandra was simply an unusually powerful young mage who came from somewhere else. And since Chandra, like so many others, didn't want to talk about her past, no one pried.

Apart from Luti, none of the Keralians knew that Chandra had traveled the Blind Eternities, bridging that chaotic interval between the planes of the Multiverse, to steal that scroll on Kephalai, a world they'd never heard of and could never visit themselves.

Chandra had heard of the scroll in her travels, and she was intrigued by its reputation. So, after some time studying and practicing at the Keep had improved her erratic control of pyromancy, Chandra decided to find and steal the scroll, which turned out to be a little better guarded than she had anticipated. That was a wild ride, to be sure. Still, she made it out with the scroll.

Since the scroll was fragile, the brothers' first act had been to make a few working copies of it. They had laboriously replicated the ancient writing by hand on fresh parchment.

Consdiering what had happened next, it was lucky they had done so. If she ever saw that mage again, she told herself, she would be ready. He would not trick her again.

Meanwhile, she knew from Luti's expression that she had better remain silent while Brother Sergil explained the problem the monks were having with their copies of the scroll.

"The script is archaic, a variant we have not seen before, so it's taken us some time to interpret its meaning. We are *sure*, though," Sergil said, with a dark glance at Chandra, "that we copied it correctly. The value of multiple brothers each making a copy means, of course, that we can compare all our results from the process and arrive at a consensus on the exact contents of the original. Right down to the tiniest brushstroke."

"Uh-huh." Chandra folded her arms and didn't attempt to conceal her boredom.

Mother Luti, who was a full head shorter than Chandra and triple her age, gave her a quelling look.

"The language of the scroll is a variant that our scholars haven't encountered, so our conclusions aren't as firm as one might wish. But it seems to be describing something of immense power, much as Chandra believed." Brother Sergil made the grudging concession to her with a little nod.

"An artifact? A spell? What?" Chandra was surprised.

"It could be either . . . or something else entirely."

"I could have told you that," said Chandra exasperated.

Φ

"You mean you could have told us that had you a memory——"

Mother Luti raised a hand to stop Brother Segril from going further, her head tilted in a gesture of contemplation. Her white hair shone brightly in the sunlight of the monastery courtyard where the three of them stood. "What kind of power?" she asked when she had their attention.

"The scroll describes either an extraordinary source of mana, or it's the key to accessing mana with extraordinary results. Either way, according to the scroll, it is something that will confer enormous power upon whomever unleashes it." He shrugged. "It's not clear to us if the text of the scroll declares this as a promise or as a warning. The intention of the author, like the its origin, is a mystery, Mother."

"And does the text strike you as fact or as fancy?" Luti asked.

"Well . . ." He cast a glance at Chandra. "That might be easier to answer if we still had the original."

Chandra scowled. "If you're blaming *me* because——"

"No, I just mean," the monk interrupted, "that the text seems to be saying the scroll itself contains the key to unlocking the mystery."

"But the location isn't in the text you've got?" Luti asked.

"No."

"And you copied the entire scroll?"

"Yes."

"So you're saying that part of the scroll was missing?" Chandra guessed.

"I don't think so," Brother Sergil said. "We're still discussing it . . . but the text seems to be complete. And, physically, the scroll itself was certainly complete. It was fragile, but it wasn't torn, or singed, or moth-eaten."

"So what *are* you saying?" Chandra asked.

"The purported location of this powerful artifact seems to be concealed in an internal puzzle," the monk said. "The answer *may* be in the text itself, it could be obfuscated by layers of magic, but . . ." He trailed off, clearly reluctant to continue.

"But?" Luti prodded.

"We've tried multiple ways of interpreting the text, various ways of scrambling the words and the letters, and numerous methods of translating the characters into numbers, various decryption spells . . ." He shook his head. "But so far, we only get gibberish. Of course, we'll keep trying, because if whatever this is does exist—if the text has any basis in fact—then this is very important information. Whoever possesses the power it speaks of could rule worlds. However . . . well, it's really starting to look as if, when the text says the key to understanding is contained in the scroll itself . . ."

"You think it means the *physical* scroll?" Luti said. "The original?"

"Perhaps, yes. We are increasingly drawn to that possibility," Brother Sergil said.

"Oh, that *is* disappointing," Luti said.

Chandra said, "Look, I did everything I could to stop the scroll from being tak—"

"I didn't mean it that way, Chandra," Luti said. "We wouldn't even have known about the scroll, if not for you, and we'd certainly never have seen it or had a chance to study it. Believe me, I'm well aware of how hard you fought to keep it from the, er, intruder. Indeed, the vegetable garden on the southern side of the monastery may never recover from your struggle with him. Well, not this year, anyhow." She shrugged. "I just mean that it's frustrating to discover something so intriguing . . . and now face the possibility of never solving the puzzle.

"Since the stranger who took the scroll from us did not have the courtesy to identify himself," Luti said to Sergil, "we'll probably never know who sent him. If, indeed, anyone did send him. He may have been a free agent acting on his own behalf, after all."

"But we might be able to better estimate the veracity of the text if we knew more about its origins," said Sergil. "That is to say, where Chandra found it."

"Where she found it and where it comes from may be completely different things, Brother. That's a subject best left alone," Luti said, "for the sake of everyone's safety. We have all witnessed first hand the destruction that so closely followed the scroll's arrival," Luti paused, letting her words sink in. "We must make do with what we have. Please continue studying the text. The answer to the puzzle may well be in our possession and just temporarily eluding us."

Looking dissatisfied, but clearly not prepared to fight about it with Luti, Brother Sergil bowed his head. "Yes, Mother."

After he had left the sunny courtyard, Luti turned to Chandra. "Well?"

Chandra shrugged. "If you're wondering whether I noticed anything unusual about the scroll when it was in my possession, I can't really answer that. And I swear by everything that burns, if I ever see that bastard again, I'll blow him so high into the sky, his ashes won't fall back down until people have forgotten he was ever born."

Luti didn't smile at her pledge. "Guard yourself, Chandra. The fire you kindle for your enemy may burn you more than him."

"Is that Jaya?"

"No, it is Luti. Listen, the Multiverse is a very big place," Luti said. "It is probable that you will never run into that mage again. It is better to think about what you can control . . ."

Chandra's attention waned as Luti went on. She was grateful for her wisdom, but she could be tedious at times.

"In a battle with another planeswalker, it's said that Jaya cunningly defeated her opponent by—"

"That stinking rat made me believe he was going to kill Brannon," Chandra said.

Luti broke off. She knew Chandra had not been listening at all, but she had hoped to penetrate the planeswalker's obvious disinterest. "As soon to kindle a fire with snow as to quench the fire of rage with words," she said, more to herself that to Chandra.

"What does that have to do with Brannon or what I said?" asked Chandra, unable to see the relevance of Luti's words.

Brannon lived at the monastery. His parents, ordinary peasant folk, had sent him here upon realizing they were increasingly unable to cope with the fiery power he had been exercising since early childhood. Because he needed instruction and supervision from people who understood his gift, his family had consigned him to the Keralians' care several years ago.

Chandra had also been a powerful child with parents who'd felt ill-equipped to deal with her explosive gifts. She felt some kinship with the boy and had become fond of him during her sojourn here.

It had been a terrible shock to see him in the clutches of the other planeswalker. And it had been a relief as much as it was an infuriating surprise to discover that it was merely an illusion.

Chandra was disgusted by the subterfuge of that planeswalker's ploys. She understood how his tactics were ultimately successful, but she didn't have to respect them. Chandra was used to dealing with conflict openly.

"Anyway, as many times as I replay the fight in my head, I don't even know if that jackass also managed to erase any other memories. If I had seen or felt anything special about the scroll, I have no memory of it now." She shrugged. "I don't even know what to think about what Brother Sergil said. I wish I remembered the scroll at all."

"I take it, then, that you don't even remember where you heard about the scroll? That you have no idea what you thought you were going after in the first place?"

"No." Chandra asked. "What do you think?"

"I believe what Brother Sergil told us. I believe that it tells of a great power, and I believe that it is old. And despite its supposed age, I'm also inclined to believe that the scroll, if it we are able to interpret it, could lead to the whatever it is."

"You really think something like this exists? That it can be found?" Chandra asked eagerly.

"Oh, yes. After all, if the text is just some ancient scribe's fancy, or if the power it speaks of has long since been seized or destroyed . . ." Luti shrugged. "Then why would the scroll be kept in a place as secure and heavily guarded as you described when you returned? What was it called again? The Sanctum of Stars?"

"Yes."

"Full of extremely valuable objects?"

"It sure looked that way to me." Chandra was not a thief by trade, however, so the valuation of objects was hardly familiar to her, particularly in the rush of stealing the scroll.

"It sounds as if they were quite prepared to kill to retrieve the scroll—and, indeed, to tear their own realm apart to find it . . . Well, their behavior certainly confirms that the scroll is important." Luti paused. "And whether the previous owners of the scroll employed that planeswalker to come after it, or whether he followed you and retrieved it for his own reasons . . ."

Chandra said, "I see your point."

"Sometimes thinking things through logically is beneficial." Luti's voice was dry.

"Yes, Mother."

✷ ✷ ✷ ✷ ✷

That night, Chandra dreamed of fire.

Not the fire that exploded from her in the battle with the mind mage. And not the intoxicating heat she drew from the red stones of Mount Keralia.

The fire in her dreams tonight wasn't the flickering seduction of a new spell. It wasn't the spine-tingling flame of her growing skill that lapped at the edges of her mind tonight. And it certainly wasn't the heart-pounding art of boom she loved so much, with its showers of fire and light.

This was the fire of sorrow and grief, the fire of shame and regret. This was the fire that consumed the innocent.

In her sleep, she could hear their screams, as clearly as if it were happening all over again. She could see their writhing bodies. She whimpered as the stench of burning flesh assailed her nostrils. Her throat burned with sobs that wouldn't come out. She tried to move, but her limbs were immobile. She wanted to scream, but her lips moved without sound.

And when the blade of a sword swept down to her throat, she awoke with a gurgled scream of horror and shot upright, gasping.

She was trapped in smothering darkness. She instinctively threw up her right hand and called forth flame, to ward off danger and illuminate her surroundings.

Squinting against the sudden light of her fire magic, Chandra looked around in confusion.

Then she realized where she was; her bed chamber in Keral Keep. Her heart was pounding. Her skin was slick with sweat. She was shaking. For a moment, she thought she would vomit. Her teeth chattered a little as she focused on breathing.

In, two, three. Out, two, three. In, two, three. Out . . .

She shook her hand to douse the flames before she wrapped her arms around her knees.

She swallowed. She would not cry. She would not think.

She would not remember.

As she rocked back and forth, trying to calm herself, she started reciting her favorite passages from the Regathan sagas, at first just in her mind, the words flowing through her brain in a rapid tumble.

Then, as she regained some control of herself, she started saying them aloud, and after a while, it worked, as it usually did. Her heart slowed to a normal rhythm. Her hands stopped shaking. Her teeth stopped chattering. Tears stopped threatening to fill her eyes.

But she wouldn't sleep again. Not tonight.

So she rose from her bed, removed her simple linen shift, and started donning her clothes as if the garments were armor against her dreams.

Chandra put on her leggings and her thigh-high boots. She pulled her calf-length tunic over her head. It was split from hip to hem to allow her free movement. Her clothes were reddish-brown, the material simple. They were the working garments of a woman with too much magical power and too much serious intent to waste time on fripperies and frills. But since it was nighttime and she wasn't going anywhere, she left off her gauntlets and the leather vest she usually wore. The armor she needed right now was mental, not physical.

Her bed chamber was small and simple, like everyone else's at the monastery. It had a narrow wooden bed with linen sheets and rough wool blankets, a small table, a single chair, and a modest trunk. And this was all she needed. People at the Keralian Monastery, whether they were visitors or permanent residents, came here in search of wisdom, knowledge, and power, not the creature comforts of material wealth.

The mountain air was cool at night, even at this time of year when the days were especially warm. Chandra welcomed the slight chill on her skin as she stepped out of her chamber, into the night air, and closed the door behind her. She moved quietly along the walkway, passing other chambers without waking anyone, until she reached the broad terrace on the eastern side of the monastery.

The moon was full tonight and shone brightly. To the west of the monastery's mountain were more mountains, but from this terrace, she gazed across the woodlands that lay peacefully below the imposing heights of Mount Keralia. And further east, past the forests, were the plains and the city of Zinara. When the air was this clear and still at night, she could see the tiny specks of light in the distance that were the flaming torches atop the great city's watch towers.

"Sleep soundly, little lambs," she murmured contemptuously.

The city was completely dominated by the Order of Heliud, a sect of mages whose dedication to an ordered society and strict adherence to law was becoming dictatorial. The city was prosperous under the Order's influence, but the number of laws had tripled under their governance so that one was scarcely able walk down a street without

Φ

breaking a rule or two. And when it came to magic, licenses to practice even the simplest of spells became necessary. Eventually, the Order became so bold as to outlaw many forms of magic, deeming anything other than their own brand of heiromancy—peacekeeping magic, as they liked to say, that emphasized law and order—as deleterious to the public health. It was even rumored that the practice of fire magic in Zinara would result in imprisonment, and any violent act involving fire magic was punishable by death.

Needless to say, these stories from the city did little to foster relations between Keral Keep and the Order of Heliud.

Chandra had been told that, during Mother Luti's lifetime, the Order had gone from being merely an influential sect in Zinara and a few other cities, to dominating the entire plains region of Regatha. Under the current rule of Walbert III and his policy of "civilization for civil welfare", it was even said their influence was spreading across the seas. But more to the point, the Order was aggressively seeking to "civilize" the mountain and woodland regions. It was clear to all that Walbert—dwelling in the massive, marble-pillared Temple of Heliud, the heart of the Order's temporal and mystical power—aspired to control the entire plane.

According to reports from Samir Mia Kauldi, a village chief of good standing among the many races of the Great Western Wood, Zinaran soldiers were patrolling the forests between Mount Keralia and the plains. Samir said that two human druids had recently been arrested for summoning creatures that the Order had recently declared "enemies of order." Creature summoning—especially for the ritual combat that settled disputes among tribes—was an accepted and eons-old practice for the woodlanders, but the Heliuds believed that the path to civilization was paved with law, and that the law was equal before all. There were inviolate truths, objective standards of right and wrong, and it was for the Order of Heliud to see that all sapient beings on Regatha benefited from the application of such standards.

To Chandra, this was so unreasonable as to seem insane. How could a group of people be so blind as to not see the shades of grey between the black and white truths they held so sacred? Surely a more relative approach was needed to accommodate the breadth of racial and cultural diversity on this great plane. However, as Samir had morosely reported to Luti, it wasn't that easy to talk sense to well-armed soldiers on horseback.

Just let them try that nonsense up here, Chandra thought. She'd send them fleeing back to Zinara with their horses' tails on fire.

In any event, the soldiers who patrolled the Great Western Wood were lucky that Samir had not been among those arrested. It would be amusing, though, if the soldiers took an elf prisoner next time they were meddling where they didn't belong. Chandra imagined the storm that such a move would precipitate. The elves would never allow their way of life to be compromised by the Order.

Oh, yes, that would be worth seeing.

"Don't mess with elves," she muttered, gazing down at the darkened forest below Mount Keralia.

CHAPTER THREE

"Ghost warden?" Chandra said. "What's a ghost warden?"

"Normally, it's a spirit from the land of the dead summoned to protect the living," said her host, Samir Mia Kauldi.

Brannon cried, "I've heard of ghost wardens! They've got flowing white hair, and white armor, and no real legs, just wispy trails of magic dust where their feet should be! They float around in silence, spying on their masters' enemies!"

Chandra looked to Samir for confirmation of this description as they walked through the forest, the dry twigs and leaves crackling under their feet.

He nodded. "'Spying' might be an exaggeration. As I said, they normally serve to protect, but the Order uses them to monitor the forest."

"They have arms without hands, and white lightning bolts shoot out of the place where their fingers should be!" Brannon said.

"I'm told that it feels more like a sharp sting than a lightning bolt," Samir said. "It startles more than anything else."

Samir Mia Kauldi was one of Keral Keep's staunchest allies in the Great Western Wood. He was well-respected among his fellow elves and shared Keralian values concerning personal freedom and the right to self determination, but, most importantly, he understood the consequences of the Order of Heliud's ever-increasing influence on the plane of Regatha. If the Heliuds were allowed to continue asserting their "civilization" agenda on the rest of Regatha, it would, sooner or later, mean an end to the elves' way of life. Their tribes would be broken up and individuals would be relocated to the camps where they would be "trained" as productive members of society. The forests, stripped of the protectors, would become resources for the cities, the trees a commodity to be managed by ministers. Samir had heard how some of the smaller forests in the distant east had been clear-cut and used for lumber, only to be replanted in neat rows so that their next harvest might be more efficient. The geometry of their placement, and the flat grid of roads laid down, cut the living spine of those groves and all but stopped the once-rich flow of mana. The elves who were able to flee the camps and cities returned to unrecognizable terrain, pine barrens, monocultures of ash or spruce. The Order had broken these forests into pieces and made sure they would not go back together.

Samir had told all of this to Mother Luti, but for years there had only been stories from far away. Now it was becoming a reality everywhere. But Luti, however her fighting spirit raged, was not getting any younger. Because the journey down the mountain to the forest below was physically demanding, she seldom made the trip herself anymore. She did insist on regular contact with the races of the woodlands that surrounded Mount Keralia, and often sent others in her place. They had to keep the Order's power in check, especially since the mountains seemed to be next in line for the Order's civilizing practices.

It was true that the Keralian pyromancers and the races of the Great Western Wood led independent existences, but they all shared this desire to limit the Order's influence to the plains and the cities of Regatha. As Luti said, they must be taught that fire and forest, much like their government, knew nothing of mercy.

Alone among the woodlanders, Samir Mia Kauldi actively agreed with Luti about this. He realized that the ghost wardens and mounted patrols were only the beginning of what was to come, but many in the forest remained unconvinced and dismissed the Order's encroachment as border skirmishes. Most believed that the stories of entire forests razed and replanted in the east would be impossible in an area as vast as the Great Western Wood.

Samir was short for an elf, with smooth skin the color of freshly-turned soil. He had a lithe build, a soft voice, and a round face that looked older than his years, possibly because of the perpetually harassed look that he carried with him like a empty coin purse: that is to say, without enthusiasm. Although he was a respected tribal chief and skilled summoner, his exhortations against the Order were met with little acceptance by other inhabitants of the woodlands. That wasn't to say he did not have support. Samir was known far and wide to summon the greatest beasts of Regatha. His status as chief had remained unchallenged because of this, and no tribe would dare question his authority, but might did not necessarily make right among the woodlanders. Much as it was with the Keralians, tribes—and the individuals who made them up—were given the right determine their own future, whether for good or bad, so long as it was not disruptive to the harmony of life in the forest.

Samir first came to the monastery as a supplicant. Since then the Keralians had been prepared to offer whatever assistance necessary. Chandra relished the opportunity to leave the monastery, so often volunteered to act as a liason to Samir and his loose association of druids, elves, and oufes.

It had been two days since her heated discussion with Brother Sergil about the scroll, and Chandra had decided to bring Brannon along as company on the long trek to Samir's small village deep in the woods.

The boy was clearly excited by the news that ghost wardens had been seen in the Great Western Wood.

"So what does a ghost warden do besides float around and sting people?" Chandra asked Samir.

"It only stings," Samir said, "if threatened."

"Whatever," Chandra said. "What good are they if they don't do anything?"

"The order uses them as spies," Samir said. "Rather than have them protect a living being, as was originally the intention of a ghost warden, they have them watch over the forest in general. The summoners share a psychic link with the warden and so are able to sense when things are out of the ordinary."

"Its summoners? You mean the Order of Heliud?"

"Yes. It is said that the summoner, once alerted by the ghost warden, will dispatch a patrol to the area in question."

"You're sure about these sightings?"

"*So* sure," Samir said, "that I have recently returned from Zinara, where I went to speak to Walbert himself. And I tell you Chandra, a more ridiculous place you will never find. They put plants in pots to decorate windows that look out on other windows with still more potted plants. They contrive *fountains*, which are absurd stone structures that trickle water in a meek imitation . . ."

"Wait, I know what a fountain is. The high priest of the Order agreed to see you?" Chandra asked in surprise. Walbert III wasn't reputed to be a very accessible man.

"Only after I spent two days insisting I would not leave the grounds of the Temple until I was granted an audience. It was a harder task than you can imagine sitting on flagstones amid those tortured trees. Can you believe they top the trees to stunt their growth? Imagine the arrogance that imposes Heliudic aesthetic values on nature. Even flowers are made to look like wounds on their hideously stripped stalks."

"So you confronted him?" Chandra said with relish.

"Yes. I demanded to know by what right the Order sent soldiers into our land to arrest us, and I said these ghost wardens must be withdrawn from the Great Western Wood."

"What did Walbert say?"

Samir made a disgusted sound. "It was infuriating, my friend. Walbert claimed that, in the interest of 'unity' throughout these lands, the laws which govern the cities and the plains are being extended to govern the woodlands, too. The ghost wardens have been summoned to patrol this vast woodland for our protection." His tone twisted the final word into an epithet. "And the soldiers are only enforcing fair and just laws that have been passed in the interest of preserving safety and . . . *order*. As if they have any understanding of protection, let alone fairness and justice."

Chandra was appalled. "Walbert is claiming the Order has authority over the woodlands?"

Samir nodded. "And he's enforcing that claim with the might of his soldiers and the skill of the Temple mages."

"He can't do that!"

"I said that to him." Samir shook his head. "In response, he offered me some pompous title in exchange for encouraging my people to abide by the laws of the plains. That, or I could remain in violation of some law and he would jail me. I decided to retreat and fight another day."

"So he's trying to take over the Great Western Wood." Chandra said in outrage. "That's unbelievable!"

"He will find it a more difficult task than he supposes," Samir said darkly. "The other tribes have been reluctant to enter into conflict with the Order, but if they continue to arrest druids for summoning hunters, perhaps I can bring others to my side."

"What will they want next?" Chandra said with contempt. "Control over Keral Keep? Do they imagine that the rule of the Order can spread to the mountains?"

"That may not be beyond the scope of their ambitions," Samir warned her. "They see the monastery as a threat. They think the Keralians are destructive and their teachings dangerous."

"It wasn't enough for them to outlaw fire magic in their own lands? They think they can outlaw it on Mount Keralia?" Chandra shook her head. "They'd have to be crazy to believe that."

"Why do they hate fire?" Brannon's red eyebrows creased in a frown on his young, freckled face. "I like it. And everyone needs it, after all."

LAURA RESNICK

"They hate it because fire takes no holiday, kiddo," Chandra said, but the boy only looked confused. Truth be told, Chandra was confused by the statement too, but she had heard Mother Luti say it so often that it seemed appropriate here.

"They don't hate fire, precisely," Samir said to the boy. "I'm not even sure they hate fire magic."

"Of course they do," Chandra said. "Why else would they punish pyromancy with *death* in Zinara?"

"They punish it with imprisonment," said Samir. "You only get executed if you commit violence with your fire magic."

"Whatever," she said. "Either way, they obviously do hate fire magic. Or more likely, they're *afraid* of it."

"I think what they don't like," said Samir, "is the nature of those who wield it. The Order of Heliud believes that no one is above the law. The law equalizes." He shrugged. "Isn't it true that you Keralians believe there is no law greater than the will of fire? You believe fire burns the criminal and the prosecutor equally, yes? The Heliuds believe that the righteous may pass through fire unscathed."

Chandra frowned. "What are you talking about?"

"I am talking about the Purifying Fire."

"The what?"

"The Purifying Fire." When Chandra and Brannon just stared at him blankly, he said, "Oh. Of course. Neither of you has ever been to Zinara?" They shook their heads. "And probably few members of the monastery have been there, either. Or know much about the Order of Heliud."

"Mother Luti tells us that relations between the monastery and the city have been tense for years." said Chandra. She knew that the woodlanders had been on civil terms with the people of the plains and the city until Walbert's ambitions had become too evident to ignore any longer.

"Yes." Samir nodded. "Those who feel the lure of Mount Keralia have little in common with those for whom order and structure are paramount. It's a very . . . *different* sort of perspective."

"It certainly is," Chandra said with distaste. "So what does fire have to do with the Order of Heliud?"

"The Order's power is said to come from something called the Purifying Fire. No one I know has ever seen it, and it is said that only a very select few within the Order have access to it, but it is believed to be a source of pure mana that dances perpetually like a flame in the ancient caverns beneath the Temple. The legend says that Heliud was a holy figure in the city of Thold across the Great Sea. He was accused of heresy, crimes against Thold, or some such thing. Regardless, Heliud was exiled along with his followers who believed his promise of a founding a shining city was indeed guidance from the Divine Will. The journey across the sea was long—they lost many of their number to sickness, and when they made landfall many more were lost to the vagaries of the wild.

"When they finally arrived at the site where Zinara was founded, Heliud's followers were beginning to doubt his plan, or even if he had one. He was facing opposition by one of his followers, a man named Zin who believed they could go no further. They should settle. Heliud was unfit to lead them. The promised land he spoke of was a fever dream. Zin had the support of the majority and Heliud, emaciated and weak from the journey, was facing exile again."

"You seem to know a lot about this, Samir," said Chandra. "You got some sympathies you aren't telling us about?" She grinned to take away the sting of the words.

"During the time I spent in protest on the grounds of the temple, an acolyte would come out and educate me on the history of Heliud. Anyway, to get to the point, Heliud returned to camp some days later. He had returned to peak physical form except that his once-lustrous black hair had gone as grey as the silver fox. When questioned about his transformation, Heliud said that he had found the physical manifestation of the Divine Will in a flickering white flame in some nearby caverns. He had thrown himself into it as penitence for failing to recognize the signs he'd been given, but rather than dying as expected, he emerged revived, stronger even than he had been before, proof of his righteousness. He claimed the fire had cleansed him of error and chosen him as the sole arbiter of Divine Law on Regatha.

"Zin still had loyal followers, many of whom believed that Heliud's revitalization was somehow demonic in its origin. Heliud challenged Zin, saying that the Fire would be the judge of right and wrong. They had to go, one and the other, to face the Purifying Fire. As you might imagine, only Heliud emerged."

"What happened to Zin?" asked Brannon.

"It's interesting that you ask, Brannon, because I wondered the same thing. Heliud told his followers that Zin's body had vaporized in the flame. The followers of Zin did not believe this explanation, but they never found his body, for as long as they searched the caverns. They were eventually mollified when Heliud named their settlement in Zin's honor. They hold Zin sacred still, saying that his opposition was divinely inspired to test the truth of Heliud's leadership."

He paused, seemingly unwilling to finish the tale, but finally added, "Walbert is the successor to this legacy and the custodian of the Purifying Fire."

"Well, doesn't that just figure," said Chandra in disgust. "The members of the Order have forbidden fire magic to everyone in their land while drawing their *own* power from fire? Or from something that's just barely similar to fire?"

A flame that was cold and white didn't sound much like fire to her. It sounded as rigid and deadly dull as she imagined the members of the Order were.

Chandra was passionate about the heat and fury of fire magic. She loved the gold, orange, yellow of explosions, the blood-red blazes of pyromancy. What was the point of something cold, white, and hidden underground? Surely there was no beauty in that. No glory, or passion, or thrill.

"The Order has forbidden fire magic in their lands," Samir agreed, "and now they want to restrict our way of life in the Western Wood, too. Certain practices are still allowed, Walbert told me, because he says the laws issued by the Order are not, in his judgment, unreasonable. But now other supposedly-dangerous practices such as summoning are forbidden to us." Samir's normally gentle expression grew thunderously angry. "And the ghost wardens are the Order's means of spying on us in our own land!"

"They have no right," Chandra said.

"None!" Samir rarely raised his voice, but he did so now.

"But at least a ghost warden doesn't sound like it can be a very *good* spy," Chandra said with a frown. "I mean, I'd sure notice it sneaking up on me, if it looks like what Brannon described."

"Me too!" said Brannon.

"Actually, it's more effective than you suppose," Samir said. "It's completely silent, after all. No feet or hands. We have many unusual things in the forest—"

"No argument there," said Chandra.

"—but we're not used to entities without any limbs. Well, apart from snakes, but you get my meaning."

"I don't like snakes," Chandra said frankly.

The shadowy forest felt claustrophobic to Chandra, who was much more used to the scenic vistas of mountain living. The woods were teeming with life, much of it strange and unnerving: carnivorous flowers whose sweet scent lured the unsuspecting, poisonous insects that posed as plants, ill-tempered beasts that resembled moss-covered rocks, and monsters that looked like trees, among many others. Dirt, noise, fungus. None of it appealed to Chandra, but it did offer time away from the other Keralians, who could become quite boring in their devotion.

Even so, sitting on the dry ground outside Samir's leafy hut, and politely pretending to drink some insipid beverage flavored with mashed plant roots, Chandra felt eager to return to the monastery and tell Mother Luti what she had learned today. If creatures of the Order were roaming the woods now, how much longer would it be before the Order tried to intrude onto Mount Keralia?

"Hardly anything moves through the forest without making a sound," Samir said. "But these creatures do. Lately, numerous woodlanders have been surprised to notice a ghost warden watching them without having any idea how long it had been there."

"That would be creepy," said Brannon.

"For example," Samir said calmly, "ever since you arrived and we sat down here together, I haven't glanced at those bushes to our left until just a moment ago." Now he turned his head and stared hard at the lush shrubbery. "So I don't know how long that ghost warden has been listening to our conversation."

Brannon gasped. Chandra jumped as if she had been bitten, leaping to her feet in the same motion as she whirled to face the bushes Samir was looking at.

She saw a white creature there, as as motionless as a rock. It didn't breathe. Its pale eyes didn't blink. It didn't even react to Chandra's sudden movement, nor to Brannon pointing at it and crying out. And its long white hair remained still, despite the breeze that made the leaves rustle gently on the bush obscuring it from Chandra's view.

She circled around the clearing, moving to get a better view of the creature. From her new position, Chandra saw that, exactly as Brannon had described, it had no hands or feet, although four appendages were attached to its torso in a disturbing suggestion of arms and legs that trailed off into whirls of glittering white dust where toes and fingers should have existed.

"How does it work?" Chandra asked Samir.

The ghost warden turned its head toward her when she spoke. Somehow, the movement was even more disturbing than the creature's stillness had been. Its motion was fluid and refined, like the passage of time.

"Work?" Samir, too, had risen to his feet. Now he pushed Brannon behind his body, shielding the boy from the creature.

"Can its master see through its eyes and hear through its ears?" Chandra asked, still staring at the ghost warden. "Does its creator see and hear us right now? Or does this thing have to return to its master to convey what it has witnessed?"

"I'm not sure," Samir said. "But, as I said, they are said to trigger an alert to patrols."

"I don't think they can do that," Chandra said decisively. "We should kill it to test the theory."

Now the creature displayed an almost eerily human reaction. It shrank away from her in recognition of the threat she posed.

"Chandra . . ." Samir said uneasily. "That might be unwise at this juncture."

But the very thought of a fight elevated Chandra's heartbeat. As her pulse quickened, so did the fire inside her. She could feel it bloom in the base of her skull as her hair became a mane of flame, and moved down her spine and out to her hands, lighting like torches.

"Be careful," Samir warned. "It has been unseasonably dry this year."

The ghost warden pointed a wispy limb toward Chandra, and a bolt of white light shot forth from the floating, shiny particles in its fingerless tendrils.

"Ouch!" Chandra staggered backward as it hit her in the stomach. The blow was enough to quench the fire that burned around her.

She doubled over, trying to catch her breath, and heard Brannon shouting her name. A moment later, she felt a hand on her back and heard Samir asking if she was all right.

"I'm fine," she croaked. "I feel like I've been . . . stung by the biggest wasp that ever lived, but I'm fine. Never mind me! *Get* that thing!"

"It's gone!" Brannon cried.

"Gone?" Chandra raised her head and looked toward the bushes. There was nothing there now but greenery. "Damn!"

"I see it!" Samir, whose eyes were far more accustomed than theirs to the shadowy forest, had spotted the creature as it fled through the trees. He pointed. "Over there!"

"Let's go!" Clutching her throbbing stomach, Chandra ran in the direction that Samir had indicated.

"*Can* we kill it?" he shouted, running after her.

"Let's find out!" she shouted back. Ghost or no ghost, Chandra thought she should be able to turn anything into a pile of ashes if she got it hot enough.

"This way!" Samir shouted behind her, veering off to the right and disappearing into the greenery.

Chandra turned to follow him. There was a broad thicket of bushes in her way, but it didn't look very thick. Rather than waste time going around it, she forced her way through it. This proved to be a mistake. The clinging shrubs and their thorns clutched at her clothes and scratched her skin. Within moments, she found she was stuck, unable to move forward. The harder she tried to free herself, the more entangled she became.

"I see it!" Samir cried, his voice significantly farther away now. "Come on!"

"I'm . . . *coming*!" Chandra winced as she struggled to free herself.

She was panting, she was in pain, she was falling behind, and, worst of all, she was trapped by a damn *bush*. Exasperated, her temper flared as a burning heat rushed through her body, erupting in an aura of flame that set the thicket alight and turned the offending bush into a charred remnant.

She had only taken a few steps when she heard shrill screeching and chattering overhead. Something heavy fell down onto her back from the overhanging branches of a tree, wrapped its limbs around her neck, and bit her shoulder.

"*Agh!*" Chandra dived to the ground and rolled over on top of her attacker. She struck the small, struggling combatant with her elbow and, as soon as she felt its grip loosen, leaped to her feet and turned to face it.

An oufe? Chandra stopped cold. She didn't like the small woodland creatures, but she had no quarrel with them either.

Graceful green limbs, tiny features, and rather immodest rough clothing blurred in a tangle of movement as her attacker jumped to its feet and launched itself at her again, baring its sharp little teeth in a growl of rage.

Chandra instinctively threw a bolt of fire at the oufe. It leaped back, shrieking in fear and pain, which made her feel guilty. The little creature was barely half her size, and the bush she had just destroyed might have been its place of worship or something. Oufes were a little strange that way.

Seeing that the frantic little creature wasn't seriously injured by her fire strike, though, Chandra said, "I'm sorry about your bush! But I don't have time for this!"

She turned and ran in the direction of Samir's distant shouts urging her to *hurry*. She heard more shrill chattering behind her and risked looking over her shoulder. Chandra saw that her attacker was being joined by two more, but tripped over a tree root and decided to keep her eyes on where she was going.

"Samir!" she shouted.

"Over here!" he shouted back.

"Chandra!" Brannon cried. "I can see it now! Hurry!"

Chandra heard more screeching behind her, but she didn't look back again, not even when the noises got more ear-splitting. She ran through a tight-knit grove of trees, jumping over fallen branches and toppled tree trunks, following the sounds of her friends' voices as they screamed for her to catch up.

When she catch up to Brannon and Samir, they were at the edge of a glade.

"There! Crossing the stream!" Samir cried. "It's just ahead of us now!"

He was breathing hard, and turned to look at Chandra as she drew up alongside him. Then he looked past her, and his sweat-beaded face underwent the most astonishing transition.

"Why," he said, "is there a load of oufes chasing you?"

"What?" Chandra looked over her shoulder. "Oh, *no*."

"Gosh," Brannon said. "They look really mad."

There appeared to be about twenty of them bearing down on her, screeching with murderous fury as they brandished sticks, spears, and daggers. Their eyes glowed with feral rage, their sharp teeth were bared, and their skin was flushed dark green with anger.

"What *is* it with oufes?" she muttered.

"This could be a problem," Samir said.

"What are they going to do?" Chandra said dismissively. "Nibble on my ankles?"

Samir said, "Well, given the opportunity . . ."

"I'm stopping that ghost warden!" Chandra spotted it floating above a narrow stream as it fled across the glade.

Samir said, "But what about—"

"You're a chief! You deal with it!"

Chandra closed the distance between herself and the ghost warden, spreading her arms wide as she felt power flow freely through her, answering her summons with satisfying heat. She shaped her will into a burning projectile and threw it at the ghost warden.

The creature flinched to escape a direct hit, a sign, in Chandra's estimation, that it could indeed be destroyed. It wouldn't expend energy fleeing or defending itself if it weren't vulnerable to her attacks. Chandra leaped over the narrow stream that her floating quarry had crossed only moments ago.

She heard a horse whinny somewhere beyond the glade as she threw another fireball that missed the ghost warden. Her next two also went wide into the underbrush that lay at the edge of the glade, where the tangle of dead twigs and leaves burst into flames.

"Hold still, damn you," Chandra muttered, trying again even as she heard thundering hooves approaching her on one side while oufes shrieked noisily on the other.

The ghost warden truly seemed to fear the fire, its entire form sliding horizontally away from the flaming projectiles with only a scant moment to spare. Then it abruptly returned two beams of white light in quick succession.

Chandra dodged the first one and met the other with a deflective ball of flame.

"Oh no you don't!" She threw another fireball, and another, and another after that. The area surrounding the glade was a wall of flame by now, each successive explosion of fire adding to the blazing fury. The oufes were in hysterics, and Samir was shouting words she couldn't quite hear.

Moving at a run, Chandra circled the glade to block the ghost warden's only remaining escape route. It hovered uncertainly, facing Chandra, surrounded on all other sides by fire.

The approaching horses were now so close that Chandra could hear the jingle of their bridles directly behind her as she threw three more fireballs at the creature in quick succession. Its rapid, evasive movements managed to dodge the assaults, but the result was a bonfire that could not be avoided and the ghost warden was soon consumed in flames.

Over the roar of the fire and the shrieking of oufes, Chandra became fully aware of the rattling bridles and snorting horses behind her, as well as the sharp exclamations of male voices. She was already turning toward the sounds when she realized what Brannon was frantically screaming at her.

"Chandra! *Soldiers!* Behind you! Soldiers on horseback!"

There were four of them. Their horses were dancing nervously, frightened by the fire. The soldiers, all wearing boiled-leather armor over pale blue tunics, looked stunned as they gazed at her. Three of them had their swords drawn. One appeared to have entirely forgotten he was armed, and just stared at Chandra with his mouth hanging open.

She grinned as she raised her arms high, a mane of fire swirling around her head and shoulders. Flames licked across her skin, surrounding her body in a flaming aura. The torches at the end of her arms grew immense as she shouted, "Leave this forest! Never come back! Tell Walbert what you have seen! The Order is finished here!"

Since they seemed to need a little encouragement, she threw a fireball over their heads. One of the horses pranced sideways, its eyes rolling with fear. Another reared up, nearly unseating its rider.

When Chandra threw a second fireball, letting this one come a little closer to hitting one of the men, they all four turned and fled. The sight of their horses galloping away made her grin with exultation.

She watched until the green woodland swallowed them up, hiding them from her view as they fled, she supposed, in the direction of the plains. She felt someone tugging at her sleeve.

"Chandra," Brannon said, his eyes wide as he looked up at her. He was still a boy, and she was tall for a woman. "Samir says we should leave before the oufes strip your flesh from your bones and feed it to wolves."

"What?" Chandra frowned as she glanced over her shoulder in Samir's direction. "*Oh.*"

The mage was holding back a mass of the woodland creatures with an undulating green net of tangled, writhing vines that he had conjured between them and the glade, Some of them were flinging themselves at the barrier, squealing as they got tangled up in it, while others were trying to climb it, in an attempt to go over the top and proceed from there.

All around them the glade burned. She had started a forest fire, one that was raging completely out of control.

"Oops."

Oufes, she knew, could be very touchy about this sort of thing. Indeed, Samir was taking quite a risk with his own people by interceding to protect her. However, she had destroyed a ghost warden and chased away four of Walbert's armed soldiers. Hopefully, when the oufes calmed down, they'd realize that she had acted for the best.

At the moment, though . . .

Chandra started toward Samir, intending to help him.

He glanced in her direction, and an expression of horror contorted his face when he saw her approaching him. "*Go!*" he ordered. "Go *now!*"

Brannon grabbed her by the shirt. "Chandra . . ."

Samir was right, she realized. These oufes were pointing at her and screaming. Her presence was only increasing their frenzy. She hated leaving Samir to deal with this alone, but that was the best choice available at the moment.

"All right, yes," Chandra said, grasping Brannon's hand. "Let's go. This way."

They ran across the glade together, their footsteps carrying them into a wall of fire. Knowing that no forest-dweller would follow them this way, they fled through the welcoming embrace of the flames.

CHAPTER FOUR

The first attack came the following night.

Chandra was lying awake in her narrow bed, torn between anger over Luti's latest lecture on self-control and a certain reluctant awareness that the mother mage had a valid point.

Fortunately, Chandra's fire—as she had been quick to remind Luti earlier tonight—had only burned down a *small* portion of the Great Western Wood. Samir had sent one of his many relatives to the monastery earlier to inform them that Chandra's forest fire had been contained and quelled after nightfall. The rains had been sporadic this year, but the elves' magic had kept the fire confined to the the glade where Chandra had destroyed the ghost warden.

"Nonetheless," Luti had said to her earlier tonight, "you did far more damage than good, Chandra."

"But I—"

"Eliminating one ghost warden may have been helpful—"

"*May* have been? That thing was a spy for the Order!"

"—or it may have been ill-advised. In either case—"

"Ill-advised *how?*" Chandra demanded.

"*In either case,*" Luti said, clearly losing patience with her.

"The possible benefit of eliminating one ghost warden from the forest cannot balance the catastrophe of *burning down* the forest."

More admonishments had followed. "Playing with fire is bad for those who burn themselves," said Luti quoting some sage or another. "But for the rest of us it is a great pleasure. I want you to be able to experience this pleasure as I do, Chandra, but until you learn to control your impulses, you will continue to burn yourself and those around you."

Chandra lay wide awake in bed thinking about that last statement and wrestling with the emotions it stirred.

She *hated* being reprimanded and lectured. It made her want to leave Regatha, Keral Keep, and Mother Luti far behind her. She was seething with indignation and felt like setting something on fire, even though that was precisely what had gotten her into this trouble in the first place.

On the other hand . . .

Chandra heaved a breath as she lay on her back, staring up into the darkness.

On the other hand, she had indeed destroyed part, however small, of the forest, enraged a tribe of oufes, and no doubt caused a lot of trouble for Samir. The woodlanders hadn't ever done her any harm. Samir considered her a friend, and the Keralians sought cooperation with the forest races against the encroaching power of the Order. It wasn't entirely unreasonable for Luti to say that making enemies in the woods by wreaking destruction had been a bad decision, or, rather, to quote her, "a stupid misstep." The actual decision had been to rid the woodlands of a spy for the Order. That was a good idea, thought Chandra.

However, given the way things had turned out, it was possible that the woodlanders found a single ghost warden among many to be slightly less disruptive to their daily routine than she had been.

Chandra kept reviewing the events of that day and wondering what she should have done differently. Capture the ghost warden instead of kill it? How could she have done that? The creature was so fast and elusive, she had barely been able to get close enough to throw fireballs at it. Should she have just let it spy on her and then go its merry way? *Out of the question!* Instead of killing it in the woods, should she have chased it to the plains and thereby accidentally set the farmlands on fire? Would Luti be less exasperated with her now if farmers were enraged instead of woodlanders?

Chandra rolled over on her side and tried to punch some shape into her flat pillow.

And why might killing a ghost warden be ill-advised, anyway? Surely Luti didn't think it was a *good* thing to have those creepy creatures roaming the woods and spying for the Order? To hear Samir talk, it wasn't long before they started appearing in the mountains to protect the Keralians from themselves and anything they might do that the Order didn't like.

Tired of chasing this subject around and around in her head, Chandra closed her eyes and tried to will herself to relax and get some sleep. She forced herself to clear her mind, focus on her breathing, and let the darkness absorb the clamoring voices in her head.

But then she realized the voices weren't all in her head. She frowned irritably as she recognized the sound of whispering directly outside her door. It was very late, but some of the Keralian acolytes were night owls who preferred to study and practice until dawn and then sleep all morning. Life at the monastery was pretty unstructured, and the residents seldom interfered with each other's habits, as long as they didn't impinge on the rights or comforts of anyone else.

Whispering and muttering outside her door, Chandra decided, especially while she was trying to sleep, counted as impinging on her rights and comforts. She heard two lowered voices. They sounded like they were arguing. She wished they'd go argue somewhere *else*. She was about to get out of bed and tell them so when the door to her chamber creaked open.

Chandra opened her eyes as her body went tense. Who was entering her room in the middle of the night?

She heard the same two voices again, now in her doorway. Chandra's room opened directly onto an outdoor walkway with a view of the mountains to the south and the sky overhead. Squinting through the dark, she saw two figures standing in her there, faintly illuminated by the moonlight.

The two intruders were short—shorter than Brannon certainly, whose head only came up to Chandra's shoulder. They were also broad and squat, with misshapen heads, and they moved in an odd, lumbering way, as if trying to keep their balance on the deck of a ship in rough waters. But it wasn't until Chandra saw their brightly glowing orange eyes that she realized what they were.

"Goblins?" she asked incredulously, so startled she forgot to feign sleep..

The closer one stumbled back in surprise when she spoke, careening into the other. The second goblin gave a muffled shriek, hopping around on one foot—his other, it seemed, had been stomped on by his staggering companion.

Chandra tilted her head back and blew a fiery breath straight upward. The resultant flame flew up to the ceiling and bounced tentatively there for a moment before it attached itself, burning like a torch to illuminate Chandra's room.

She got out of bed and looked at the intruders with unconcealed revulsion. *"Goblins."*

The red skin that covered their misshapen, bald heads had the texture of lumpy dough. Hair sprouted from their fungal ears and their scaly hands had claws as long as the yellow fangs that protruded from their mouths, dripping with saliva.

"You're drooling on my floor!" Chandra said in disgust.

They also, she noticed, smelled *terrible*.

The goblin hopping around on one foot gibbered at its companion in a tongue Chandra didn't recognize. The other goblin hissed at her.

"I'll say this just once," she told them, letting flames ripple boldly along her skin in an effort to intimidate them. "Get out of my room. Get out *now*."

The goblin that had hissed at her nudged its companion, who was still obsessed with the pain in his foot. Getting no reaction, the hissing goblin nudged again. This annoyed the second goblin, who put down his aching foot and irritably swatted the first goblin. The first one growled in annoyance, turned around, and hit him back.

As if oblivious to Chandra's presence, they were suddenly clobbering each other with vehemence, growling and gibbering. Chandra watched them for a few moments, but her amusement quickly palled, and she interrupted them with a stinging bolt of fire that got their attention.

"What in the Multiverse are you two doing here?" she demanded.

They blinked, as if startled to be reminded that they had invaded a woman's bedchamber in a monastery where they had no business being. Although goblins practiced fire magic, they were unwelcome here. The Keralians had no interest in studying and working alongside creatures who had the manners, values, and sanitary habits of rabid animals.

ⵁ

One of the goblins, evidently remembering the business at hand, bared its chipped yellow fangs and snarled, "*Kill woman.*"

In unison, the two goblins gave a guttural little war cry, before launching themselves at Chandra.

She moved her hands forward, calling golden heat into her palms, and warded off her attackers' claws by throwing a large fireball into their faces. However, the goblins were perhaps more competent then they'd originally appeared. It was clear they had some moderate protection against fire, whether from a charm or spell. Chandra's opening salvo left them unsinged, though slightly disoriented.

Taking advantage of that moment, Chandra picked up the lone chair in her room, and brought it crashing down on the confused goblins. One of them screamed and clutched his bald head, staggering. Apparently rethinking his commitment to murder, he dashed out the door.

The other goblin merely seemed to be enraged by the heavy blow. It snarled viciously and, doubling over, flew straight into Chandra's knees. The chair flew out of Chandra's grasp as she lost her balance and fell against the wall, propelled by the speed and surprising weight of her attacker.

The goblin tried to tear out her throat with its fangs, but Chandra gouged the beast's fiery orange eyes with one hand and pulled its hairy ear as hard as she could with the other, trying to pull its head away from her neck. While the beast was temporarily blinded, she balled her fist and transferred all her energy there. Her knuckles superheated like molten lava and she punched the goblin in the stomach. As the wind and a considerable amount of spittle was knocked out of her assailant, she pushed with her fist again, twisting it from side to side in an effort to cook the thing from the inside out.

She squirmed beneath her adversary, trying to shift her weight so that the goblin's dripping saliva and revolting breath weren't in such close proximity to her face.

"Chandra? Chandra!"

She risked glancing away from her opponent and saw Brother Sergil standing in the doorway, blinking at her. There were a couple of other Keralians behind him, also attracted by the commotion.

"There's a second goblin!" Chandra shouted. "It got away! Stop it! Get it!"

"A second . . ." Sergil gasped, still staring at her. "Fires above! What are you doing to that *goblin*?"

"Get the other one!" Chandra shouted, as the goblin took advantage of her distraction to throw its weight. She was suddenly rolling around on the floor with her gruesome opponent.

"Do you want some help with that?"

"*Sergil!* Get the . . . *Agh!*" She cried out in sudden pain when the beast's claw drew blood from her thigh. ". . . other one!"

"There's *another* one?" Brother Sergil said, sounding appalled, but he and the other monks disappeared before she could reply.

Trying to keep the goblin's fangs away from her throat, Chandra kept pressing her molten fist into its muscular belly. Her magic was much stronger than anything claimed by this stinking *thing*, she knew. She just needed a little more time . . . And, sure enough, a moment later, she felt the goblin's skin start to sizzle. The stench of burning cloth arose from the spot, followed by the sickly smell of roasting flesh. The goblin quivered, snarled again . . . then let out a howl of pain and released its hold on Chandra, intent now on getting away from her. She tried to cling to it, telling herself to take it captive, but really wanting to kill it. However, its fight or flight instinct had taken a distinct turn toward flight and Chandra released it rather than have her arm chewed off.

The goblin scrambled to its feet and ran out the door. Chandra leaped up and followed it out of the room. The claw wound on her thigh stung sharply now, slowing her down. She tried not to think about what sort of horrible, festering infection she would get from a filthy goblin claw.

On the walkway outside, the goblin barreled into a startled woman, who screamed, but the collision didn't stop the goblin's flight. Other Keralians were running around and shouting, apparently looking for the goblin that had previously fled. Chandra followed *this* goblin down the walkway and toward the eastern terrace.

"Chandra!" a familiar voice cried.

She looked over her shoulder and saw Brannon running toward her, trying to catch up. "Stay back!" she ordered.

"I'll help you!"

"Stay *back!*" Chandra doubted the goblin would have any scruples about killing a child.

"Brannon!" Brother Sergil shouted. "Stay with me!"

Chandra kept after the goblin.

Moving awkwardly, but quite fast nonetheless, the hideous assassin ran across the eastern terrace and straight for the stairway that led down to the herb garden below, from which it could escape over the red stone wall and into the dark night.

Chandra stretched out her arms, incredibly angry that this whole thing was happening. But anger was good for Chandra. Anger tapped that part of her that made the fire hot. Anger was the accelerant that took fire to inferno. That little beast was not getting away. Chandra raised a wall of fire around the fleeing goblin. He tried to run through it, but the wall grew thicker, moving with him as he ran, the circle shrinking in on him so that he couldn't escape. Shrieking in panic now, the goblin hesitated, unsure if any direction were better than another. And the flames closed in on him, no matter which direction he turned as he sought to flee the fire's destructive hunger.

Chandra's magic was much stronger than whatever pathetic power this lumpish assassin could claim. She only needed another moment . . . And sure enough, the goblin screamed in pain as he was consumed by the fire, his thrashing discernible even through the shifting wall that closed on him like a molten iron maiden.

When the glowing remnants of the dying goblin vanished and all that remained was her own fire, Chandra let go of her spell. The flames calmed, no longer moving and shifting to imprison her enemy. With nothing fueling it, the fire she had called forth began to die. Within a few moments, it would disappear altogether.

Chandra was breathing heavily, but she was no longer angry. Only her throbbing leg served as a reminder of the rage that had beaten so furiously in her heart moments ago. She wiped perspiration from her face, smoothed away the lingering flames from her long red hair, and leaned over, resting her hands on her knees as she tried to catch her breath.

Her head turned quickly when she heard footsteps approaching her, but she relaxed when she saw Luti, wearing a long, copper-colored robe. The mother mage's white hair was loosely braided and hanging over one shoulder. Her dark eyes were alert as she gazed at Chandra's dying fire on the eastern terrace.

"A goblin attack, they're saying," Luti said.

Chandra nodded. "Two of them."

"Yes, I heard. Unfortunately, no one can find the other one. It must have got away."

"Oh." Chandra steadied her breathing and stood upright again. "I don't think it'll come back. It didn't seem to be the persistent type."

Luti noticed her bleeding leg. "You're hurt."

"Goblin claw."

Luti grimaced. "We'll have to clean it and keep an eye on it. Fortunately, it doesn't look serious. But it'll sting for a few days."

"Chandra!" Brannon called, running toward her. "Are you all right?"

"I'm fine," she assured him as he reached her side.

"Was that really a goblin, like they're saying?" he asked eagerly.

"Yes."

"I wish I had gotten a good look. I've never seen one!"

"They're disgusting," she said. "I can't believe that female goblins actually . . . well . . . whatever they do."

Luti asked her, "Did you know your attackers?"

"Know them?" Chandra blinked. "They were *goblins*."

"You never saw them before?"

"You've seen one, you've seen 'em all, I guess."

"I wish you'd take this seriously, Chandra," Luti said. "But if you don't think they were personal enemies of yours, and considering we haven't had a goblin attack here in many years . . . I think we can guess who sent them."

"Who sent . . ." Chandra realized what she meant. "You mean the oufes? They can sure carry a grudge for little guys."

"Yes," Luti said. "Even though it was, of course, only a *small* portion of the forest."

✳ ✳ ✳ ✳ ✳

"No, no," Samir said, sitting in Mother Luti's private workshop in the monastery five days later. "Not *all* the woodlanders. There's some ill feeling about the fire among other factions, of course, but it's only the oufes who are calling for your execution, Chandra."

Samir, who looked more harassed than usual, had made the trip up the mountain that day to update Mother Luti and Chandra on the situation in the Great Western Wood.

"Only the oufes," Chandra repeated, shifting her position to stretch her sore leg. The claw wound was healing well, but it still ached a little.

Luti said, "I suppose we can regard that as good news."

"Actually, it's one particular tribe of oufes." Samir added wearily, "A big tribe."

"Presumably the tribe in whose territory the fire occurred?" Luti said.

"Yes. I've tried reasoning with them. To explain that Chandra was fighting a ghost warden who had invaded our lands to spy on us." Samir sighed. "But you know what oufes are like."

Luti said, "Not amenable to reason."

"Not really." He shrugged and added, "To them, the forest is sacred. What happened in the woods that day has offended them deeply. Imagine what the Keralians would do if some came in and set your monastery on fire . . . Okay, bad example, but you get what I mean.

"They insist that nothing less than Chandra's death will atone for the destruction of the forest. They're calling for her assassination."

"We supposed so," Luti said, "since as of now there have been three energetic attempts on Chandra's life."

Samir said, "And since those attempts failed, this morning the tribe increased the size of the reward they're offering for her death."

"What sort of reward do oufes offer?" Chandra said with a frown. "Most of the killers I've met aren't so keen on pussy willow trees."

"Well, I wouldn't know what they are offering," Samir said. "But you've seen the caliber of assassin they are attracting."

"Thank goodness for small mercies," Luti said dryly. "Even so, we must resolve this matter."

Chandra said, "Maybe if I talked to them—"

"*No*," said Luti and Samir in unison.

Chandra blinked.

Samir said more gently, "Oufes don't leave the forest, so they certainly won't come here. And if you entered the forest, my friend, there's nothing I can say or do that would protect you from the tribe's wrath. Not in their current frame of mind, anyway."

"I can handle a little oufe wrath," Chandra said dismissively.

"And burn down *more* of the forest?" Luti said. "*No*."

"Mother Luti is right, Chandra," said Samir. "While the tribe remains this angry, I feel sure that a confrontation would only worsen the situation. We don't want that. Especially not at a time when cooperation between the monastery and the woodlanders is vital."

"So what's the solution?" Chandra said in frustration. "I just keep fighting off the assassins that come after me every day or two?"

"No, of course not," Samir said. "We must find a way to resolve this matter peaceably. You mentioned there were other attacks?"

"Yes," Luti said, "and you know about the goblins. But there was also a very large man with an axe outside the walls of the monastery. Luckily, he was more accustomed to chopping wood than people or he might have hurt Brannon."

"Brannon was attacked?" Samir repeated, clearly horrified.

"Perhaps not intentionally, but he was with Chandra when the idiot tried to take her down. Then, most recently, an archer sent a few arrows from that rock outcropping near the west wall. Fortunately," Luti said, "the archer had poor aim and lacked stealth, so he didn't survive even until midday. But what next? How many attempts on her life must Chandra endure? And how long before someone *else* gets injured in one of these attacks? Or even killed?"

"That's an excellent point," Samir said with a nod. "I will appeal to the tribe on the basis of justice. If they persist in their quest for vengeance, they could be responsible for the death of an innocent person. Even a child!"

"Will that argument sway them?" Luti asked.

"Not immediately," Samir admitted. "Empathy is not an oufe characteristic."

Luti shook her head in exasperation. "*Oufes*. Even the smallest spark left unattended can make a fire."

"Have patience for now," Samir urged, "and give me time. I believe I can persuade them to call off these attacks. Oufes also tend to have short memories."

Luti sighed, then nodded. "All right, Samir. I have faith in your leadership and your powers of persuasion. We will try to be patient. Meanwhile . . ." She frowned down at her folded hands.

"Meanwhile?" Chandra prodded.

"Meanwhile, inform the tribe that Chandra has left the monastery."

Samir shook his head. "If I tell them a falsehood and they find out, then I will lose—"

"It's not a falsehood," Luti said. "At least, it won't be by this time tomorrow."

"I'm not running away!" Chandra said.

"Of course you're not," said Luti. "You are, at my request, leaving on a mission on behalf of the monastery."

"I am?" Chandra said suspiciously.

"Yes. A mission that only you can accomplish." Their eyes met. "We'll discuss the details later."

A mission that only you can accomplish . . .

Did Luti want her to planeswalk? Chandra's curiosity was kindled, but planeswalking wasn't something they could discuss in front of Samir, so she nodded in acceptance of Luti's statement.

"So . . ." Samir looked from Luti to Chandra, then back to Luti. "If I tell the tribe tomorrow that Chandra has left the monastery, I will be speaking the truth?"

Luti nodded. "And if you think it will help cool their rage, tell them Chandra has been sent away as punishment for what happened. That's not our way here, of course, but I rather doubt that oufes know—or care—what our ways are."

"Tell them I'm being *punished*?" Chandra was insulted. "I don't want a bunch of oufes thinking—"

"Does it really matter what oufes think of you, Chandra?" Luti said impatiently. "If it means these disruptive attacks cease, so be it. I just want to resolve this matter as quickly as possible, so that we can give our full attention to dealing with the Order!"

Chandra shrugged and folded her arms. She didn't like it, but Luti had a point, so she let it go.

"And speaking of the Order," Luti continued. "Killing that ghost warden has attracted Walbert's attention."

"What?" Chandra said in surprise.

"How do you know?" asked Samir.

"The soldiers from Zinara who saw you in the forest," Luti said to Chandra, "reported what they saw. And the tale was carried all the way to the ears of the high priest of the Temple."

"To Walbert?"

Luti nodded. "I received a letter this morning from Walbert himself, brought by courier." She gestured to a sheaf of papers sitting on the table next to her. "A *long* letter."

"What does he want?" Chandra asked.

"His ultimate goal is to shut down Keral Keep and to outlaw fire magic as we practice it throughout Regatha."

"He wants *what*?" Chandra said in outrage.

"Of course that's what he wants," Samir said. "The rule of the Order can't spread to the mountains while Keral Keep stands."

"Precisely," said Luti. "Oh, Walbert's letter—which is so long-winded that one can only pity his scribes—he goes on about wanting peace, harmony, and unity; seemingly harmless aspirations. But his righteous language can't hide the fact that what he really wants is unchallenged rule over all the lands of Regatha. What he wants is total power." Luti scowled as she added, "He wants power over *us*."

"And us," Samir added.

"Yes," Luti agreed. "Over everyone."

"And to have such power," Samir said, "to rule over all of Regatha unopposed, to ensure that the Order holds sway over the forests and the mountains, as well as the plains . . . Walbert must eliminate all *other* power. Or at least nullify it."

"Particularly fire magic?" Chandra guessed.

"Yes," Luti said. "If Walbert can quell fire magic, then all the other undesirable practices—the ones he doesn't like—will become easier for him to control, too."

"What about this Purifying Fire that you told me about, Samir?" Chandra asked. "Is it really that important to the Order?"

"So people say, in Zinara."

"Can it be . . . I don't know—destroyed? Damaged? Eliminated?"

"What is created that cannot be destroyed? I suppose the answer is yes, but that would mean entering the Temple of Heliud and infiltrating the caverns. One would assume that it is heavily guarded. I can't imagine they let just anyone in there."

"It was just a question," Chandra muttered.

"You're not going to Zinara," Luti said firmly.

"What else does the letter say?"

"Exactly what you might expect. Walbert decries the 'irresponsible' teachings of the monastery and the 'dangerous reign' of pyromancy in the mountains."

"All because I killed a ghost warden?" Chandra said.

"His letter goes on at some length about the *undisciplined* nature of fire mages and the *destructive* influence of pyromancy in magic." Luti scowled, her intonation emphasizing those of Walbert's words that she particularly disagreed with. "Well, if I may paraphrase the great Jaya Ballard: others have criticized destruction, and you know what? They're all dead."

Chandra asked, "Is Walbert's reaction what you meant when you said that destroying the ghost warden might have been ill-advised?"

"Yes," said Luti. "I've never seen one, but I know those creatures are supposed to be hard to eliminate. I thought you might attract Walbert's attention when you killed it. But I've changed my mind about that being ill-advised."

"Why?"

"Walbert has been looking for an excuse to confront the Keralians openly." Luti shrugged. "Now that he has found one . . . I realize that it's a relief. The growing tension has been exhausting. I, too, am ready for confrontation."

"But will this . . ." Chandra frowned. "Mother, have I endangered the monastery?"

"No. Oh, you've burned down part of the Great Western Wood, turned the monastery into a target for inept assassins, and made Samir's life a nightmare of frenzied oufes and disgruntled woodlanders," Luti said. "But if Walbert didn't have the destruction of that ghost warden to use as an excuse, then he'd find something else. So I don't believe that *this*—" Luti picked up Walbert's letter from the table beside her and waved it at Chandra. "—is your fault. It was going to happen eventually."

Samir said, "I agree, Chandra. Walbert has been preparing to challenge the monastery for years. If he didn't feel ready to try to impose the rule of the Order here, he wouldn't have used the ghost warden's demise as an excuse." He added, "Remember, I've met Walbert. Nothing he does is done without a great deal of thought."

"What's he like?"

"He's about Luti's age, tall, gray-haired, thin. He holds himself erect and is very well-groomed. His smile is cold, like his eyes. He speaks in a calm, civilized tone, yet manages to be threatening." Samir thought for a moment. "The things he says are outrageous and self-serving, but listening to him talk, I'm sure he really believes what he's saying."

Luti made a sound of disgust. "Then he must believe that that I can be moved by the transparent posturing in his letter. Does he imagine that the mountain cares, for even one moment, about the shade it casts on the plain? If he supposes that his absurd rhetoric will somehow curb our belief in the power of fire, then he is in for a rude awakening."

"Oh, I doubt Walbert thinks a letter will cause you to cooperate with his demands," said Samir. "Instead, I think he hopes the letter will incite you to rash behavior."

Luti's angry frown changed to a look of surprise. And then she smiled ruefully. "This is why you're such a valuable friend, Samir." She nodded. "Yes. Of course you're right.

Walbert isn't just arrogant and power-hungry. He's also shrewd and manipulative. He will need popular support so he is trying to provoke us."

"But it's important," Samir said, "to give careful thought to your next move. Because careful thought is not what he's hoping for."

"Actually, my next move doesn't really call for that much thought," Luti said.

"Oh?"

"Walbert demands that I turn over Chandra to him— or, rather, 'the red-haired female pyromancer who attacked four soldiers of the Order after criminally destroying a ghost warden.'" Luti looked at Chandra as she added, "Which is why I think the first thing I should do is send you away for a while. Someplace where Walbert won't look for you."

"So it's not the oufes you were worried about, after all," Chandra said.

"Oh, I'm worried about them, too," Luti said. "Never underestimate just how vengeful an oufe can be."

CHAPTER FIVE

There actually *is* a mission I'm asking you to go on for the monastery," Luti said to Chandra as they strolled through the herb garden, having just said farewell to Samir at the eastern gate. "Considering the danger that I suspect is involved, I'd be reluctant to send you, under normal circumstances. But since it's obviously a good idea for you to be absent for a while . . ."

"You want me to planeswalk?" Chandra guessed. "That's not dangerous."

"According to Jaya," Luti said, "it *is* rather dangerous. There aren't roads or signs or maps among the planes of the Multiverse, are there? There are no convenient doors indicating where to enter and leave the Blind Eternities. And I assume there aren't any heralds helpfully crying things like, 'Welcome to Regatha!'"

"Well, I guess it's a *little* dangerous," Chandra said with a shrug. "But nothing I can't handle."

"A place without time or logic. Without physical form or substance. No ordinary person can survive in the æther that exists between the planes. Only a planeswalker can," Luti mused. "And they say that a planeswalker can only survive there for a limited time. If you become disoriented and get lost in the Blind Eternities, you might never emerge. Before long, you'd be consumed there and die."

"*They* say? *They*, who?" Chandra said dismissively. "Besides you, who around here knows anything about planeswalkers?"

"Is it true?" Luti demanded.

Chandra looked out over the vast forest below the mountain, and to the plains that lay further east. "All right, yes. I could get lost and die in the Blind Eternities. So what? You, or Brannon, or Samir, could get lost and die in the mountains. The first time you sent me to meet with Samir, I thought I'd get lost and die in the Great Western Wood!"

"Yes, I remember. When you finally made your way back here, you were . . . irritable about your misadventure in the woods."

"But the only alternative to taking that sort of risk is to stay home all your life."

"And staying home isn't that safe these days, either," Luti said dryly as she sat on a bench under one of the garden's ancient olive trees. Her glance surveyed the vegetation. "Goodness, that rosemary really needs trimming! It's taking over the whole place."

Not remotely interested in gardening, Chandra sat next to her and asked, "So where do you want me to go?"

Luti folded her hands in her lap. "Kephalai. Which is also part of the danger I'm worried about."

"Keph . . ." Chandra laughed. "I get to steal the scroll again?"

"That all depends."

"On what?"

"On you, I suppose." She frowned again at the over-grown rosemary, then said, "Brother Sergil and the other monks working on the scroll believe they've solved the riddle. I don't suppose you remember the decorative border surrounding the text in the original scroll?"

"No. Like I said . . ."

"Yes, the planeswalker who stole it from us played tricks on your memory." Luti nodded. "Well, after more days of studying the text, the brothers believe that the decorative border—which they did not copy or study during the brief time that we had the original here—contains the clue to where the artifact can be found."

"The border? In what way?"

"They're not sure. It may be a map, it may be hidden text, it may be a spell . . ." Luti shrugged. "So if you can *look* at the scroll again, you may be able to see the information concealed within the decorative border."

"And to look at the scroll, I need to go back to Kephalai."

"If it's still there. If the planeswalker who stole it from us didn't take it somewhere else entirely."

"Even if the scroll is back on Kephalai now, I might not be able to interpret what's in the border," Chandra said.

"In that case, the monks would like an opportunity to study it themselves. So you'll need to bring it back here again, if you can." Luti looked at her. "If the scroll is back in the Sanctum of Stars now, it will certainly be under increased security. Stealing it a second time will be very dangerous."

"Fortunately," Chandra said, "I enjoy a challenge."

"Yes, I thought you'd say that. Even so, please be careful. If only for the sake of an old woman who has become rather fond of you, even though you're an awful lot of trouble to have around."

"Yes, Mother."

"I think it would be—" But Luti's comment ended on a shocked gasp as the rosemary plant lifted itself from the soil and attacked them.

Chandra saw claws and fangs hiding amidst the plant's spiky leaves as it suddenly turned into a tall, moving creature, with arms and legs that ended in the same spikes.

Heat flowed through her in immediate response to the danger, and she amputated one of the plant's attacking limbs with a bolt of fire that she swept downward as she was assaulted. The creature hissed in pain, swayed, then doubled over and re-formed itself into some sort of small, leafy wolf-looking thing.

"How did it do *that*?" Chandra blurted, staring in surprise.

Luti gasped again. "Watch out!" She hurled a fireball at the creature as it crouched to attack. The projectile hit the growling four-legged bush in the face, but the leafy wolf easily shook off the blow and leaped for Chandra.

Her fireball was considerably more powerful than Luti's, and when it hit the creature, the thing fell back with a screech, rolled over into a ball, and reshaped itself into the form of a giant spider.

"I *hate* spiders," Chandra said with feeling.

She raised her hands to call forth a hot flow of lava, and dumped it all over the disgusting creature that was scuttling toward her with murderous intent. The massive spidery *thing* was smothered beneath the lava and incinerated by the liquid fire.

The two women stared at the glowing pile of cooling lava that had destroyed their attacker.

"Well." Luti was panting. "That was . . . different."

"Ugh! Did you say you know what that thing was?"

"Yes. I'm pretty sure it was a woodland shapeshifter," Luti said, still breathless. "I've heard of them . . . but this is the first one . . . I've ever . . . ." She sat down shakily on the bench again. "I'm too old for a shock like that."

"Even *I'm* too old for a shock like that." Chandra's heart was pounding after the brief fight.

"No *wonder* the rosemary looked so overgrown," Luti murmured.

"That was pretty clever, I have to admit."

"Not that we won't miss you, Chandra," Luti said, her hand resting over her heart on her heaving chest, "but how soon can you go?"

✽ ✽ ✽ ✽ ✽

Chandra talked with Brother Sergil that evening, trying to get some idea of what to look for in the decorative border if she saw the scroll again. She didn't learn much. As Luti had already told her, it might be a pattern, it might be artfully concealed text, it might be an ornate map. Or it might be none of those. But he did tell her enough so that she would be able to identify the scroll, considering she had no memory of it.

Wonderful.

She decided to go to Brannon's room while he was getting ready for bed to tell him she was going away again, but that she would be back before long.

"You're not running away from *oufes*, are you?" he demanded.

"No, of course not," she assured him.

"Because we're better sorcerers than a bunch of elves and weird woodland creatures."

"Yes, we are." She tucked him into bed and said, "But the brothers want to know more about the scroll I brought back—you remember the scroll?"

"Yes. The one that the stranger stole."

"Right. So Mother Luti asked me to try to find it."

"I should come with you." He started to get out of bed. "I can help you!"

"I need you to stay here and protect the monastery," she said firmly, nudging him back onto his narrow cot. "There was another attack today. That's the fourth one. And if I hadn't been there, something awful might have happened to Mother Luti."

"I heard! A woodland shapeshifter!" Brannon's eyes glowed with excitement. "I kind of wish you hadn't killed it right away, Chandra. Mother Luti's never seen one before, and she's really *old*, so maybe I'll never get another chance to see one."

"I'm sorry about that," she said. "It was pretty interesting."

"But you weren't scared?"

"I was a little scared," she admitted. "Especially when it shaped itself like a *spider*."

"Ooh! I wish I'd seen that! Was Mother Luti scared?"

"Yes, I think she was pretty scared. And now, even though I won't be here after tonight, it might take Samir a little while to convince that oufe tribe to stop sending assassins to the monastery. So who knows what could happen next?"

"They might even send a spitebellows!" he said eagerly.

Chandra didn't know what that was, but she said, "*Exactly*. So while I'm away looking for the scroll, I need to know that someone is here protecting Mother Luti and the monastery. Someone I *trust*. Someone I can count on."

Brannon sighed, the weight of the world on his shoulders. "Oh, all right. I'll stay."

"Good. Thank you."

"But just this time. Next time, I'm coming, too."

"We'll see, kiddo."

"*Chandra*." The unfairness of her equivocation clearly incensed him.

"It's getting late," she said hastily. "Try to get some sleep."

"When will you be back?"

"Soon," she promised. "Goodnight."

"Here, take this." Brannon handed Chandra a small piece of flame quartz on a string. "It's for luck."

"Thanks, kiddo."

Chandra left Brannon, knowing he'd lie awake for a while thinking about the exciting things that had happened and that might happen again. She went back to her own room and began preparing to planeswalk.

Ideally, she'd rather do this outside, alone in the mountains. That was where she felt the most centered and focused, the best prepared for planeswalking. But it would be a little difficult to concentrate on entering the æther if she had to keep both eyes peeled for assassins outside the comparative safety of the monastery walls.

Even *inside* the walls, she needed to be alert, considering that goblins had invaded her room and a small bush had tried to kill her in the herb garden.

A death sentence from oufes was a nuisance, she decided.

But alone in her room, with the door closed and the table pushed in front of it to keep out intruders, she could prepare in safety and depart unseen.

Of course, in an emergency, she could planeswalk without as much preparation, but it was dangerous. Also pretty nauseating. The first time had been like that. She hadn't known what was happening, and the disorientation had been like some horrific combination of being poisoned, beaten, dropped down a well, and scalded. With no idea what was happening or where she was going, she'd thought she was dying. Indeed, she nearly *had* died. It was just luck, survival instinct, and some innate, previously unrecognized talent that had led her through the Blind Eternities to find the relative safety of another plane.

There, she learned what she really was, and had also learned how to travel more safely between the planes of the Multiverse. And, with practice, she was getting better at it.

She sat down on the floor of her dark room and began by focusing on her breathing.

In, out. Slow. Even. Relaxed. Inhale, exhale.

Each time a thought intruded, she banished it and focused again on her breathing.

Innnnnn. Outtttt.

With each cycle of her slow, rhythmic breathing, her bond grew stronger with the eternal flow of mana throughout the Multiverse and its infinite planes. Her bond to mana, that ethereal fuel for all magic, was strong on Regatha, and she would use it to carry her through, but there were other planes and other sources of mana ready for those who understood the use of the power.

Chandra felt a welcome tingle of heat begin to flow through her. She opened herself further, accepting the intense flow. She felt fire in her blood, in her bones, in her belly. She heard the roar of flames around her, and she felt their glow all through her body.

Still concentrating on maintaining a deep, relaxed breathing pattern, she sensed her physical presence on Regatha beginning to dissolve into flames as she slipped into the Blind Eternities. As she disappeared from her humble bedchamber into the hot blaze of a fiery chasm, she recognized the formless void that existed outside of time and space.

Green, blue, white, red, black. Undulating rivers of vibrant, multi-colored mana swirled around her in a dizzying whirlwind. Overhead. Underfoot. On all sides. Tumbling like waterfalls, twining like ribbons. Vibrating like the strings of a harp, filling her senses, flowing endlessly . . .

She moved as if swimming in invisible lava, pushing her way through something rich and heavy that she could neither see nor touch, but which surrounded her, engulfed her, and melded itself to her. Its fiery heat both energized and drained her, consorting with that Spark inside her, that innate quality that kept her from being devoured by the void.

She spread her hands wide, palms facing outward, and concentrated, trying to sense the energy of the planes echoing throughout the Multiverse. She had been to Kephalai once before, so this journey was easier than the other. Even though there was no path, she recognized the way. She sensed where Kephalai lay in the tumult of her surroundings, and she willed herself to journey toward it. There was no herald, no marker. She sensed the energy flowing from a particular source, and she recognized it with comforting certainty as Kephalai.

She sought entry to the plane, a way through the shifting veils in her path, coming between her and her goal. Calling on all her power, she propelled herself toward the plane like a flaming arrow, shooting herself into physical reality once more.

"*Ungh!*" Chandra grunted as she was flung physically against something very *hard*, flat, and broad. She bounced off it and fell down to an equally hard surface. She lay there limp, breathless, trying not to pass out.

All right, the journey had gone well, but the arrival was a little bumpy.

She lay facedown on the stony ground, her ribs heaving as she gasped for breath, and a chill creeping across her sweat-drenched back and arms as the cool air of Kephalai washed over her.

She opened one eye and saw that she had bounced off a stone wall. No wonder it had hurt. The building nearby and the stone paving beneath her cheek were both a cool, pale gray. She thought she smelled dead fish, an odor so rank that even the gulls she saw circling overhead might decline a free meal.

"Mummy, look!" cried a child.

"No, dear, stay away from her," said a woman's voice.

Chandra rolled over and looked up at the woman and small child who were walking past her. They were both fair-skinned, with the blonde hair and blue eyes that were common on Kephalai. The woman was holding the little boy's hand, and she had a well-bundled sleeping baby nestled in her other arm. She and the boy both wore cloaks over their clothing.

"Is it morning or afternoon?" Chandra asked, shivering a little. The cloud cover made it impossible to tell.

The woman scowled at her. "Women like *you* should stay off the streets by day and leave them safe for decent folk and innocent children!"

Chandra stared after the woman as she stomped away, dragging her little boy with her. "Some things don't change, wherever you go," she muttered.

She took a steadying breath and slowly hauled herself to her feet, wincing a little as she did so. She'd definitely have some bruises as souvenirs of her arrival on this plane. She rubbed a hand over her thigh and was glad that the claw wound there hadn't split open as a result of her crash landing. It might leave a scar, but it was still healing well.

Chandra looked around to get her bearings. She recognized the place, having been there before. Rising above the water on the other side of the harbor was the bridge where she'd had to seriously blow some things up so that she could leave Kephalai. She grinned when she saw there was still a heap of tumbled stone from the damage she'd done, including some hideous statue she'd destroyed. That hadn't been intentional, but there was no denying that Kephalai was a better looking place without it.

Chandra tensed when she heard screeching overhead. Looking into the sky, she relaxed when she saw only birds flying above. One of the nastier surprises of her previous adventure here had been the gargoyles from the Prelate's palace. Two of them had captured Chandra and carried her above the city, hauling her off to captivity. If she was going to steal the scroll again, she'd need to do something about those creatures.

Getting her bearings, Chandra turned away from the harbor and started making her way along the city's crowded flagstone streets. The first order of business, obviously, was to see if the scroll was back in the Sanctum of Stars. Then she could decide what to do next.

The Sanctum of Stars was a sort of combined museum and treasury in the heart of the city. It was a repository of such rich, diverse, and rare objects that its renown extended beyond the plane. She spotted the Sanctum easily, though she was still some distance from it. Its pale stone spire rose majestically above the domed buildings surrounding it. Chandra crossed another bridge that stretched over one of the city's many canals. While walking in the direction of her goal, she considered how to approach this situation.

She had been seen by some of the Prelate's guards when she eluded capture during her previous visit there. And for all she knew, that tricky mage who'd followed her to Regatha could be lurking under a rock somewhere near. Obviously, she should avoid being recognized by anyone who had seen her before, or to whom a description could have been circulated. The problem was how to know who that might be. Chandra's appearance was distinctive, especially on Kephalai. She was taller than most of the inhabitants of Kephalai and her red hair, golden skin, and amber-flecked eyes stood out in a society where most of the people were fair-skinned, blue-eyed, and blonde-haired.

Since the air was chilly, she decided to confiscate a hooded cloak. If she covered her hair with a hood and kept her eyes shyly downcast, she ought to be able to enter the Sanctum of Stars without arousing much suspicion. It was a much-visited place, after all—and although her height and coloring were unusual here, Chandra didn't think these features alone would attract attention.

She found the garment-makers' district by asking a passing stranger for directions. Once there, she soon found her opportunity to acquire a cloak when a couple of careless lads took a break while loading up a cart with garments. Chandra didn't want to waste a whole day earning enough local coin to *buy* a cloak by performing fire tricks in a city square. With silent apologies to the merchant from whom she was stealing, she stealthily took a cloak from the back of the cart.

As she approached the Sanctum of Stars on foot, Chandra scraped the hair away from her face, tucked it under her collar as best she could, and pulled the hood of her cloak over her head. She was glad for its warmth in the chilly air.

If there were extra security here now, it wasn't obvious from the outside. The building still looked exactly the way it had looked before. Chandra admired the round stained-glass window in the center of the pale gray spire. The sapphire-blue glass had a large, glowing, eight-pointed white star embedded in it. She looked warily at the gargoyles squatting strategically around the spire, since it seemed likely that they, too, could turn into dangerous pursuers if given the command. But at the moment, at least, they were still.

She knew from previous reconnaissance that admission to the Sanctum of Stars was open to all by day, though visitors were prohibited from bringing weapons into the building. There was no body search at the door, just a death penalty and prompt execution for anyone who violated the rule, a deterrent that had kept the Sanctum murder-free for nearly a century.

Keeping her eyes downcast, Chandra added a slight stoop to her posture and started limping a little. Overall, it was a weak disguise, but her hair was covered and she might be taken for an invalid of sorts.

She limped up to the entrance and, with her gaze on the stone steps at her feet, spoke in a bashful, age-weary voice to ask for permission to enter to the museum. The bored guard at the door granted it and let her enter. She went inside and, rather than make a beeline for the display case where she hoped to find the scroll again, she made herself meander around the exhibits for a while, pretending to admire the many exotic objects and rare artifacts in which she had no interest.

Moving slowly and maintaining the outward appearance of a bashful invalid, she gradually made her way to the big glass case where, on her last visit, four precious scrolls had been displayed. Originally, she had simply smashed the case and removed the scroll she'd wanted. She could see as she approached that the case had been replaced and that there were four scrolls inside it.

Chandra's heart thudded. *Yes.* The scroll was there! With Brother Segril's description, she could identify it easily. There was also a distinctive scorch mark on the leather casing, and a big dent in the gold end piece.

Unfortunately, she still had no idea what it contained. Given that it was rolled up, its contents firmly hidden, she could not understand why it was displayed to the public.

What was interesting about a rolled piece of paper? It could be some scribe's to-do list for all anyone knew.

Still, there was no question: she'd have to steal it a second time.

She was still gazing at it, trying to think of a plan, when two pairs of strong hands seized her from behind—one assailant for each arm—and a deep, booming voice said, "Chandra Nalaar, by the authority vested in me, I arrest you for crimes against the Prelate, the Sanctum of Stars, and the people of Kephalai!"

CHAPTER SIX

Chandra was stunned speechless. She raised her head as her two captors whirled her around with brute force; her hood fell back, and a rough hand yanked her long red hair out of her collar so that it fell freely around her shoulders.

There was a fairly good-sized crowd of visitors here. Most of them were staring in surprised fascination at Chandra, who was held firmly by two guards, one of whom had pressed the blade of his sword against her throat. She stared in bemusement at the third guard, a stocky, middle-aged man who didn't look remotely familiar. He had just *used her name* when arresting her.

How could he possibly know . . .

Oh, no.

The planeswalker who had come to Regatha! He had known her name, too. Had she really thought he'd have just returned the scroll and left again?

She looked quickly around the Sanctum, but she didn't see the planeswalker. She froze in appalled surprise, though, when she *did* see . . .

"Telepaths?" she guessed.

There were two of them. Both women. They emerged

from their concealment walking arm in arm. Their bald heads reflected the lights of the Sanctum as their hairless brows cast shadows over unnaturally bright eyes. She saw that their skin was eerily white, and they wore identical pale blue robes with an unfamiliar dark blue symbol embroidered on the left shoulder. They stared hard at Chandra.

She nodded, answering her own question. "Telepaths."

Chandra realized that her physical disguise had been pointless. These two had probably been reading everyone who entered the building!

Fine, read this: drop dead you creepy, bald hags!

The two women blinked in unison.

Well, this was just *great*. The intruder had returned the scroll to the Sanctum of Stars, told them her name, and told them she might be back. They had obviously prepared for this. She had just as obviously walked into a trap.

That fact became even clearer as about two dozen soldiers now poured into the hall, moving with swift, well-rehearsed efficiency.

Damn, damn, damn.

Eight of the soldiers took charge of organizing the departure of the gawking visitors. The rest of them surrounded Chandra, weapons drawn. In addition to swordsmen, there were six archers among them who drew their bows and pointed their arrows directly at her.

"Now, now, let's all stay calm," she said. "I'm sure we can discuss our differences like reasonable adults."

One of the mind mages warned the guards, "She intends to fight."

Chandra scowled and tried to block their probing. She knew she was stronger, if she could concentrate. But for Chandra it was actually the opposite. Her mind was racing with possibility. Thoughts were moving in her head with such imprecision, that *she* barely knew she was thinking. She did know, however, that this whole situation was making her very mad.

They sensed it, or rather they sensed that Chandra's fuse was short. The telepath who had spoken before told the head guard, "We can't read her. She's too erratic."

The other one said, "Keep hold of her."

The head guard said impatiently to one of his men, "Where are the Enervants? They're supposed to be here!"

"Enervants?" Chandra said. "That's some nerve showing up late for the party." This was no time for jokes, but she couldn't help it.

"The Prelate told me you'd be back," the head guard said. "I said no one was that reckless, but she said that *you* might be.

So the Prelate of Kephalai had indeed enlisted the planeswalker to retrieve the scroll from Regatha. And he'd reported to the Prelate.

"All right, so I've come back," Chandra said, assessing the situation. "Now what?"

"Now I turn you over the Enervants."

"Sounds like fun."

"Actually," the guard said, "I don't think you'll like them. They are particularly suited to breaking the will of even the most headstrong. It is said they enjoy torturing their subjects in the way most would enjoy a fine meal. They savor it. They take time over the courses, but are not so gluttonous that they don't leave a helping for the rats. I should imagine they will have a particularly good time with you."

There were more than twenty armed guards, a closed space, no visible exits, a scroll to liberate, a couple of mind mages who might have other tricks up their floppy blue sleeves . . . And whoever the Enervants were, they didn't sound like a crowd Chandra really wanted to meet.

"You're right," she said. "The Enervants are late. I don't like anyone who isn't punctual."

She was worried about the fragility of the scroll. She hadn't come all the way to Kephalai to destroy it by accident. However, like it or not, she only saw one viable option now.

"Have you ever heard of Jaya Ballard? No? No, of course not. My teacher's always quoting her, and I get a little tired of it. But I have to admit, once in a while, there's some good advice there."

She made her decision. Fire, scroll, fire.

"For example," Chandra said, feeling heat pour through her. "Jaya said, 'when in doubt . . .'" Fire licked her veins, her skin, her fingertips. "'Use the biggest boom you know.'"

The sound of steel being drawn from scabbards was decisive. The guards were poised for attack, arrows were knocked and drawn, but they hesitated as a small ball of white-hot flame emanated from Chandra's core. It didn't seem like much to them.

Chandra, meanwhile, concentrated on the on the ball as best as she could. As magical energy flowed into her, the ball expanded rapidly to the size of a human head and Chandra sagged a bit, as if the spell had failed. The ball remained where it was, quivering impotently like a mass of gelatin.

"That's not much of a boom," said one of the guards and the tension drained from the room, as many lowered their weapons laughing.

As they did so, Chandra sharpened her focus and the ball collapsed into an infinitesimal point before exploding with such force that it knocked everyone in the room off their feet. Arrows were incinerated, clothing set afire, and the swords of the guards were suddenly searing the flesh of their palms. Luckily the telepaths had no hair to burn, but the stench from the others in the room was more than Chandra had bargained for.

Immune to the blast herself, Chandra turned to smash the glass case but saw that her blast had already done so. She reached inside and grabbed the scroll, which seemed unharmed.

She heard screams all around her. People in panic, burning. People in pain.

"Kill her! *Kill* her!" someone shouted hoarsely.

Calling on all of her power, on everything she had left, Chandra formed another ball of fire in her free hand and cast it at the wall. The fiery explosion blew out an entire wall of the Sanctum. She squinted against the flying dust and debris, coughing as she inhaled. She ran through the burning chaos and out of the building. Four guards who had survived the explosions were hot on her heels, shouting, "*Stop that woman!*"

People in the crowded streets were screaming, too terrified by the explosion to pay any attention to one fleeing woman and the bloody, dirty soldiers running after her.

The Sanctum's structure was more precarious than it looked. Without that wall supporting its fourth side, the building began to cave in on itself.

Chandra heard the tremendous crack of splintering stone and the crash of collapsing walls and floors. Despite the soldiers right behind her, she turned to look. What she saw was so startling, she stopped running and just stood there and stared in shock at her handiwork. So did the soldiers who, moments ago, had been so intent on killing her.

The tall spire of the Sanctum, high overhead, had started to sway. The gargoyles that squatted around it reacted slowly, their wings shuddering uncertainly as they unfolded from their hunched positions and prepared to take flight. Inside the building, all the soldiers and both mind mages were probably already dead; if not, then they would die within moments.

The massive spire toppled and fell. The Sanctum of Stars completely collapsed. It seemed to happen with a horrific slowness. The immense weight of cracking, falling stone created a terrifying roar. People in the streets were screaming in panic and fleeing to safety. Chandra turned and fled, too.

The enormous impact of the Sanctum collapsing on itself hurled rocks, flames, ashes, dust, and debris across the main square and down the length of every surrounding street. Chandra was knocked off her feet when the ground shook and a wave of rock and ash hurled her forward. Someone trampled her prone body as they ran headlong from the disaster. Winded and in pain, Chandra was lying face down in the street, debris still showering down on her as the dust of pulverized stone filled her lungs.

Coughing and bleeding, she lay there in a daze.

Fire above, the whole thing! The whole building! I didn't mean to do that.

The screams of children filled her ears. She heard a woman wailing. A horse was whinnying in terror.

She had just wanted to escape alive with the scroll.

Dead soldiers? Sure. Dead telepaths? Fair game.

But she hadn't meant to destroy a whole section of the city, terrorizing all of its citizens and perhaps killing innocents.

Pull yourself together. Come on! Get up. Get out of here—or you'll be joining the dead.

Coughing and shaking, she rose to her feet. The scroll was still in her hand. She looked down at it, trying to think.

She couldn't planeswalk. Not under these circumstances.

And not with her strength so depleted. She didn't have anything left right now. She needed to regroup and get a handle on things.

Still coughing, she staggered down the street, away from the Sanctum, going in the same direction as the fleeing crowd. By the time she felt she really needed to sit down, she was well beyond the dust, debris, and milling panic. Many people were filling the market street where she stopped to rest. News of the disaster, as well as varied explanations for it, circulated quickly.

Someone who saw her sitting in a dazed slump on the street kindly offered her food and water. Chandra realized she was shaking with fatigue, and accepted gratefully. She hadn't really thought she was hungry, but once she started eating, she discovered she was ravenous. She consumed the food as greedily as a growing boy who hadn't eaten in two days. She was thirsty, too, after all the dust that had coated her throat when the Sanctum collapsed. She drank her fill, then poured water over her head, neck, and hands, washing away blood, dust, and filth.

Only then did she look skyward and realize that the hunt was already on for her.

She saw gargoyles flying overhead, their big wings spread wide and their spindly legs trailing behind their pudgy bodies as they patrolled the sky. She could see two of them directly above. Just as one would expect from creatures made of stone, they were remarkably thorough and methodical in their work. The two of them moved back and forth across the sky in an even, intersecting pattern, switching each other's route to double-check a section of ground with another implacable set of eyes.

Chandra moved slowly, so as not to attract their attention as she scooted beneath a street merchant's canopy to shield herself from their view.

She wondered just how well those gargoyles could see; if they could spot her red hair from overhead. She needed to cover it up again even if they did they have some other means of detecting her. How many of them were hovering over the city? She was too weak right now to deal with them if they plucked her off the street.

Within moments, she noticed something even more alarming. The woman who had given her food a little while ago was now pointing her out to a man. Or, rather, pointing to the spot where Chandra had been sitting a moment ago. The woman was frowning in perplexity as she scanned the street, looking for where she might have gone.

"She was *just* there, so she can't have gone far," is what Chandra guessed the woman said to the man as she searched the street with her eyes.

He wasn't wearing the uniform of a Sanctum guard, or of the Prelate's soldiers, but he looked far from innocuous.

He was older than Chandra, but he was still young, late twenties, maybe thirty. He was taller than average, but only by a little. He had fair skin, blue eyes, and black hair. When he turned his head, she saw that his hair was long and wavy, and tied neatly at the back of his neck. He was dressed simply—tan pants and top, with scuffed leather boots and a well-worn dark leather vest. There was a small coin purse attached to his belt, along with something else that looked like a tool or a weapon. It was shiny, like metal, and coiled like rope—or a like a whip.

He looked lithe, agile, and fit. More than that, he looked as alert as a wild animal scenting prey. His movements were economical—even something as simple as the turn of his head, when his gaze sought her out under the merchant's canopy. He didn't waste motion or squander energy.

And his face didn't give away any reaction when he saw her.

He nodded politely to the other woman without taking his gaze off Chandra, as if aware she'd use the slightest opportunity to bolt. His eyes held hers as he approached her. He didn't hurry, but his walk was direct and purposeful.

She rose to feet, her heart racing as she tried to summon the power to defend herself. But she was still too weak right now. She hadn't paced herself or conserved any strength. Back there in the Sanctum of Stars, she had thought only about living through her confrontation. She hadn't thought about what she would do afterwards.

Several oft-repeated lectures of Mother Luti's floated briefly through her mind. She needed to pace herself, control her power, and manage her emotions with more discipline. She needed to learn the limits of her strength and ration it intelligently in her magic.

And not just the limits. She needed to learn the extent of her power, too, and how to master it. She thought of the collapsing Sanctum and the chaos in the streets of Kephalai, and she felt the weight of that deed.

Chandra's gaze remained locked with that of the approaching stranger. She couldn't enter the æther and escape him that way. She couldn't call forth fire and fight him. She felt naked as he stopped and stood before her.

His gaze released hers as he took in her appearance, looking her over from head to toe. It wasn't insolent, insulting, or sympathetic. He simply seemed to acknowledge her bedraggled condition and the event that had caused it.

Then he said, "Chandra Nalaar." It wasn't a question.

She shifted her weight. Since he was obviously looking for her, she wasn't really surprised that he knew her name. It seemed everyone did these days. But it made her uneasy, even so.

She asked, "Who are you?"

"My name is Gideon."

"And what's that to me?"

"I think we should get you out of here."

"What?" she said.

He glanced around. Just a slight turn of his chin, a quick flicker of his eyes to encompass the street scene and the gargoyle guardians overhead. "This situation is volatile. We should leave."

"Who are you?"

"We have very little time."

"Then answer my question quickly," she snapped.

"What happened back there," he said quietly, tilting his head to indicate the disaster at the Sanctum of Stars. "That was you."

She didn't respond.

He prodded, "Wasn't it?" When she remained unresponsive, he said, "Of course it was. Who else *could* have done it?"

"You'd better back up and tell me how you even know who I am." She was starting to think he wasn't working for the Prelate, or the ruined Sanctum.

"You've been making yourself conspicuous," he said.

"Maybe so. But *you* haven't. So I suggest you start explaining."

"What was it?" He lowered his voice so they wouldn't be overheard, but some emotion showed now. Tension? Disdain? She wasn't sure. "A explosion of that size? Inside the Sanctum?" She didn't deny it, and he whispered, "What were you *thinking*?"

She admitted wearily, "I was just thinking about surviving."

His gaze dropped to the scroll clutched in her hand. "And also about stealing?"

"All right, fine, so I'm a bad person," she said. "I had a troubled youth."

"You're *still* having a troubled youth."

"All the more reason to stay away from me, Gideon." She turned to go.

His grip on her arm stopped her. "Hunting you down has been troublesome. I don't intend to go through it twice."

She stared at him. "Why have you been hunting me down?"

He looked past her and, though he didn't move, she sensed his tension increase sharply. "Never mind that now. I think we both know why *they're* hunting you down."

She turned to follow his gaze and saw half a dozen soldiers heading this way. She turned to escape in the other direction, only to see soldiers approaching from there, too.

"Are you their scout?" she demanded.

"No, *I* was hoping to avoid this." He looked up at the gruesome sky patrol. "And I think you may have been spotted from above, as well."

"Now what?"

"They're going to take you into custody." He added, "I hope you have a high threshold for pain."

Adrenaline surged through her, and she felt herself getting her second wind. "I think I can fight."

"No!"

"Will you help?"

"*No.*"

"Then get out of the way!"

Chandra felt stronger. She was thinking about survival again, and fear had a wonderfully energizing effect.

As the soldiers approached her from both sides in the crowded street, she felt heat start to flow through her, welcome and inspiring. She felt the fire moving through her blood once more.

Gideon moved swiftly. He grabbed the thing hanging from his belt—that coil of metal. It unfurled in his hand, glowing so brightly that Chandra was distracted. He swung his arm, and then the thing was twining around her.

"No!" she said, shocked and caught off guard. "Stop!"

It had broad, flexible blades and sharp edges, and it was cold . . . so *cold*. It tightened around her, constricting her, stifling her breath. And its terrible cold trapped her fire, contained her heat, smothered her rage . . . As she struggled for air and shivered with cold, the weapon robbed her of consciousness.

But just before everything went black, she thought she heard him say, "I'm sorry."

CHAPTER SEVEN

When Chandra opened her eyes, she found herself staring into the beady eyes of a black snake.

Its tongue flicked out at her.

She flinched and tried to move back, but couldn't.

Her back was flat against a wall, her limbs uncomfortably chained in a spread-eagle position. Bound by her wrists and ankles, her movement was almost totally restricted.

As the snake's big face moved even closer, Chandra turned her head and made a stifled sound of protest. She really didn't like snakes.

"Ah." Someone spoke in a low, breathy voice. "It'sss awake."

She gaped at the snake. "Excuse me?" Her voice was a dry croak.

But the snake said nothing more for the moment.

Chandra blinked and tried to focus her vision. That was when she realized the "snake" was standing upright on a set of legs and wearing a black robe with a hood.

"Oh." She groaned as the realization penetrated her confusion. "You must be one of the Enervants I've heard so much about?"

"Yesss."

Her mistake was understandable. It was standing so close to her that its head almost entirely filled her field of vision. And from the neck up, this thing looked exactly like a snake. A *big* one.

She looked down and saw that it had hands; hands that were thin, almost delicate, and scaly black with long wrinkled fingernails. Strangely a snake with hands made sense to Chandra at this point. *Actual* snakes were pretty limited in their activities, after all; and none, so far as she knew, spoke or practiced magic.

Chandra wasn't sure what to make of these creatures, but she was sure they wouldn't like the inferno she was going to bring. But as she struggled against her bonds, she realized that she could barely move. And it wasn't because the chains were that tight. She felt absolutely exhausted, as if she hadn't eaten or slept for days.

Blinking a few times to clear her foggy vision, she looked at her surroundings. She was clearly being held in a dungeon. Stone walls, floor, and ceiling. No windows. No torches, either. No candles, no fire, no flames of any kind.

The only illumination in the room came from slimy-looking phosphorescent things clinging to the walls here and there. Chandra guessed that the snakelike sorcerers had brought them here from whatever swamp they called home.

With such faint light and no windows, the room was dark, stuffy, and dank. And it stank.

The odor of damp decay, she suspected, was coming from her companions. There were seven Enervants in the room with her. One was still peering into her face; its tongue flicked in and out every few moments, as if testing Chandra's scent. The other six, who all looked just like the first one, were gliding silently around the room in a figure eight. Their bodies were evenly spaced as they followed the pattern at a steady pace. Their paths steadily intersected without ever bumping into each other or pausing in their flow.

Chandra found it eerie. "What are they doing?"

She coughed a little as she spoke. Her throat was dry and she was dying of thirst. But she'd be damned if she'd ask for anything.

To her surprise, her captor answered her. "Gathering ssstrength."

"Oh. Can't they do that elsewhere?"

The Enervant didn't answer. It just kept staring at her.

She tried another question. "Where am I? The Prelate's dungeon?"

The snake nodded, its head moving on its muscular neck in a slow, sinewy motion.

She tried to think of what else she wanted to ask, but she was so tired. It was hard to pull her thoughts together or make the effort to speak.

Chandra tried to remember what had happened to put her in this position.

She remembered the man, Gideon, and his weapon. She had never seen anything like it, but she was reasonably certain that he had used some form white-mana based magic to subdue her. Even in her weakened state, the weapon alone could not have pulled her into unconsciousness like that.

As if the Order back on Regatha weren't burden enough, she was in a dungeon on Kephalai because of some interfering heiromancer? But why would he be in league with these creatures? It didn't seem right.

Chandra remembered the feel of those coldly glowing white blades wrapping around her, constricting her, and trapping the flow of her fire. Imprisoning her power within her, so that she couldn't fight or defend herself. Or even breathe . . .

It surprised her that this Gideon wielded magic. She hadn't taken him for a mage. He looked like a warrior to her. Or maybe a tracker of some kind; one with special skills for an unusual quarry.

Chandra frowned, puzzled.

In that case, where was he now? Had he given her over, or had he abandoned his prey to superior forces?

Admittedly, Chandra hadn't been at her best just then, but Gideon's strength was impressive. Given that he was powerful, as well as quick with his hands, surely he didn't have to back down in the face of a few soldiers?

Perhaps he had decided he couldn't take on the soldiers *and* the gargoyles at the same time.

As Chandra watched the Enervants silently gliding through their pattern over and over in the dark dungeon, she realized that if Gideon had been ordered to kill her, then letting the Prelate's men have her might accomplish his goal.

But she wasn't sure he would leave such a thing to chance.

Chandra tugged against her chains, testing their strength as well as her own, and started thinking about how to get out of there.

She reached out with her senses, hoping to tap into the flow of mana. Even though she could feel its presence, she was having trouble concentrating enough to establish a solid bond.

What was *wrong* with her?

The Enervant who was guarding her suddenly hissed and turned its head away from her, which was something of a relief. She didn't enjoy being the object of its unwavering, beady-eyed stare. Its attention was focused on the narrow metal door across the room. Chandra looked that way, too, wondering what had drawn its interest.

A moment later, the hinges whined a little as the door opened.

"Oh, goody," Chandra said. "Visitors."

Two of the Prelate's soldiers entered, accompanied by another who she assumed was a telepath. Based on her physical appearance, Chandra assumed the woman belonged to the same order as the two mages who had died in the Sanctum of Stars earlier that day. Or had it been the day before? Come to think of it, Chandra had no idea how long she had been chained unconscious in this room, although the stiffness in her limbs suggested it had been a while.

The Enervants didn't look up at the newcomers, didn't even pause in their perambulations. They just kept moving back and forth silently, tracing their figure eight on the floor, over and over and over.

"Just watching them makes me tired," Chandra said as the mage, moving around the snake-headed wizards, approached her.

"No," said the woman. "It is not the watching. It is what you are watching."

"That is not a very encouraging start to this conversation," Chandra muttered.

"We are not here to encourage. Quite the opposite, really."

Chandra eyed her.

"They are Enervants." The mage nodded toward the six individuals moving steadily in their pattern. "This is their work."

"Yes, I've been told. They're gathering sssstrength," said Chandra imitating her captor. "I don't see why they have to gather it *here*, though."

The woman nodded. "They are gathering *your* strength."

"I thought they were having a little snake dance in my honor." Chandra scowled.

But Chandra understood. This was dark magic. These strange creatures were sapping her strength. She could feel the direct assault on her energy now that she knew about it.

And they were effective. Considering how exhausted she felt, she suspected they could quickly turn an ordinary mage into a useless husk.

Chandra glared at the telepath. "Your friends tried to read me, and they died for their efforts. Quit while you're ahead."

"I can be patient," the woman said coldly. "You may still be strong enough to resist now. You may even be strong enough to resist on my next visit. But you're much weaker now than you were yesterday, and tomorrow you will be weaker still. And when you are weak enough, we will succeed. You will not be able to conceal it from me then. I *will* find out what you did with the scroll."

"The scroll? That's what you want? I don't . . ." Cold surprise washed through Chandra.

The scroll.

"I don't know where it is," Chandra said, baffled by how they couldn't know this.

"You seem convinced of that, yes. But there are many corners in the mind, many places for things to hide," said the telepath, her clear blue eyes radiating in the dark of the room. "You didn't succeed in killing everyone who was in the Sanctum of Stars, you know. Four soldiers survived. They saw you flee into the city streets with the scroll."

"Uh-huh." She wouldn't let herself think about what had happened. Truth be told, she was too tired to think about it, anyway.

"If you want the scroll back," Chandra said, "why not talk to the man who got it back last time?"

"The Prelate says he's gone." It was obvious the woman was only answering because she was curious to see what Chandra's reaction would be.

"Gone where?"

"I do not question the Prelate."

"No, *of course* not," said Chandra, using the same tone of voice the telepath had used moments before.

"Where is the scroll?" the mage demanded, realizing she was being mocked.

"Why does it matter so much to you?"

"You risked death *twice* to acquire it. Why does it matter so much to *you*?"

"If I tell you where the scroll is," Chandra said, "what then?"

"You destroyed the Sanctum of Stars, a holy place filled with Kephalai's most precious artifacts. You killed soldiers, guards, and mages dedicated to its protection. You damaged more than property. You damaged the will of the people of Kephalai. You created a city-wide panic. The death toll has not yet been measured." The mage's gaze was hostile. "But if you cooperate now and tell us where the scroll is, your sentence will be lenient."

"*How* lenient?"

"You will be executed. Quickly and humanely. Otherwise, we will leave you to the Enervants, and they are not know for their humanity."

"Well," Chandra said. "It's always nice to have choices."

"If you do not cooperate," the mage said, "if you force me to wait until you are weak enough for me to probe your mind for the answers we seek, then you will no longer have a choice. We will learn all that we want to know. I, personally, hope you decide to help us find the scroll. The Enervants' ways are are repellant to me. No one deserves what they have in store for you."

"*All* that you want to know?" Chandra said. "What answers are you looking for, besides the location of the scroll?"

"For starters, who are you, and what did you plan to do with the scroll?"

"I don't really like to talk about myself," Chandra said.

"Where were you born? Who are your people?"

"And I especially don't talk about my past."

The mage looked at her for a moment longer, then said, "It doesn't matter. Soon, I will know all that I want to know."

"You won't find out where the scroll is," Chandra said truthfully.

"Yes, I will. But, in any event, you have made your choice. I will inform the Prelate: death by slow torture."

"I look forward to it."

"I'm sure you do," she looked at Chandra with what seemed to be pitty. "These guards will remain outside the door should you decide to give us the answers we seek."

"How will they know when to come in?"

"This one is Dirk," she said indicating one of the guards. "Call his name, and he will come."

Only after the mage left the dungeon did Chandra risk dwelling on what the woman had told her.

They don't know where the scroll is.

It had been in Chandra's hand when she lost consciousness in the city streets, and she had woken up in captivity. She had assumed her captors had reclaimed possession of the scroll.

There was obviously more to Gideon than she thought. She'd seen for herself that he was fast, that he moved quickly. So he must have had time to conceal the scroll from the soldiers after incapacitating her.

Things were in chaos at the time, after all. Perhaps Gideon had claimed, when turning her unconscious carcass over to them, that she didn't have the scroll on her, and had planted the notion that she had hidden it somewhere.

Was that why he had let them capture her? So he could make off with the scroll?

I will *kill* him for this.

The rage felt good. It woke her up, cleared her head, and refreshed her senses.

She focused on her anger, on the fury in her heart at being duped by that man. She berated herself for the way he had taken her by surprise and overpowered her. She imagined him enjoying himself somewhere now, with her scroll, having a good laugh over her predicament.

Because of *him*, she was chained to a wall in a dungeon and being drained of energy by these snakes! *Get mad, this is good. Anger is accelerant. Rage is fuel. Fury is fire.*

She had to escape. Death by slow torture was no way for a planeswalker to die. More to the point, she couldn't hunt him, she couldn't get revenge on Gideon, if she died here.

A big boom would go a long way toward solving her current problem. But even with the reassuring glow of rage coursing through her now, she knew there was no way she could summon that kind of power. Not until she recovered from the sapping sorcery of the Enervants. And she'd only start recovering once she got away from them.

She had to act now. Immediately. The longer she was in their custody, the weaker she would get.

Chandra closed her eyes and focused on her breathing, concentrating, centering herself on the rage. She embraced the anger, nurtured the hot thirst for retribution. With each steady inhalation, she felt her tenuous mana bond become a little stronger, a little more within her reach. With each inhalation, she felt power coil firmly within her.

She targeted her attention on the seventh Enervant. He had moved to the side of the room where he was reaching into a box. From it he pulled what seemed to be a black, wriggling string. It was about a foot long and thin. He held it out with one hand and came close enough that Chandra could see that it was actually a snake.

"What are you going to do with that?" she asked.

The Enervant's eyes seemed to glitter in response.

"It's going to take more than that to crack me." Chandra was trying to put up a brave front, but, truthfully the snake was terrifying. Suspended by its tail, it moved purposefully, as though it was slithering toward the ground, its sharp head intent on reaching a target. The Enervant held the snake higher and pinched it again beneath his other hand. He slowly drew his hand down the snake, stretching it taut. When he got to the head and let go, it remained as straight and stiff as a splinter of wood.

The black wizard held it out again, showing Chandra what he had done, perhaps taunting her with it, the dim phosphorescent light reflecting sickly in his eyes.

"Now we begin," he said with obvious pleasure.

Chandra steeled herself, not knowing what to expect. The Enervant went to her right hand and inspected it for a moment, his tongue flickering gently from his mouth. Chandra balled up a fist in response, but in retrospect it was the wrong thing to do. The creature leveled the straightened snake at her knuckles, placed its head directly between her index and forefinger, and pushed. The thing's head cut into her flesh easily, burning with a pain more intense than anything she had ever known.

Chandra screamed as the entire snake went into her hand,

its form bulging beneath her skin as it began to slither up her arm. The pain was like nothing she had ever known.

"DIRK!" she screamed as loudly as she could. "Get in here now!"

Without any further promting, the two guards entered the room. "Get this thing out of my arm," she cried. "I'll tell you anything you want to know."

The guard called Dirk gave the command to the Enervant to do as she said. He produced a knife and made a small inciscion just above the snake's head, which emerged without prompting. The Enervant took hold of it with his withered nails and pulled it out, spilling blood and interstitial fluid heedlessly. Both guards' faces went ashen. Chandra was sure the one behind Dirk was on the verge of fainting. For her own part, the only thing that kept Chandra conscious was a fury as pure the heart of the volcano. But she knew she could not let this show. Instead she let her head drop as though she'd fainted.

The guard called Dirk collected himself. "Well, out with it, then. Where's the scroll?" When Chandra didn't answer he nudged her, but she still gave no response. "Get some water," he told the other.

Dirk unshackled her right wrist and let her wounded arm hang. Although it was throbbing, Chandra didn't feel like there was lasting damage. She remained motionless with her head hanging until the guard came back with a pail and ladle. At that, Chandra raised her head weakly and looked at the guard. He held the full ladle out to her and she cupped the bowl in her hand, bending her head over it as though to drink, her hair falling around it to obscure the ladle from view.

Chandra focused her rage on the water and called on her power to heat it. Within seconds, the small amount of water had come to a boil, and she threw it into the guard's face, blinding him and scalding his flesh. He stumbled back into the Enervant, who dropped his knife and fell back, disrupting the path of the other enervants. The effect was immediate. Chandra could feel her strength returning, her power blossoming like a flower at the base of her skull and racing out to her extremities.

When the fire came to her like this, it was as if time slowed for Chandra. Everything around her moved in slow motion, while she was able to think and move freely. Even as the others in the room were still trying to make sense of what was happening, Chandra grabbed the knife on the ground with her free hand and used it to pry the shackles on her left arm loose. Before the Enervant knew what was happening, she had released herself and was on top of it, driving the knife into his neck in the soft spot beneath its jaw. The snakeman went slack like a bag of grain.

She turned to deal with the other soldier, but he was was on his knees like a penitent, pleading for his life. Chandra ignored him and shifted her attention to the remaining six Enervants.

They were hissing noisily, their heads weaving and bobbing on necks that were much longer than they had originally seemed. They were moving to surround her, but Chandra noticed they were regulating their spacing and their movements were synchronizing again. She sensed they were trying to begin another ritual to drain her of her power. She had to act fast.

Chandra realized she was sweating and panting. The brief use of her power had already tired her far more than it should have, thanks to the Enervants' work. Searching for one act that would affect six adversaries, Chandra called on her remaining power to produce a sheet of fire between herself and the hissing snakes. As she had hoped, it halted their advance toward her.

However, they were still between her and the door. Not only could they prevent her escape, they could also leave the room and summon help. Fortunately, they were wholly focused on her, and they were obviously unwilling to pass through her fire. She needed to move quickly, though, before they were able to act in concert again to sap her strength.

Fighting exhaustion and struggling hard to call forth more power in her weakened condition, Chandra spread her arms, then uttered a short spell that Mother Luti had taught her. She simultaneously clapped her hands together as she stared hard at the six wizards, keeping them all in focus. Her sheet of fire sprang around them like a trap, coiling to encircle them.

Their menacing hissing grew panicky as the fire closed in on them. Chandra clasped her hands together and squeezed hard, commanding her flames to embrace and consume her enemies. As the giant hooded snakes and their robes caught fire, their bodies writhed frantically. They clawed at each other, and their gaping jaws opened wide in agony, exposing their terrible fangs. The stench was unbelievable, and Chandra found it somehow disturbing that they didn't scream or make any noise beside that tortured hissing.

The burned soldier was still howling in pain, and the cowed one wept, openly terrified. The Enervants were still alive, but writhing in their death throes as the flames consumed them.

With her captors all but vanquished, Chandra fled past her fatal fire and out the door of her cell. Fortunately, the soldiers had left it unlocked when they entered.

Beyond the door was a narrow corridor that led in two directions. She looked to her right and could see a dead end. She had no choice but to go left. When she reached a corner, she was spotted by two soldiers standing guard in the intersecting hallway.

"Prisoner escaped!" one of them cried.

She ran straight into them, hurtling her full body weight at them before they could unsheathe their swords. Her best chance of staying alive now was to planeswalk out of Kephalai, and she needed to conserve what was left of her power if she was to enter the æther. She knocked one of them against the wall as hard as she could, and stomped on the other's stomach when he fell. Hoping that would at least slow them down, she ran onward.

She saw a stone staircase at the end of the corridor where four more guards waited.

Behind her, the soldiers she had just knocked down were shouting, "Prisoner escaping! Prisoner escaping!"

The soldiers she was approaching clearly heard. One of them, at the top of the stairs, shouted this same phrase through the bars of the door up there and called for help.

Another of the soldiers guarding the stairs saw her and warned her in a loud voice, "Within moments, thirty soldiers will come through that door! Surrender *now*!"

He was wrong. It didn't take moments. He had barely finished speaking when the door opened and armed soldiers began pouring through it.

And, if anything, he had underestimated their number.

Chandra turned around and ran back the way she had just come.

CHAPTER EIGHT

Fortunately, the two soldiers she had just knocked down hadn't expected her to turn back and trample them again. This time their feeble interference barely slowed her down as she dashed past.

Chandra knew she couldn't deal with all those reinforcements. As Gideon so obviously had understated, she had made herself conspicuous. She had to assume this was just the first wave. Now that the alarm had been sounded, the Prelate's entire army would be devoted to keeping her a prisoner or dispatching her. And in her current condition, they would succeed—not immediately and not without pain, but they would succeed.

She didn't have time to search for another way out of the prison. There might well not be one. And even if there were another way out, she had no chance of evading dozens of soldiers while she looked for it.

Her only remaining choice wasn't a good one, but at least there was a chance she would survive.

She turned a corner and ran back to the large cell where she had been held captive. Behind her, she could hear the footsteps, rattling swords, and shouts of a lot of soldiers.

In front of her, blocking the door to the cell, were the the two original guards, the coward supporting Dirk. When the coward saw her, a new look of horror washed across his puffy, sweating face.

"Out of my way!" Chandra snapped as she moved forward. They might have fully obliged had she not reached them before the two could move, shoving them to the floor outside the door.

Once inside she slammed the door shut. No lock on this side. Of course not. Dungeons were built to lock prisoners in, not to lock soldiers out.

A fetid cloud of smoke hung in the cell. The Enervants were dead, but their smoldering remains filled the room with an odor so foul Chandra could scarcely bear to breathe.

Coughing as the smoke and stench assaulted her, Chandra pressed her back against the door and heard heavy footsteps approaching. She had only moments now. A short controlled burst of fire welded the door to its jam. It wouldn't hold for long, but it would have to do.

She concentrated with all her might as she forged a path to the æther. The soldiers were pounding on the door, but Chandra was able to reach the meditative state she needed. *Breathe steadily and regularly.* At her first glimpse of the void, she hurled herself recklessly into it.

Behind her, on Kephalai, two guards—one an emotional wreck, the other gruesomely burned—would insist they had seen her enter the chamber. Their account would be dismissed as attempt to cover up incompetence when she wasn't found inside the cell. Nevertheless, there would be a thorough search of the whole prison, and that would take time. In the end, they'd never know how she had disappeared. And when the Prelate received the report of Chandra's escape, she'd only be able to guess what had happened. In any case, without the mage who had followed Chandra back to Regatha last time, they'd never find her. She was out of their reach the moment she entered the æther.

Which wasn't the same thing as being *safe*.

Chandra fell through a tunnel of flame. And, having had no time to prepare herself for planeswalking, she was unprotected from the raw, red, furious force of this fire. It scalded her so brutally that she cried out in agony, feeling it burn through her flesh, her blood, her bones, and sink into her soul with angry, destructive heat.

Disoriented and in pain, she kept plummeting through the endless reaches of the void between the planes of the Multiverse. Her whole body felt consumed by fire and torn apart by her relentless fall. She had entered the Blind Eternities in sudden desperation, without sufficient power or focus, and now she was paying the price for such a rash act.

She had only entered the æther without preparation once before—the very first time she walked—and it had come close to killing her. Then, as now, she was fleeing death. But now, at least, she knew what was happening. This time, she didn't feel the blind, animal terror she had felt then. This time, she struggled to take charge of her planeswalk, rather than simply succumbing in helpless fear to its effects.

Chandra tried to focus on her breathing, her heartbeat, her body's rhythms . . . but the air in her lungs felt like boiling water, fire scorched her belly, and ice filled her veins. She tried to concentrate on her mana bonds to maintain her power, but the Blind Eternities flowed around her with the brilliance of a billion suns, blinding and stunning her, while at the same time soaking her in dark fatigue. She tried to reach out and sense the energy of different planes, to seek out a physical reality where she could anchor herself, but everything around her tumbled in a multicolored chaos.

The channel through which Chandra plunged became fearfully black, an entropic void sucking at her life force. Just as she thought she would lose consciousness, fire became water, cold and viscous. Chandra panicked as a drowning sensation enveloped her before everything became white, binding and smothering, and surrounded her like an unbearable weight. A shift to green created pain she didn't understand, as if her bones were trying to push through her skin. And when fire engulfed her again, she welcomed the familiar agony.

When the pain became so familiar that it ceased to register, Chandra was so disoriented and exhausted, she couldn't move or think or react. She floated erratically in the whirling mana storm that surrounded her, dazed and inert for what seemed a very long time. Consciousness had become a relative state: it was becoming harder for her to separate herself from her surroundings. She told herself many times to gather her senses and find a way out of here before she died, yet she remained still, unable to move, as if her mind had become disconnected from her body. She had to focus on something tangible.

Kephalai . . .

Memory penetrated the haze of chaos. Chains on her hands and feet. Combat with other beings. Running. Panting.

She focused on these memories, coaxing them into vivid life in her scattered, confused mind.

Kephalai . . . *Sanctum of Stars* . . .

Knowledge of her physical reality, of her life on the planes of the Multiverse, started returning to her. And with this knowledge came the fervent, forceful desire to rejoin the dimensions of physical existence. To overcome

her gradual absorption into the æther. To escape the Blind
Eternities and find a plane on which to reclaim her power,
her physical life, and her mental coherence.

She concentrated on the most vivid of the memories
that were dancing around the edge of her consciousness.
Memories of fear, anger, pain, urgency. She didn't remember the details now, but she vaguely knew she had lost the
scroll, had failed to achieve her goal. This infuriated her,
and she welcomed the rage, letting it warm her blood and
sharpen her senses.

But she still wasn't strong enough. She instinctively recognized that she needed even more visceral connection to
her physical life. So, with foreboding, she opened herself
to the old memories, to her past, to the sensations she had
banished to the realm of nightmare, to the events she never
thought about, recalled, or acknowledged.

She opened herself to the fire of sorrow and grief, of
shame and regret, to that which consumes innocence.

In the echoing corridors of her memory, she listened to
their screams, hearing their agonized cries now as clearly
as if it were happening all over again. In her mind's tormented eye, she watched their writhing bodies now, just as
she had watched them then. Helpless. Horrified. Consumed
by guilt. She forced herself to dwell on the memory of what
their burning flesh had smelled like. She felt the pain of the
sobs that wouldn't come out of her mouth.

And when the blade of a sword swept down to her throat,
to end her life . . .

Chandra sprang into awareness.

How long had she been wandering here, falling and
floating between the physical planes of the Multiverse?

She banished the question. All she must think about
was escaping the chaotic, sense-warping maze of the Blind
Eternities. Until she was safely on a physical plane again,

nothing else mattered, and no other thought could be allowed to penetrate her vulnerable focus.

She spread her senses and tried to find something familiar to orient her. She felt the flow of mana, which was reassuring, but it mingled with so many other forces in a bewildering whirlwind of color that she felt wrung out and frustrated as she tried to bond with it. Still, with no other way to survive and escape, she concentrated, summoning all her will, all her rage and heat and passion, and focused on channeling the magical energy.

When she finally felt ready, Chandra propelled herself through the undulating, swirling colors that consumed her, seeking the solid energy of a physical plane. She was vaguely aware that there was someplace she wanted to return, a place where she had a community and a purpose . . . but she couldn't even recall it well enough to look for it, let alone control this planeswalk to that extent. Right now, *all* that mattered was finding a plane, any plane at all. Later, she would think about where exactly in the Multiverse she wanted to be.

Then she sensed it. A dark, bitter energy . . . but blessedly physical, solid, and tangible. And because she could sense it, because her will drew her toward it, a path to it began opening before her in the æther.

She hesitated. The plane she was approaching didn't feel at all familiar, and it certainly didn't feel welcoming.

Should she travel further? The next plane might be a better choice.

No. The next plane she encountered might just as easily be a worse choice. Or, in her weakness and confusion, she might not find another plane at all. Not before she succumbed to the consuming whirlwind she was trying to escape.

It must be now. Here. Go.

She moved through the æther, following the path that beckoned her to the physical plane she sensed. She let the plane's sullen energy lure her forward as she focused with all her might on making the transition away from the eternal flow surrounding her to the finite, solid reality that lay ahead of her.

Her body, her senses, her mind, all felt torn apart, stretched to the breaking point between two realities. She fought fear and struggled for control. She reached for the dark plane she sensed, stretching toward it with all her will.

Chandra's feet touched solid ground.

The sensation was so startling, the weight of her own body so unexpected, that she fell down, collapsing into an awkward heap with a choked gasp.

Then she lay there, eyes closed, her face pressed into the damp earth with grateful relief. She spread her palms against the ground, reveling in its solid, unyielding presence.

I'm alive. Alive!

The worst was over. She had escaped Kephalai and the Prelate's dungeon; escaped death by slow torture at the hands of the Enervants.

Right now, being lost on some wholly unfamiliar plane that radiated dark energy didn't matter. Even losing the scroll to that mage didn't matter. She was just very, very happy she wasn't dead.

Lying on the ground, soaking up the wonderful feeling of being alive, Chandra gradually became aware of a scuffling, scurrying sound nearby. When she opened her eyes to see what had made the noise, she realized that it was nighttime. She pushed herself to a sitting position and looked around, blinking as her eyes adjusted to the dark shadows of her surroundings.

High overhead, a full moon glowed white in the endless, starless black of the night sky. Its cool, silvery light shone down brightly on an eerie landscape of twisted trees, squatting bushes, dark expanses of emptiness, and the tumbled ruins of crumbling stone structures. The trees and bushes that Chandra could make out in the moonlight looked strangely stark and bony.

She realized none of them had any leaves.

That seemed odd. The temperature was mild. The air was cool, but not uncomfortably so—certainly not enough to suggest winter or a season of dormancy. The damp ground suggested preciptation. Indeed, the air itself felt humid. Obviously, drought hadn't caused the absence of leaves on all of the trees and bushes around here.

She wondered what *had* caused it. Had there been a fire here recently?

Curious, she rose to her feet, intending to examine some of the denuded branches more closely. The act of rising, however, made her so dizzy she almost fell down again. Her vision swam darkly, and she felt light-headed.

That was when she realized she was desperatcly thirsty. She recalled now that she had been thirsty even back in the dungeon on Kephalai. And who knew how long ago that was? What seemed like days could also have been minutes—or even longer. Regardless, her physical needs were reasserting themselves now.

Chandra took a steadying breath and realized she must find water. Her stomach rumbled, and she realized that finding something to eat would be a good idea, too.

The air was heavy with damp and decay. Not the fetid odor of the Envervants in her cell back on Kephalai, but the rich, dark smell of sodden soil, of decomposing vegetation mingling with fog. This seemed like a plane where quenching her thirst shouldn't be too difficult. There must surely be substantial water here.

She heard scuffling again in the nearby undergrowth. The rustling sound of dead plants being brushed aside by some small creature's passing struck her as strange. Like the barren trees and naked bushes, the rustling of dead vegetation didn't seem to go with the damp richness of the soil and the air.

With her curiosity reawakened, Chandra walked past the tumbled, moss-covered stone walls surrounding the spot where she had entered this plane, and went over to a dark, twisted tree that was silhouetted by the moonlight. Her feet encountered a denser, softer surface as she got close to the tree, and she looked down.

Mulch, she realized, all around the tree where the leaves had once fallen. She wrapped her fingers around a slender tree branch and gave it a slight squeeze. She was no expert, but the wood didn't feel right. It was slightly soft, as if the tree were rotting.

Chandra wondered whether the tree had become diseased and shed its leaves in its initial stages of dying.

She looked around at the moon-swept landscape, where all she saw were bare branches drooping in the silvery light.

It seemed that all the trees in the area had become infected with the same disease. Chandra started to wonder whether this was a local phenomenon, or whether the whole plane was covered with dying vegetation.

She started to feel uneasy, increasingly aware of the dark, bitter energy that permeated this place. Instinct warned her that whatever was killing the plant life here, the cause was more likely magical than mundane.

With her senses restored and her mind functioning again, Chandra realized that she was more than ready to return to Keral Keep. She would report that she had failed to get the scroll and didn't even know where it was now.

Well, presumably it's in the hands of some opportunist on Kephalai, she thought with a scowl.

She found this *infuriating*.

It would also be difficult for her to return to Kephalai and hunt down Gideon. Impossible, really. She might not be a shrewd strategic planner, and she *hated* losing, but she wasn't a fool. She knew that she had very little chance of moving freely on Kephalai ever again. *No* chance, actually. She had destroyed the Sanctum of Stars, wreaked havoc in the city, and stolen the scroll a second time.

Because of her actions, she would be hunted on Kephalai for a long time. There would certainly be a price on her head. Descriptions of her would circulate. If there were any tall, red-headed women in the Prelate's realm, they'd be harassed. She might even become the most notorious criminal they had ever known. In spite of what she knew was right, this gave Chandra a giddy feeling. She would go down in legend, or at least she hopped so.

Chandra moved over to a hedge of bushes and absently examined their branches, wondering whether she could have escaped with the scroll if that black-haired mage with his glowing, daggertail whip hadn't interfered. She'd never know for sure, but it was easier to blame him for the way things had gone. And she reveled for a few moments in a vision of roasting him alive in the fires of retribution.

Acknowledging that this dream would likely never be realized, she sighed. Meanwhile, her examination of the bushes revealed that they, too, were dying.

She decided that, ravenous though she was, if she came across any trees or bushes bearing fruit, she wouldn't eat it. Whatever was killing these plants could have easily infected other, seemingly healthy, foliage.

Chandra gazed around the darkened landscape again and realized that, in fact, she was skeptical about finding any healthy-looking plants, at all. The sullen shroud of dark magic she sensed earlier seemed to stretch far and wide across this place.

She needed to get out of here and return to Regatha. There were problems to be faced and solved back there. Hopefully, the oufe tribe that wanted her dead had calmed down a bit by now. And as for the Order of Heliud, and Walbert's demand that Chandra be turned over to his custody . . . Well, just let Walbert's soldiers *try* to come take her from the mountains. She'd make sure it didn't take long for them to rethink *that* plan.

Even so, as much as she wanted to leave this plane immediately, she knew—particularly after her recent experience—that she needed to recoup some of her strength before trying to re-enter the Blind Eternities. She had to search for some water, then get some rest. The syrupy darkness of the night sky and the full brilliance of the moon suggested that morning was still a long way off. By then, Chandra should be ready to planeswalk back to Regatha.

"All right," she said, looking around at the eerie landscape. "Water."

Despite her driving thirst, her surroundings were so creepy that it was with some reluctance that she set out in *any* direction. Although it was unquestionably better than being chained to a wall with her power being sucked away by seven giant snakes as a prelude to death by torture, wandering alone through the darkness was still a less-than-enjoyable endeavor.

She had not gone far when she heard noise coming from a cluster of bushes that she was passing, the rustle of dead vegetation under stomping footsteps, some faint, high-pitched squealing, some growling.

Chandra crouched down and crept closer to the commotion. The intensity of the squealing increased sharply, scraping at her senses. The growling was replaced by satisfied grunting and the noisy smacking of . . . robust chewing?

Chandra pushed further into the thicket, taking care to move silently. Peering between leafless branches, she spotted her quarry.

She found herself looking at some sort of goblin. It was squat and ungainly, with lumpy gray skin, hairy legs, and arms so long they would surely drag along the ground when it stood up and walked. Its bald head was immense, and its long, pointy ears flopped sideways in a ridiculous manner. It was hunched over and grunting, while something in its grasp squealed. Chandra saw a tail and flailing little paws . . .

When she realized the beast was eating a small animal *alive*, she gasped aloud in revulsion.

The goblin heard her and whirled around to face her. Its fangs dripped with blood and entrails as it growled at her. The little animal in its grasp continued squealing in agony. Chandra's appalled gaze flashed to the animal's eviscerated torso and wiggling paws.

"Ugh! What are you *doing*?" she demanded. "Even for a goblin, this is unbelievable!"

The goblin stared at her for a moment, crouching frozen while its agonized prey flailed and squealed. Then, as if afraid Chandra would try to steal its treat, the creature stuffed the entire mole into its mouth and crunched down hard. Chandra winced at the mole's final, shrill scream, followed closely by the sound of its splintering bones. The goblin's cheeks bulged as it chewed, still staring at Chandra.

Then the creature swallowed its meal in one huge gulp

and went completely still. The goblin and Chandra stared at each other in silence.

"Well," she said at last. "That may not be the single most disgusting thing I've ever seen, but it's definitely on the list."

"List?" The goblin's voice was deep and husky.

"Never mind."

"Don't kill," it said.

"Agreed. You don't kill me, and I won't kill you."

It nodded. Its ears flopped a little.

"Where are we?" Chandra asked.

The goblin looked around for a moment, then returned its gaze to Chandra. "Bushes."

"I meant, what's the name of this realm?"

"Diraden."

"Never heard of it."

The goblin pointed at her. "What name?"

"Chandra. And you?"

"Jurl."

"Jurl, show me where there's water." When the goblin didn't move, just continued to stare at her, she added, "I don't like to brag, Jurl, but I'm a powerful fire mage. If you take me to water, I'll be nice. If you don't, I'll be mean."

"Water." The goblin looked over its shoulder. "Maybe not safe."

"Not safe? Is the water bad?" That might explain why everything around here was dying.

Jurl shook his head. "Water good."

"Then what's the problem?"

"Maybe guarded."

"By who?"

"Prince Velrav. Sometimes."

"A prince guards the water?" Chandra said skeptically.

"Servants."

"Oh, *servants* of the prince guard the water." That made a little more sense. But not much. "Why guard water in a place as wet as Diraden?"

"See who come. Maybe take."

"Take? You mean, the prince's servants capture those who come to the water?"

"Sometimes."

"Do they take everyone? Or just goblins?"

"Everyone."

"So far, you're the only, er, person that I've met. Who else lives on Diraden?"

"Some like me. Some like . . ." Jurl shrugged. "Others. Many others. And some like you."

"And Prince Velrav's servants take them all?"

"Take *some* of all."

"Why?" Chandra asked.

"Hunger."

That was disconcerting. "They're taken when they're near the water?"

The goblin shrugged. "Near water. Near wood. Near ruins. Near hill. Near village. Near castle. Near——"

"So you're saying that the prince's servants have taken individuals from everywhere?" What a lovely plane she had stumbled onto.

"Yes."

"In that case, I might as well get water." And then maybe she'd try leaving Diraden straight away, without bothering to pause for rest. The situation here sounded deranged and deadly—and perfectly in keeping with the atmosphere she had sensed. If she felt better after drinking her fill, then perhaps leaving while she was still fatigued—but with proper preparation this time—would be better than sticking around here until she felt stronger. "Jurl, I'll bet you know this place well. Do you know how to get water without being bothered by Prince Velrav's servants?"

The goblin stared at her silently. Although its grotesque face showed no expression, she sensed it was suspicious of her request.

"If you take me there," Chandra said, "I won't tell anyone. I won't betray you. I'm thirsty. I just want to get water, and then go away."

"Go away?"

"Yes. You'll never see me again." It was a promise she intended to keep.

Jurl studied her. "Go away soon?"

"*Very* soon."

"How soon?"

"By morning."

"No." The goblin shook its head.

Chandra frowned. "Why not?"

"No morning."

"What?"

"Morning never come," Jurl said. "Not here."

✳ ✳ ✳ ✳ ✳

After some discussion, Chandra guessed that Prince Velrav was some sort of necromancer who had pulled a veil of eternal night across this plane. There was presumably a good reason for this, but Jurl didn't know what it was. Nor did Jurl remember an era when things had been different, so this had apparently been going on for quite some time.

When Chandra asked how long the trees had been naked and dying, he said, "Always."

She supposed perpetual darkness explained *why* they were dying. And black magic probably explained why they were dying so slowly that, as far back as Jurl could remember, they had looked exactly the way they looked right now.

But it was possible that this was just what normal trees looked like on the dark plane of Diraden, swamped in black magic and ruled by a demented mage who occasionally had his subjects captured and brought back to his castle to satisfy "hunger." Jurl seemed to know no more than that about the "taking" of various individuals over the years; nor did he seem to think anything more *needed* to be known about it.

A goblin's life revolved around pretty simple interests, after all: hunt, eat, drink, reproduce, make merry, fight, kill, be killed. It seldom got more complicated than that.

It was a welcome relief that the water that Jurl led her to wasn't far away. They passed through a moonlit copse of tall, thin, trees with thick, spidery roots that had snaked across the surface of ground, covering the path in long, lumpy twists of rotting wood and thick, sickly vines. Beyond the wood, they came to a lagoon. Silvery light from the moon glinted off the still surface of the water, which was rimmed by a dense thicket of vegetation.

Chandra surveyed the sinister-looking pool of water. "How long have you been coming here?"

"Always."

Because some species of goblin matured fast, growing to adulthood within a couple of years of their birth, "always" might only mean a year or two. On the other hand, some goblins lived a very long time. Chandra was unsure which category Jurl fell into, but couldn't bring herself to ask.

"Water good," Jurl said encouragingly. He lay face down beside the lagoon, stuck his head into the water, and began drinking.

Chandra walked a few judicious steps away from his noisy gulping, then knelt down, reached a cupped hand into the lagoon, and scooped up a small quantity of water, which she studied in the moonlight. It was clear and cold.

When she brought it close to her nose, it had no odor. She bent over her hand to cautiously take a sip. It tasted fine.

With a shaky sigh of relief, she lay face down at the edge of the lagoon, bracing her hands by her shoulders, and drank her fill. After slaking her thirst, she rested briefly, then drank some more. When she was done, she realized how dehydrated she had been. Already, thanks to the water, Chandra's thoughts felt clearer, her body more responsive, her senses sharper. She was still tired, but she was in complete command of herself again.

Suddenly, the goblin made a hissing sound.

Chandra glanced at him and saw that he was frozen in position and staring across the lagoon. She followed his gaze, but she didn't see anything, which wasn't surprising. Jurl's eyes were probably better accustomed to this dim light than hers.

She whispered, "What's wrong?"

"Bog Wraith," the goblin growled. "*Bad*."

Chandra froze, peering into the darkness and trying to see the creature that Jurl saw. "Is that what takes people?"

"No. Can't take. Can tell."

"Can tell?" Chandra repeated. "It will tell its master it saw us here?"

"Yes."

And presumably its master was Prince Velrav. "Great."

"Kill," said Jurl.

"Kill it? I can't even see it."

"There." One long, lumpy arm pointed to a twisted tree that leaned out over the water, its barren branches touching the surface of the lagoon.

Staring hard, Chandra was able to make out something that looked like pale white skin gleaming in the moonlight. Then she realized that some of the shapes she had assumed were branches were actually the long, dark tendrils of the Bog Wraith's hair, floating eerily in the still air. The creature itself floated, too; a pale, transparent figure veiled in black shadows.

"Bad," Chandra agreed, aware of a chill in her blood as she studied the silently watchful creature.

"*Kill,*" Jurl repeated.

This thing seemed familiar . . . She realized that it reminded her of the ghost warden she had destroyed on Regatha.

That wasn't the sort of incident she wanted to repeat here. She intended to leave Diraden unnoticed, not create a commotion and attract attention. And she wanted to enter the æther in a sane and steady manner, not to reenact her frantic and nearly fatal departure from Kephalai.

"No," she said to Jurl. "I won't kill it. All that thing has seen is a woman and a goblin drinking water. So what if it tells? Let's go quietly now."

As she turned to go, the goblin grunted, obviously dissatisfied.

When they had traveled some distance, Jurl said, "Now eat?"

She thought of his recent meal, which she had interrupted, and said truthfully, "I'm not that hungry."

"Sleep?"

"No, I'm going to leave," she said decisively. Diraden was no place to linger.

"Leave where?"

"It's complicated."

"Leave now?"

"Soon." And since she didn't want the goblin asking questions while she prepared to planeswalk, it was time to bid him farewell. "Thank you for taking me to water, Jurl. You've been, um, a good host."

"Still hungry." Jurl nodded at some nearby bushes. "Hunt."

"Enjoy." She tried not to think about it. "Goodbye."

"Wait here. Jurl bring food."

Jurl turned and entered the nearby thicket. Chandra had been wrong in her initial assumption that his long arms would drag on the ground. He walked with them bent sharply at the elbows, shoulders wide and forearms dangling at his sides, and he could move with surprising speed and silence.

Chandra turned away and continued walking as she considered her options. Not wanting to be there if the Jurl did return, she decided it would be best to return to the ruins where she had arrived, since the crumbling walls offered a little cover. It also made sense to her to open a path to the Blind Eternities at same spot she had entered the plane.

Fortunately, the journey to water had not taken her very far from the place she sought. She retraced her steps without difficulty and arrived back at the ruins before long. The crumbling, lichen-covered walls looked stark and foreboding in the eerie, eternal night.

As her gaze traveled over her stony destination, Chandra was surprised to see a flash of bright white light explode silently from within the ruins, although she couldn't see what had caused it. A stone wall stood between her and the source of the sudden, bold flare.

She froze in her tracks. She didn't think this source of bright light had anything to do with this dark Prince Velrav, but wanted to be cautious, none the less.

She stretched out her senses in order to call on the mana of the Keralian Mountains as a means to protect herself. A flash of panic washed through her when she realized she could scarcely feel it.

Breathe, she told herself, smothering the fear. Breathe.

She concentrated. She focused on her memory of other planes, of other sources, but she still couldn't feel that flow of red mana. How was that possible? She was feeling stronger, better than she had a while ago, but she couldn't establish a mana bond.

Stop. Think.

She squared her shoulders and moved forward, her footfalls silent on the damp ground. Whatever was going on inside these stony ruins, she needed this space to commence her planeswalk back to Regatha. And, if necessary, she would make her temporary claim on these ruins clear to others. With or without the use of magic.

She crept up to the walls of the ruins, stepped quietly over some fallen stones, and peered around a corner, looking to the spot where the burst of light seemed to have originated.

She saw a man rising slowly to his feet as he seemed to gather himself and reconnoiter his surroundings.

Chandra saw two dark smudges on his tan leggings where he had been kneeling in the mud. His long, tousled hair hung in his face as he turned toward Chandra.

When the man saw her staring at him, he went still.

After a brief pause, he said, "Hello, Chandra."

Cold shock washed through her. "*Gideon.*"

CHAPTER NINE

I wasn't sure you'd still be alive. That was some walk you took." Gideon's voice was dry.

"How did you . . ." Chandra's heart was pounding as she realized what the answer had to be. "You *followed* me? You followed my trail through the Blind Eternities?"

He nodded. Just one small, downward movement of his chin. No motion wasted.

"*Planeswalker,*" she breathed, still stunned. She hadn't forgotten the promises she'd made to herself about what she'd do if she ever found him again, but this revelation changed things a bit.

There was no wonder he had been able to catch her off guard and capture her so easily in that street back on Kephalai. *A planeswalker!* He would be at least as powerful as she was. And he was a little older than she, so he was probably more experienced, more skilled at using his power, given that he'd had more time to learn and practice.

Gideon's gaze traveled over her. "I see that you're all right now."

Apart from looking like he'd taken a tumble when he entered this plane, his appearance was exactly the same as it had been.

She said, "Apparently that walk didn't do you any harm."

He gave a small, dismissive shrug. "I had time to prepare."

And he evidently knew that she hadn't.

Chandra was impressed that he had been able to follow the erratic trail of her confused wandering through the Blind Eternities. That had certainly taken skill.

Impressed—and disturbed. Why had he bothered?

She doubted she'd like his reasons, whatever they were.

"Where are we?" Gideon asked.

"You don't know?"

"I was following *you*," he reminded her.

"I got lost," she said irritably.

"I could tell." He looked around. "So you don't know where we are?"

"It's called Diraden. What are you doing here?"

He walked past her, moving beyond the ruined stone walls to look out over the landscape. "Like I said, I followed you."

"Why?"

"Everything's dying here," he observed.

"Where's my scroll?" Chandra demanded, noticing that he didn't have it on him in any obvious place.

"It's not your scroll." Gideon walked over to a tree, examined the naked branches, and used his foot to brush aside some loose dirt.

"It's not yours, either!" Chandra said.

"No," he agreed absently as he knelt down to touch the ground. He picked up a handful of damp soil, closed his fist around it, and inhaled deeply as he looked up at the sky.

"Where *is* it?" Chandra demanded.

Gideon was scarcely paying attention to her, which

irked her. He stood upright again, looked into the distance, and said quietly, "Everything is wrong here."

"I asked you a question," she said with gritted teeth.

Ignoring her comment, he brushed past her and walked back into the ruins. Chandra followed him. When she started to speak again, he held up a hand to silence her. He was circling the spot where he had arrived on this plane. There was a frown of concentration on his face.

Chandra decided she'd had *enough*. "You tricked me! You helped the Prelate's soldiers capture me! You *stole* my scroll—"

"You stole it, too," he said dismissively, still frowning as he looked up at the sky again. "And it's not yours."

"I was imprisoned because of you! Enervants tried to drain all my power!"

"Enervants?" That got his attention for a moment. He glanced in her direction. "Do they smell as bad as people say?"

"Yes."

"Enervants," he murmured. "That explains why your planeswalk went so badly. You were weakened."

"In part," she snapped. "The other part is that I had to enter the æther just moments ahead of dozens of soldiers! They tortured me to find out where the scroll was, and they would have done it until I died because I didn't know where it was!"

"Yes, I heard." Gideon seemed lost in thought, his mind scarcely on the conversation as he said, "All things considered, you did well to survive. But it's a pity you chose *this* place to end your walk."

"So sorry you don't like it," Chandra said acidly. "But since you weren't invited in the first place, why don't you just leave?"

He looked at her. "You haven't figured it out."

His face was in shadows and his expression guarded, but something about his bland tone infuriated her.

"If you followed me to take me prisoner and drag me back to Kephalai, then you made a big mistake, Gideon!" She threw her hands out to encircle him with a ring of fire . . .

And nothing happened.

He stood there calmly, not moving a muscle, not reacting physically at all. His voice sounded faintly amused when he said, "Indeed."

Chandra stared at her hands in bewildered shock, turning them over and studying her palms as if she could read the answer there to her sudden absence of power.

"But I feel much better now," she muttered. "So what . . ."

"You may feel better," Gideon said, "but surely there's something you *don't* feel?"

"I . . ." She frowned, realizing what he meant. "*Mana.*" Suddenly, her difficulty in feeling it earlier made sense.

He nodded. "Something's blocking our access to mana.

She stared at him in surprise. "Blocking mana?"

"It's not completely effective," he said. "That's why you feel *something*. But it's effective enough to be a serious problem for us."

"Us?" She realized the full import of what he was telling her. "You're without power, too?"

"As much as you are," he confirmed.

"I noticed it was hard to feel the flow," she said, thinking back. "Hard to bond. But I thought that was because I was still weak."

"No." He shook his head. "If you concentrate long and hard, you can probably call on enough mana here to start a small cooking fire. But that's about all, while it's being blocked so well."

Chandra had never heard of such a thing. "What could do this?"

"I'm not sure. Something very powerful, obviously."

"Or some*one*?" She thought of the hungry prince.

Gideon shrugged. "It would take constant focus and a lot of strength. The effort would be enormous. A big drain on just one person."

"So he probably has help," she mused.

"He?" Gideon repeated.

"There's a necromancer named Prince Velrav who rules here."

"Of course," Gideon said. "Black mana would be abundant here."

"Is that why it's always nighttime here?"

He looked at her sharply. "Always?"

She told him what she had learned from Jurl.

"A goblin," Gideon mused. "I suppose you couldn't get any sense from him of whether this phenomenon is recent or has been going on for centuries?"

"No."

Jurl had been pretty typical of goblins, in Chandra's experience: neither bright, nor articulate.

Gideon looked up at the night sky. "No clouds. But no stars."

"I noticed that, too," she said. "I've never seen that before."

"I doubt that's the normal night sky here."

"You think Velrav pulled a . . ." Chandra shrugged. "A *shroud* over this plane?"

"That's one way of putting it," Gideon said.

"Is that what's restricting the mana?"

"I don't know. But I've never experienced anything like this, and I've never been anywhere where *that* had happened." He jerked his chin skyward. "Perpetual night attributed to the local necromancer king . . ."

"Prince."

"My guess is, the two things are related. What else did your goblin friend tell you?"

"'Friend' would be an exaggeration."

"He led you to water. He didn't try to kill you. For a goblin, that sounds pretty friendly."

"Yes," she said pensively, reflecting on the encounter. Her first impression of Jurl, when she saw him eating his squealing prey alive, was that he was like all other goblins she had encountered—only more so. "He *was* surprisingly nice to me. I wonder why?"

"I don't suppose you threatened to set fire to him?" Gideon said dryly.

"Oh, yeah. Maybe that's why."

"What else did he tell you about Velrav?"

Chandra recounted Jurl's vague comments about Velrav's servants abducting individuals from every race living on Diraden, in order to satisfy the "hunger." She concluded by describing the encounter with the Bog Wraith.

Gideon said, "So you didn't kill it and alert Velrav's entire army to your presence?"

"No," she said stonily.

"It's nice to see you're learning from your mistakes."

"What do *you* know about my—"

"Before we go to all the trouble of destroying this . . . yes, *shroud* is a good word for it, we should make sure—"

"Hold on, what do you mean 'we'?" she said. "If you're determined to meddle in local problems, that's your choice. Enjoy yourself! But this has nothing to do with me. All *I* want to do is get the blazes *off* this creepy plane and . . . " The full weight of the problem facing them hit Chandra like a physical blow. She swayed a little as she realized exactly what this meant.

"Ah," Gideon said. "Therein lies the rub."

"We can't leave," she said, appalled by the realization.

"Not until we can establish proper mana bonds. As long as it's restricted . . ."

"We're stuck here."

Fleeing Kephalai in a weakened state, Chandra had risked dying in the Blind Eternities. And here, without access to any real power, she risked living the rest of her days in perpetual night.

"I'm stranded." She gazed at her handsome companion in horror. "With *you*."

"Well, if you get bored with me," he said, "there's always Jurl."

"I suppose you're going to suggest that you and I . . ." She swallowed, so revolted by the idea that she had trouble even saying it. "That we . . . work together. To get out of here."

"I can manage alone, if you'd rather just give in and settle down here. But, yes, I—"

"Give *in*?"

"I imagine it will be easier to escape this plane if both of us are working on the problem." His lips relaxed momentarily into what might have been a slight smile. "Together."

She thought it over. "There are certain conditions, if you want my help."

"By all means, let's pause to negotiate the terms under which we'll cooperate."

"*I* didn't ask you to come here," she reminded him. "Your being here is entirely your own fault. You shouldn't have followed me. While we're on the subject, you also shouldn't have stolen my scroll or helped the Prelate's soldiers capture me!"

"I think we're digressing."

Chandra said, "My conditions are as follows."

"Go on."

"I won't return to Kephalai. You will not take me back there. You will not trick me or manipulate me into going there again."

"Agreed."

"Nor will you inform the Prelate, her forces, or any other inhabitants of Kephalai where I go when I leave here."

"Agreed," he said.

"You will not betray me to Prince Velrav or his minions in order to secure your own escape, and you will not prevent me from leaving this plane."

His black brows rose. "You *do* have a low opinion of me."

"If you don't like my terms," she said, "that's fine. We don't have to work together."

"No, your terms are fine. I agree to them."

She searched his face to see if she trusted his word on this. His expression gave away little. But she refused to be afraid of him . . . and she recognized, however reluctantly, that it made more sense for them to cooperate here than to be at odds with each other.

He said, "As long as we're negotiating our partnership . . ."

"We're not partners," Chandra said sharply. "We're just . . . um . . ."

"I have some conditions, too."

"Oh?"

"You will—at least, insofar as you are capable of it—*think* before you act, while we are here."

"How dare—"

"I don't want to spend the rest of my life here—and probably a very short life, at that—because you didn't use your head." When she just glowered at him, he prodded, "Well?"

"Insofar as I am *capable*," she said darkly, "I will think before I act."

"Good. Next condition: You will not kill anyone who isn't a danger to us."

"How are we deciding who is or isn't a danger?" she asked suspiciously.

"Let's agree you'll trust my judgment on that."

"*No*." She turned away.

His hand on her arm stopped her. "Chandra."

She turned her head. Their eyes met. His were very serious. To her surprise, he didn't look angry. She wasn't quite sure what she saw there, though.

He said softly, "We could die here."

Gideon was a little taller than she. Chandra tilted her head up and said, "Then I'll die because of *my* judgment. Not *yours*."

His hand still held her arm. "I don't want to kill any innocents while I'm trying to get out of here."

The thought of innocents bothered her.

"I don't, either," she said, aware of how close together they were standing. So close that she noticed now he needed to shave. The dark shadow starting to darken his jaw would become more obvious by morning . . . which wouldn't come, of course. Not on Diraden.

Gideon said, "You can be a little . . . reckless that way."

His gaze dropped, and his dark lashes lowered. Chandra had a feeling he was staring at her lips. She licked them, and she felt the grip on her arm tighten ever so slightly.

"I was trying to survive. They'd have killed me on Kephalai." She heard the breathlessness in her voice and didn't like it. She jerked her arm out of his hold and stepped away. "Anyhow, what makes you think we'll meet innocents? So far, I've talked to a goblin, seen a Bog Wraith, and heard about a black mage with a sinister appetite."

"The night is still young."

He looked at her impassively, as if that odd moment hadn't happened between them.

Maybe it hadn't for him.

She scowled at him. "So. Are we working together?"

"Yes."

"Fine," she said. "Since you're an advocate of *thinking* before you act, what's your plan?"

"First," he said, "I think we should find out who's watching us."

"Watching us?" She frowned. "What makes you think we're being w—"

"*Yaaagggh!*"

The wordless bellow was accompanied by something big and heavy careening into Chandra's back. At that same moment, she saw Jurl leap over a tumbled stone wall and attack Gideon, who whirled around to defend himself.

Chandra hit the ground with considerable force, and had the wind knocked out of her. She heard snarling right by her ear and felt a heavy body lying on top of her. Then a powerful grip seized her shoulders and started banging her against the ground. Over and over. *Hard.*

She called on fire, intending to incinerate her attacker . . . and then realized that she couldn't.

Damn, damn, damn.

While she fought to retain consciousness, Chandra saw a hairy, clawed hand out of the corner of her eye. Lumpy, gray skin. Another goblin.

Jurl? she wondered in confusion.

It kept banging her into the ground, as if trying to tenderize her.

That does it!

Without enough physical strength to gain the advantage, in her current position, she tried a different tactic. "I . . ." Fortunately, the ground wasn't hard: but even so, this was painful. ". . . surrender!" She was smashed into the ground again. "I surrender! I surrender!"

"What?" the goblin said, pausing in its assault.

"I surrender!" Now that she wasn't being pummeled against the ground, she could hear the grunts and blows of Gideon and the other goblin fighting each other.

"Surrender?" the goblin said, breathing on her neck.

"Yes! I surrender! I give up!" Chandra cried. "You win!"

The goblin's weight shifted. It was evidently surprised, and perhaps a little confused. Since goblins weren't known for their mercy, it might never have encountered this reaction to an attack before. Typically, a fight with a goblin was a fight to the death.

The pause in the goblin's assault and the shifting of its weight was all Chandra needed. She used the muscles of her legs to buck the goblin off of her with a powerful scissor kick, before she rolled over and reached for one of the rocks lying at the base of a nearby ruined wall. Rock in hand, she threw herself at the goblin and smashed its massive head. The goblin shrieked and stumbled backward. Chandra jumped up and hit it in the head again right at the temple. The beast hit the ground hard. Unmoving, blood trickling from its ear, Chandra left the it where it lay and staggered away, unsure if it was dead.

"*Ugh!* I hate goblins! I *hate* them!"

Chandra turned around, intending to go help Gideon. He and the other goblin were rolling around on the ground together, their bodies wallowing frantically in the mud around the stone walls.

Chandra picked up another rock and moved toward them. The goblin lost its hold on Gideon, who rolled away

and raised his foot to kick the goblin in the face with considerable force. It fell backward, then staggered in a circle
and turned toward Gideon, who rolled across the ground
rapidly and stretched out his arm, reaching for something.
The goblin saw Chandra approaching them and froze. It
turned its head and saw its companion lying prone on the
ground.

The goblin gave a shrill little cry—then turned and
fled.

"Stay back!" Gideon ordered as Chandra dashed across
the ground.

"It's getting away!"

"Get down!" Gideon raised an arm to make wide, rapid
circles over his head.

Chandra saw something glint brightly in the moonlight
as it spun over Gideon's head, making a menacing *whooshing*
sound. She realized it was that daggertail of his, unfurled
and swirling above them with deadly speed.

Remembering that the thing had three very long,
sharp blades, Chandra threw herself to the ground and
covered her head. Without his magic guiding the weapon's
steely tendrils, who knew whether Gideon's aim was
any good.

She heard the *whooshing* sound change to a long steel
sigh as Gideon unleashed the whip. She peeked between
her fingers and saw that he had released the entire weapon,
letting it sail through the dark night, handle and all. The
goblin was speedy and had already covered some distance,
but it couldn't outrun the flying weapon.

As Chandra rose to her knees, gaze fixed intently on
the fleeing goblin, Gideon set off at a run. Chandra saw
something glint briefly in the moonlight, then she saw
the goblin fall down. She rose to her feet and ran after
him, too.

When she reached Gideon's side, the goblin was lying on the ground, grunting and snarling as it struggled in the sharp tangle of flexible blades that were constraining its short legs.

"I shouldn't have doubted your aim," Chandra said to Gideon, breathing hard from her exertions.

"Lucky shot," Gideon said. "To be honest, I could scarcely see him."

"Chandra!" the goblin said in a familiar-sounding voice. "Don't kill!"

She sighed. "Hello, Jurl. We meet again."

CHAPTER TEN

Gideon seized the handle of the whip and jerked it sharply. Jurl's eyes bulged and he made a horrible groaning sound from the pain inflicted on his trapped limbs.

Chandra asked Gideon, "How did you know they were watching us?"

"The one that attacked you was casting a shadow on the stone wall near you. I realized it when he moved."

She hadn't seen the realization dawn on Gideon's face. She should remember that he was good at hiding things.

Gideon gave Jurl a light tap with his foot. "But I didn't know there was one behind me, too. They move quietly, don't they?"

"Don't kick!" Jurl said.

"Explain why you just attacked us," Gideon said to the goblin."

"Chandra go away soon."

Gideon glanced at Chandra, then said, "You attacked her because she was leaving?"

"Because no time."

"I think he means," Chandra said, "he attacked *now* because I had told him I was leaving very soon."

"Yes!" Jurl was apparently pleased with her interpretation. "No time."

"Why attack her at all?" Gideon asked the goblin.

"Take to Prince Velrav."

"What?" Chandra scowled. "You were going to turn me over to Velrav? To feed the hunger?"

"Yes."

"Now I see why you were so helpful, Jurl. You wanted me for yourself."

"Yes," Jurl confirmed.

"To think I was beginning to like you," she muttered.

"So you're one of Velrav's takers?" Gideon asked Jurl.

"Yes."

"I see," Gideon said. "Why?"

"Take gift to Velrav. Velrav give something."

"Ah. And if you took a beautiful fire mage to Velrav," Gideon said, "you'd get something good, wouldn't you?"

"Yes." Jurl looked as crestfallen as a writhing, captive goblin could look. "But not now." He looked at Gideon and added, "Don't kill."

"Why not?" Gideon gave the handle of his weapon another sharp tug.

Jurl gasped. "Give me life. I give you."

"Give us *what*?"

"Tell me what," Jurl said. "I get."

"What I want," Gideon said, "is someone who can answer all my questions."

"Questions?" Jurl repeated.

"My questions about Velrav. About Diraden. About why morning never comes."

Jurl thought it over, then suggested, "Wise woman?"

"Yes," Gideon agreed. "I want to speak to a wise woman."

"Village wise woman," Jurl said eagerly. "Know things."

"How far?" Gideon asked

"Not far. I bring you."

Gideon said to the goblin, "I'm going to remove the *sural* from your legs."

"What?"

"The weapon."

"Good!"

"And then I'm going to use it to tie your hands behind your back."

"*Bad.*"

"If you resist or try to get away while I'm doing this," Gideon said, "I will catch you again, but I won't be nice."

"You could end up like your friend, Jurl. You don't want that, do you?" Chandra prodded.

"Not friend," Jurl said dismissively.

"Then why did you bring him along?" she asked. "Wouldn't you have to share with him whatever Velrav gave you?"

"Need help now," Jurl said. "Kill later."

"No honor among goblins," Chandra muttered.

"I guess the prospect of attacking a woman alone was too daunting," Gideon said dryly.

"Intimidated by my beauty, no doubt," she said, recalling Gideon's earlier comment.

"Maybe so." There was no mockery in his voice. He was looking down at the goblin as he began untangling his weapon from its legs. His expression was hidden in shadows. Chandra stared at him in bemusement. Until he said, "Hold the rock where he can see it."

Gideon finished removing the sural from Jurl's legs. "Roll over."

Jurl said, "Don't tie hands."

"Roll over," Chandra said, "or you'll die right now, exactly the way your friend died."

"Not frien—"

"Shut up and do as you're told," she snapped.

With blatant reluctance, Jurl rolled over and allowed Gideon to seize his arms and start binding his hands together with the flexible blades of the sural.

When the goblin cried out in pain and protested, Gideon advised him to stop resisting. "This will hurt less if you cooperate."

When Gideon was satisfied that the restraint was secure enough, he rose to his feet, holding the handle of the sural. The lengths of steel that stretched between the handle and the goblin's bound wrists served as a sort of leash.

"Get up," Gideon said.

"Cannot," Jurl said.

Chandra moved to put her hands under the prostrate goblin's shoulders, and pushed him—with some effort—up to a kneeling position. From there, she and Gideon each took one arm and hauled Jurl to his feet.

"Now take us to the wise woman," Gideon said.

"Yes."

"Oh, one more thing." Gideon twitched the handle of the sural. Jurl protested as the sharp bands of steel tightened around his wrists and pulled his arms backward at a painful angle. "If you try to trick us, or betray us, or take us to anyone else . . ." Gideon tugged the handle again. "I'll pull on this thing so hard, it will cut off your hands."

"No!"

"Without hands, the rest of your life will be helpless and miserable. On the bright side," Gideon added, "it will no doubt also be very, very short."

"No trick!" Jurl promised. "Just wise woman!"

"Good," said Gideon.

"This way," Jurl said.

They left the stone ruins behind and set off in a different

direction than Chandra had gone before. As they walked through the quiet, dying landscape, following their reluctant guide, Gideon said, "You're pretty useful when there's trouble, even without the fire magic."

So was he. But she was reluctant to pay him compliments. Instead she asked, "Where did you get your . . ." She pointed to the weapon whose handle he held.

"The sural?"

"Yes, your sural."

"My teacher gave it to me."

"Did he . . ." She hesitated, then asked, "Did he know about you?"

He didn't have to ask what she meant. "Yes."

"Was he a . . ." Chandra glanced at the goblin trudging ahead of them. "Was your teacher one of us?"

"No, but he knew about our kind."

"How?"

"His teacher was one." Gideon added, "And his teacher gave him the sural."

"Where did it originally come from?" She had never seen anything like it.

"I don't know." Beside her in the dark, Gideon said quietly, "His teacher died without telling him where he'd gotten it."

"Do you know how he died?" For a planeswalker, there were so many possibilities.

"A pyromancer killed him." His voice was calm, without expression.

There was a long silence between them.

The ground they were walking over was particularly damp. It squished under Chandra's feet as she kept pace beside Gideon in the dark, neither of them speaking.

Ahead of them, Jurl trudged along, his shoulders stooped. He started to pant a little, and his steps got slower.

Apparently the goblin was feeling fatigued. At one point, he asked to rest. Gideon refused the request.

The continuing cool silence between her and Gideon gradually got on Chandra's nerves. After all, it wasn't *her* fault that his teacher's teacher had been killed by a fire mage. For all she knew, he deserved what happened to him.

"So did you know him?" she asked abruptly.

"Know who?" He sounded mildly puzzled, as if he'd been thinking about something else entirely.

"The pla—" But before she could finish the word, she recalled that Jurl could hear them. The goblin was stupid and ignorant, but nonetheless capable of plotting and scheming. The less he learned by eavesdropping, the better. "The one who owned the sural. The one who died."

"No. He died many years before I met my teacher."

"How did you meet your teacher?" she asked.

Chandra had encountered very few planeswalkers. In her experience, they were a rare breed, and they were loners. They didn't congregate, and they weren't necessarily friendly to each other.

"He . . . found me," Gideon said.

"After you . . ." She phrased it in a way that would make no sense to the goblin, in case the creature was feigning fatigue and listening to them. "Crossed over?"

"You mean after I traveled?" Gideon sounded a little amused by her attempt to question him without being understood by their captive.

"Yes."

"No, we met before that."

"How did he find you?"

"Jurl, you said it wasn't far," Gideon reminded the goblin. "This seems far."

"Yes," Jurl agreed wearily. "Seems far."

"If you've lied . . ."

"No." Jurl added, "Don't take hands."

"Well, maybe I'm just little tired," Gideon admitted to Chandra. "Does it seem far to you?"

She couldn't see his expression. Instead of answering him, she prodded, "You were about to tell me how you met your teacher."

"Was I?"

"Yes."

"Why do you want to know?"

"I'm bored." When he didn't respond, she said, "Of course, we could talk about something else. The scroll, for example."

"Then *I'd* be bored."

"So how did your teacher find you?"

"Well, *you'll* identify with this," he said. "I was a criminal."

"Somehow that doesn't surprise me." She asked, "What did you do? Attack women and take away their valuables?"

"Very funny. As a matter of fact, we sacrificed the cutest animals we could find and drank their blood from our victims' skulls by the light of the moon."

"Then this place should bring you back to your roots."

"To be serious, we mostly broke into rich people's homes—"

"We?"

"There was a group of us. I was the leader, more or less. We stole money, goods, valuables. And, uh . . ."

He seemed reluctant to continue his story. "Yes?" she prodded.

"Then we gave it away." When she didn't respond, he added, "To the poor."

She frowned. "Why?"

"We were . . ." He seemed to search for the right word. "Idealistic."

"That's a far cry from drinking animal blood."

"I was very young. I wanted to change things," he said. "But I didn't know how. I was good at stealing. Good at fighting. Pretty good at handling a group of wild boys my own age."

"That's easy to believe."

"But I had a lot to learn."

"Where were your parents? Didn't they try to rein you in?" Her own parents had certainly tried, back when she was a girl.

"My mother was dead by then," he said.

"And your father?"

"Who knows?" He sounded indifferent. "I never met him."

They all walked in silence for a while. Chandra really started to feel, deep in her bones, how helpless she was here without her power. Even if they did get some answers from this wise woman Jurl was taking them to, what would they do to get away from this plane? She tried to stop thinking it.

Finally she broke the silence: she had to find something to distract her from these thoughts.

"Your teacher," she said suddenly.

"What?" She could tell by Gideon's reaction that he had been far away. Perhaps lost in thoughts similar to her own.

"How did your teacher find you?" she said urgently. "How did he get you to give up your life as an outlaw?"

There was a pause. Then he said, "What makes you think I gave it up?"

She released her breath on a puff of surprise. Then she

smiled—and felt grateful to him for making her smile. "I stand corrected."

In fact, for all she knew, he *was* an outlaw. She had assumed he followed her here to capture her and take her back to Kephalai. She had vaguely supposed he was some sort of inter-planar bounty hunter. The Prelate had employed someone with extraordinary abilities to go after Chandra last time. Why not this time?

But since the Prelate's forces didn't know where the scroll was, *this* planeswalker obviously hadn't returned it to them.

Perhaps Gideon was still an outlaw. Or at least playing all the angles and working on both sides of the fence. The thought warmed him to her.

"As long as you stick to our bargain and don't try to deliver me to the Prelate," she said aloud, "I make no judgments about the path you have chosen in life."

"That's very kind of you."

"So were did your teacher find you?"

"I was in prison," he said.

"We *do* have a lot in common."

"He was respected, and the prison wasn't well equipped to hold someone with my abilities," Gideon said. "So I was released into his custody."

"And that's how your education began?"

"Yes," Gideon said. "More easily than he expected, I suppose. After my initial resistance—and an attempt to escape his custody—I became a dedicated student. Eager."

"You liked the power," she said, remembering her own obsession with it when she had started discovering some of the things she could do, things that no one in her community had understood or condoned.

"Yes, I liked the power. I liked developing and honing it. Mostly, though . . ." Gideon paused pensively. "Mostly,

I realized that my teacher was the first person I'd ever met who could help me find what I was looking for."

"Which was?"

"Direction. Focus. A path for my life."

"Direction . . ." Chandra hadn't thought about direction before. She had gone to the Keralian Monastery to learn more about her power. How to access more of it, but also how to control it better. And her recent experiences demonstrated that she still had much to learn in that respect.

She didn't want to think about any of that now. Besides, she didn't even have access to her full power at the moment. And that wasn't a subject she wanted to dwell on, either, just now. So she asked Gideon, "When did you find out what you really were?"

"When the time came," he said. "When my Spark was ignited."

The Spark, Chandra had been taught, was a suffusion of the Blind Eternities within a planeswalker's soul. It was what gave an individual protection against the entropic forces of the æther. Although it happened differently for everyone, the ignition of a planeswalker's Spark was the trigger for their first walk.

Gideon added, "But my teacher knew before I did."

"How did he know?"

"Because of my power. As I dedicated myself to my training, my strength grew. To me, it just seemed to be the result of studying and learning. But later, after I knew the truth about myself, he said that he had known for some time, because he'd only ever seen one other hieromancer as powerful as I was."

"Ah. The one who had given him the sural all those years ago."

"Yes. A long time before it happened, he believed my

Spark would be ignited and I would become . . . what I became." Gideon said, "So he prepared me."

"He told you what you were?" she asked.

"No. He told me about our kind, and about the one that he had known. He related what he knew about the Multiverse, the æther, and the Blind Eternities. How to prepare for a walk. How to survive it."

"So you knew what was happening?"

"Yes. I was fully conscious of what was happening."

"Did you know *before* it happened?" she asked in astonishment.

"Not exactly. But when I *felt* my Spark ignite, I understood. It was . . ." He hesitated. "I killed someone," he said quietly. "Someone very powerful. Very dangerous. I knew I shouldn't have lived through that confrontation. Not logically. I was shocked at how much power I had accessed. I sensed a clarity in the world around me. I felt an intensity of experience, an awareness of simply being that I had never known. I had a moment, however fleeting, where I understood everything around me. I understood the Multiverse on a fundamental level, if you can imagine such a thing, so that when I slipped into the æther I knew where to go."

"Is it like that every time?"

"No," he said. "As soon as I had landed on another plane, it was gone. I have tried to achieve that state of awareness for most of my life since then, but I have yet to come close." He let out a slow breath. "But the planeswalk worked. Very much the way my teacher had described it. And also by following his teachings, I found my way back. So that I could tell him what I was."

Chandra felt a mingled surge of wonder and envy. "I can't imagine . . ."

"Imagine what?" he asked.

"What my first walk would have been like, if I had known those things. If someone had told me."

"You didn't have any idea what was happening to you?"

"None," she said. "I'd never even heard of a planeswalk."

Chandra blinked as she realized they'd become indiscreet. She looked uneasily at the goblin walking ahead of them, its hands bound behind its back. But Jurl seemed to be paying no attention to them. Instead, he seemed jumpy, anxious, and wholly focused on their surroundings, as if expecting an ambush at any moment.

"That must have been hard," Gideon said.

"I didn't experience anything like you. I thought I was dying," she admitted. "Or dead. Or . . . I don't know. It was very painful. And, um, terrifying."

She didn't know why she was telling him this. She had never told anyone, not even Mother Luti. She'd never had a teacher except for Luti, and she had not known her long. Chandra had never even met another planeswalker before her most recent encounters. All that she knew about planeswalking, she'd taught herself, and all that she learned about her kind, which wasn't a lot, she learned from Mother Luti.

"Some combination of desperation, survival instinct, and . . ." Chandra shrugged. "Sheer luck, I suppose, helped me find my way out of the æther and onto a physical plane that first time."

"And will," he said.

"What?"

"Will," Gideon said. "You have a very strong will. That makes a difference in who survives a walk like your first. And also like the one that brought you here."

"How did you follow me?" She knew it couldn't have been easy.

"Actually, you leave a pretty bright trail."

She supposed that was why that mind mage with the cerulean cloak had been able to find her on Regatha.

"But the trail was erratic and seemed to . . ." He searched for the right word ". . . *bounce* all over the place. I could tell it had been a rough journey." He added, "And to come *here* of all places . . ."

"I didn't exactly choose it," she said.

"I knew even as I approached that it was a bad destination."

"So why did you follow?"

"Why did you steal that scroll?" he countered. "*Twice?*"

"Why did *you* steal it?"

"I didn't exactly steal it."

"Then where *is* it?" she demanded.

"I don't know," he said. "Now that there is no Sanctum of Stars to keep it in, I suppose it's somewhere in the Prelate's palace, under lock and key."

"No, it's not," Chandra said. "The Prelate's pets were going to torture me to find it."

"That was before you escaped. Since then, the scroll has been found."

"*What?*"

"Don't even think about it, Chandra," he said. "If it's in the palace, you *might* get inside alive, but you'd never get back out. Not even you. They'll be watching for you. And now they know they made a mistake by not killing you the moment they identified you. They won't be that careless again."

"You *gave back* the scroll?"

"Yes."

"I don't believe you!"

They walked along in silence for a few paces.

"You gave it back?" she demanded.

"Yes."

"No, you didn't!"

He said nothing.

Her thoughts whirling, she said, "*Why* did you give it back?"

"It seemed like the most sensible thing to do. You know, to calm things down after you left."

"That's *it*?"

"More or less," he said.

"More or less of a reward?"

"Well, there was a reward."

"So *that's* why."

"Not exactly."

"What do you mean?"

"Well, I didn't precisely *give* it back."

"If you didn't give it back, then what did you do. *Precisely*?"

"I left it where it would be found by someone who would recognize it and turn it in for the reward."

"I don't understand," she said. "You stole it from me. You didn't keep it. You didn't sell it. You didn't take credit for retrieving it, and you didn't collect the reward."

"Actually, you seem to understand perfectly."

"If you didn't want it," she said, "why take it in the first place?"

"I thought that if the Prelate didn't have the scroll and didn't know where it was, then she wouldn't execute you immediately. She'd want to find it before she killed you. And since *you* didn't know where it was, there would be some delays." Gideon concluded, "I thought that would give you time to try to escape."

"You *wanted* me to escape?" She felt bewildered. "Why

didn't you help me instead of manipulating me with your passive little ploy?"

"I didn't know about the Enervants," he said. "Or I might have been a bit more proactive."

"If you didn't want them to execute me, then why did you help them capture me?"

"Because you were about to start a battle with those soldiers in a street full of innocent people."

"In a . . . I was . . ." She realized what he was saying.

"You were thinking about yourself," he said. "I was thinking about the dozens of people who might get killed."

"Whatever." After a few long moments of tense silence, she said, "So you didn't want the scroll." When he didn't bother responding, she said, "And you don't want me to go back to Kephalai."

"I think it would be stupid." He added, "And fatal."

"Then what are you doing here?" she demanded. "Why did you follow me? Why were you looking for me on Kephalai? Who *are* you?"

Jurl said, "Stop talking."

"What?" Chandra snapped.

The goblin raised his head, his pointy ears perked alertly.

"He hears something," Gideon said in a low voice.

Their captive raised his head and sniffed the damp night air, apparently oblivious to their presence.

Chandra looked at Gideon. The grove of twisted, leafless trees that they were walking through cast so many shadows in the silvery light that she couldn't see his face well. But she sensed that he was as tense as she was.

Then Jurl's demeanor abruptly changed. He flinched, crouched low, and turned toward them, panting and making little noises of distress.

"What's wrong?" Gideon asked in a low voice.

"Riders," the goblin rasped.

"Riders?"

A moment later, Chandra heard the distant pounding of hooves. Approaching fast.

"*Bad*," Jurl said, "Hide!"

CHAPTER ELEVEN

Jurl scurried toward a thicket of bushes. The steel leash prevented him from going more than a few steps before he stopped, grunting in pain.

"*Hide.*" The goblin sounded terrified.

Gideon took Chandra's arm. "Come on."

Moving fast, they followed Jurl into the bushes. The thundering hoof beats were already much closer. As the three of them crouched down low behind the bushes' naked branches, Chandra was grateful for the dark. These shrubs were thick, even without leaves, but she knew that she and her companions would be visible in the light of day.

She leaned forward and looked off to the left, past Gideon, where the hoof beats were coming from. As she swayed slightly in that direction, unsteady in her crouching position, her shoulder came into contact with Gideon's.

He turned toward her. It was too dark to see his expression, but she could see his eyes looking directly into hers. Neither spoke. Then he, too, looked in the direction of the approaching riders.

Chandra heard a sharp whinny as the galloping horses entered the grove. Peering into the darkness, Chandra could

Φ

see them faintly now. Fortunately, they weren't coming this way. They passed through the withered grove at some distance from where they crouched in the bushes, moving diagonally away. She counted three riders . . . No, four, she realized, as they galloped into a pool of moonlight.

They were racing through a dense, low cloud of fog . . .

No, she realized a moment later, the fog moved *with* them, surrounding them and traveling in their company, flowing swiftly across the landscape. It made the horses look as if they were running atop a shifting white cloud, galloping through the air rather than on the ground. Yet their hooves must be touching soil, because they made a sound louder than thunder.

Watching this spectacle, Chandra felt chilled. The horses were all dark, and they galloped through the night with heedless speed. Perhaps, like Jurl, their eyes were well accustomed to this perpetual night. Or perhaps, she thought, as she watched the fog move with them, they didn't really need to see where they were going.

The lead horse appeared to be carrying two riders, one of whom was struggling, seemingly held captive by the other. She saw pale limbs fighting for freedom and dark-clad arms restraining them. Chandra thought she could hear a terrified wailing as the horses galloped out of sight. A few moments later, the sound of the riders had faded completely.

Now she heard only the pounding of her heart and Gideon's rapid breathing.

"What *was* that?" she asked Jurl.

"Fog Riders."

"Good name," she muttered.

"Who are they?" Gideon's voice was low. His body, so close to Chandra's, was still tense. "What are they doing?"

"Someone run away," Jurl said. "They find. Bring back."

"Back where?" Chandra asked.

"Velrav Castle."

She listened to Gideon's breathing and knew they were both thinking about the captive on that horse.

After a long moment, Gideon said, "Let's keep moving."

"Fog Riders, bad," Jurl said with feeling.

"Yes, I think we grasped that." Gideon rose to his feet and turned to help Chandra extract herself from the clinging arms of the thicket.

Something tugged on her hair. She winced as she pulled against it.

"Wait," Gideon said softly. He reached out to untangle her hair from a slender branch. Then he smoothed the rescued strand over her shoulder. "There."

"Thanks."

Feeling somber and sickened after what she had just witnessed, Chandra turned in the direction they had been heading before hearing the Fog Riders. Jurl grumbled a bit, but then he did the same. Gideon seemed preoccupied and didn't even bother tugging on the goblin's makeshift leash to get him to pick up his heel-dragging pace.

After a few moments walking in silence, Jurl nodded. "Village, near. You walk first," the goblin said.

"Why?" Gideon asked suspiciously.

"Not like goblin," Jurl explained, nodding in the direction of the village.

"What a mystery." Chandra said to Gideon, "I'll walk ahead. You keep a tight hold of his leash. If anything happens to me, cut off his hands." She added, "Did you hear that, Jurl?"

"Yes." He sounded morose.

Chandra moved past Jurl and walked ahead of him. Within moments, she saw a thatched hut. Then several others. They were part of a small village, nestled in the side of a hill and bathed in moonlight. It looked like there were about twenty dwellings here.

As she drew closer, she saw several people standing in the doorways of their huts, peering at her. By the time she reached the first few huts, she heard gasps and excited voices exchanging muffled comments. People were coming out of their huts and standing in the moonlight.

She thought at first that the gasps and the excitement were because of the goblin entering the village. But then she realized, as she stood surrounded by people, that they were all staring at *her*. And she thought she could guess why.

Although no one here looked like Gideon—they were too frail and hollow-eyed to resemble him—they had similar coloring: dark hair, dark eyes, fair skin. As Chandra looked around at the dozens of people who were emerging from their huts and gathering to stare at her, she saw, even in the light of the moon, that she was the only redhead present. Perhaps the only redhead they had ever seen.

"Hello," Chandra said, looking around at the gathering crowd. "We've come to speak to the wise woman."

A young woman, a girl by some standards, stepped forward, separating herself from the crowd. She approached Chandra hesitantly, and slowly reached out a hand to touch her red hair.

Her voice was soft and shy as she said, "You're so beautiful!"

"Thank you," said Chandra.

Behind her, Jurl said, "Wise woman."

"My name is Gideon. We'd like to speak with the wise woman."

The girl said, "You're welcome here."

Gideon said, "Thank you."

Jurl said, "Wise woman."

"Yes," Chandra said, "if someone would tell the wise woman we've come to see her? It's important."

Sounding impatient now, Jurl repeated, "*Wise woman.*"

"Oh." Gideon said, "Chandra..."

"Yes," she said slowly. "I think I understand." Chandra looked at the girl standing before her. "You're the wise woman?"

She smiled sweetly. "Yes, I am the village menarch. Why have you come to see me?"

⚹ ⚹ ⚹ ⚹ ⚹

The wise woman told them her name was Falia, and she led them to a hut where they could sit and talk.

As they entered the doorway of the small thatched hut, Jurl hung back, tugging a little on his leash.

"Free Jurl," he insisted.

"So you can attack us again?" said Chandra. "And trade us to your hungry prince in exchange for goblin goodies? No."

"Jurl bring here. Now set free." The goblin added with reproach, "You *promise.*"

"No," said Gideon, "I promised I wouldn't kill you if you brought us here. *Freeing* you is a whole different subject."

Jurl snarled in outrage.

Looking bored, Gideon tugged the leash sharply.

Jurl gasped in pain, went silent, and trudged into the hut with them. The interior was lighted by short, thick candles.

"Sit in the corner and be quiet," Gideon told the goblin.

Jurl's gaze searched the round hut. "No corner."

Gideon sighed. "Sit out of the way."

"Hungry," Jurl said sullenly.

The wise woman said in her soft, high voice, "We can provide food and drink for all of you."

"What food?" Jurl asked, sounding skeptical.

"Oh, don't pretend you're fussy," Chandra said.

"Thank you," Gideon said to Falia. "Whatever you offer us will be much appreciated."

The girl's gaze traveled over Chandra's bloodied, smeared appearance, the mud on Gideon's clothes, and his darkening jaw. "It seems you've had a long and difficult journey. After we talk, perhaps you would also like to wash, and then to rest."

Wash, Chandra thought with longing. Since they were stuck here, rest was obviously a good idea, too, even though she didn't relish the thought of closing her eyes on this grim and sinister plane.

"Yes, thank you," Gideon said. "We're grateful for your hospitality."

Falia's gaze went back to Gideon and lingered there. The expression of dawning fascination Chandra saw on her face belied Falia's girlish appearance. Gideon was a handsome man, beautiful without being pretty, strong without being bulky. His predatory grace was evident in every movement, and his expression was friendly and reassuring as he returned the girl's unwavering gaze.

But Chandra didn't see a frightened girl in need of reassurance looking back at him. Falia wore the expression of a woman encountering an attractive stranger in her drab little village where everyone knew everyone else, and where the choice of marriage partners was very limited.

Falia gave a little start, evidently realizing she'd been staring, and said to them, "Please, sit now." The girl stuck her head outside the door of the hut to give instructions to someone while Gideon and Chandra helped Jurl sit.

"Free hands," said Jurl.

"Don't be ridiculous," said Chandra.

"He can't help it," said Gideon. "He's a goblin."

The two of them sat down side by side on the woven mats that covered the earthen floor.

Falia re-entered the hut and sat down facing them. Despite her frail appearance and sickly pallor, she was a pretty girl, with a delicate, ethereal quality. Her dark, hollow eyes seemed too sad and haunted for someone so young, but they gave her a world-weary hint of tragic beauty and inner wisdom.

Looking at her now, Chandra thought it seemed a bit less strange that this girl was the village wise woman.

Gideon said, "Please believe that I mean no insult or disrespect when I say that you seem very young to be a wise woman."

Falia looked puzzled. "I do?"

Gideon asked, "How is the wise woman—I mean menarch chosen here?"

"It's the calling of my family," she said. "When I showed first blood, my mother knew that I was ready. Someday I will marry and bear children. My daughter will one day assume this duty."

"That seems like a pretty short time in which to gain wisdom," Chandra said.

Gideon glanced at her, but didn't tell her to be quiet. So apparently he had a little wisdom, too.

"My wisdom was passed to me by my mother. Her wisdom is mine. She was given hers by her mother, and so it has been for generations within us."

"How do you pass it?" Chandra asked.

"We share our blood in the ritual passing of our power," the girl said pleasantly.

Chandra decided she didn't want details. This wasn't

what they had come here to talk about.

"Ah, here is your meal," Falia said.

A woman entered the hut, carrying a large pot. A boy followed behind her, carrying wooden bowls and spoons. The woman smiled kindly at Gideon and Chandra as she set the pot down in front of them. Falia ladled soup into the two bowls the boy had brought, then handed the bowls to Chandra and Gideon.

The boy, who also placed his wares in front of them, paused to gape with wide-eyed curiosity until Falia put a hand on his shoulder to get his attention.

"Please give the goblin food. We must show him our appreciation." The boy picked up the pot, and carried it over to Jurl. He set it down in front of him, turned away, and left the hut.

With his hands still bound behind his back, Jurl wiggled around into a kneeling position, then stuck his whole head into the pot and started slurping noisily.

Chandra looked down into her bowl. It contained a translucent, pale gray broth with lumpy, white things floating in it. It didn't look remotely appetizing, not even to someone as hungry as she was.

"How nice," Chandra said politely, trying not to let her face contort when she took a whiff. The stuff smelled ghastly. "What is this dish?"

"Grub soup," said Falia.

Chandra focused on keeping her expression courteous. "Ah."

No wonder everyone here was so thin! Who would ever eat more than they absolutely had to, if this was a typical local dish? She suddenly missed Regatha.

"It looks delicious," Gideon said in an admirably sincere tone. "Thank you."

"You're our guests, and guests are a gift from the gods!"

Falia said with a bright smile as she rose to her feet. "That silly boy forgot to bring water for you. I'll go get it."

As soon as the girl disappeared through the doorway, Chandra said quietly, "I don't think I can eat this."

"It may be all we'll get for some time," Gideon said, looking into his bowl without enthusiasm. "And when was the last time you ate?"

"I can't even remember," she said. "But suddenly I'm not as hungry as I thought I was."

"Listen, it's meat. More or less." He sounded as if he was trying to convince himself. "It'll give you strength."

"I don't suppose many things grow in a land of constant darkness," she said, noting the absence of vegetables in the soup. Chandra filled her spoon with the broth, which was much more viscous than she had anticipated, and lifted it to take a sip. The closer she brought it to her lips, the harder it was was. She dropped the spoonful back into her bowl, untasted.

"Eat. We have been given this food. We can't refuse it," Gideon said, also lifting a spoonful of soup from his bowl.

Chandra reflected irritably that Jurl's noisy slurping wasn't making the soup seem any less disgusting, either. She said loudly, "I think I'd have preferred roasted goblin."

"The village looks poor," Gideon said, "so they probably only serve goblin on special occasions."

Jurl gave a surly grunt before he returned to gobbling the grub soup.

Gideon said to her, "Eat."

"You first," she said.

He sniffed the thick, shiny, gray broth filling his spoon and evidently decided that inhaling was a mistake. Looking like he was holding his breath now, he took a sip. "It's . . . fine."

She knew he was lying, but Chandra used her spoon to scoop up a boiled grub. Gideon was right on one thing. It was meat. She needed strength. Summoning her will, she put it in her mouth and chewed on the rubbery morsel.

Falia re-entered the hut, carrying a clay pitcher and two cups. "Are you enjoying the soup?"

"It's excellent." Gideon took a big spoonful.

Falia smiled. "Good!"

"We have some questions, Falia," Gideon said.

"Eat first," Falia said. "Then we'll talk."

"Of course." Gideon nodded.

Chandra steeled her resolve and ate some more grub worms, washing them down with a generous quantity of water. Since Gideon was sipping the broth without expiring on the spot, she consumed some of it, too. The texture was disgusting, and the flavor could best be described as aquatic. She wondered what the grubs might have grown into.

The thought nearly made her gag, so she tried to empty her mind, and continued eating in silence—all while Jurl kept eating in noisy, voracious gulps.

The goblin finished his meal first. He gave a satisfied sigh, and shifted his position so that he could lean against the wall of the hut. After a few minutes, he fell into a peaceful doze. Chandra knew this because he snored.

When she could endure no more of the grub soup, Chandra set her bowl aside and looked at Falia, intending to thank her. That was when she realized that the girl was staring at Gideon again—this time, with a look that could only be longing.

From what Chandra had seen, there were few men in the village. Undoubtedly, Falia was evaluating Gideon's fitness as a mate. Though seemingly young for it, Falia clearly was ready for marriage. Chandra realized abruptly that the girl could well be several years older than she looked. Who knew what effects this blood ritual for the passing of wisdom had on an individual, to say nothing of her diet.

Even supposing that Falia was the same age at which girls on Chandra's native plane typically married, it was unsettling to see how she looked at Gideon.

Chandra wondered whether he was aware of her keen interest in him. Gideon simply ate, his gaze lowered all the while on the food. If he was aware of the girl's perusal, he didn't acknowledge or return it.

When he finished eating, he set aside his bowl, and thanked Falia, who seemed to awaken from a trance.

She smiled. "Now what have you come here to ask me?"

"Has it always been nighttime on Diraden?" Gideon asked. "Forever?"

"Ah." She nodded. "You've come to ask about Prince Velrav's rule."

"Yes. Did the endless night begin with him?"

"It did."

"What happened?"

"When my grandmother was a child," Falia said, "there was day *and* night here. King Gelidor ruled Diraden. He had three sons. The youngest, Prince Velrav, was wild and dissolute."

The girl was a good storyteller, and the tale flowed smoothly, but the heart of the story was simple. The young Prince Velrav had engaged in various scandalous and destructive indulgences until his father banished him from castle and court.

Furious over his exile, and more ambitious and vengeful than anyone had ever guessed, Prince Velrav studied black magic and consorted with the darkest blood demons of the realm to plot against his father.

"You tell the story well," Chandra said when Falia paused.

"Thank you," said Falia, smiling at Gideon as if *he* had delivered the compliment.

Jurl snored peacefully as the girl continued her story.

"When he felt ready to carry out his nefarious plan, Velrav returned to his father's castle. He presented himself as a humbled, penitent son, reformed in his ways and seeking forgiveness. The king welcomed home his wayward son, and never thought to protect himself from him."

"Which was evidently a mistake?" said Chandra.

Falia nodded. "In the dead of night, while the whole castle slept, the prince crept into his two brothers' bed chambers and murdered them both, along with their wives. Then he went into the nursery and slaughtered the three children whom his brothers had sired."

"He slaughtered the children?" Chandra repeated.

"Then he went to his parents' chamber," Falia said, "where he beheaded his mother with one heavy blow of his sword."

"He killed his *mother*?" Chandra blurted.

"He's very wicked," the girl said prosaically.

"He beheaded her," Gideon mused. "Interesting."

"It's not *interesting*," Chandra said. "It's disgusting! His own mother!"

"And then he murdered the king?" Gideon asked.

"No." Falia shook her head. "He fed on the king."

"He *ate* his father?" The grub soup churned unpleasantly in Chandra's stomach.

"No, he fed on him," Falia said.

Chandra said, "What's the diff—"

"And that didn't kill the king?" Gideon asked.

"It might have, of course," the girl said. "But he also fed the king of himself."

"Fed him of himself?" Chandra said with a frown. "What does that mean?"

Gideon asked, "Is the king still alive?"

"Of course not," Chandra said dismissively. "This happened when Falia's grandmother was a child." A man who'd had grown sons and grandchildren that long ago wouldn't still be alive now.

"Yes." Ignoring Chandra, Falia nodded, holding Gideon's gaze. "The king lives still. And since the night Prince Velrav killed his family and turned his father into a sickly shadow of what he himself had become," Falia said, "daylight has never again come to Diraden."

"How can the king still be alive after all this time?" Chandra wondered.

"Blood magic," Gideon said.

"*Fierce* blood magic," Falia said, her nostrils flaring. "Wicked. *Dark*." She made the words sound . . . seductive.

Gideon said to her, "That's what the 'hunger' is."

They looked to Falia for confirmation. She nodded.

"Why did he feed his father his own blood?" Gideon asked. "He'd killed the rest of the family. Why keep the king alive?"

"To curse him," said Falia. "The king lives in the darkest, deepest dungeon of the castle. He is fed only blood. He is left alone, in terrible solitude. No one speaks to him or sees him, except for Velrav, who visits him once in a great while and tells him about all the torment and suffering he is inflicting on the king's realm."

"And this has been going on since your grandmother was a child?" Chandra asked, appalled.

"So that's why Velrav made it perpetual night here," Gideon mused.

"I don't understand," Chandra said.

"Some blood drinkers don't like daylight," he said.

"You mean they don't want to be *seen* drinking blood?" she said in puzzlement.

"No, I mean the sunlight burns them," he said. "Like fire. Those who choose blood magic, those who decide to embrace the power it holds must guard themselves at all cost against the powers of light."

Fire. The word reminded Chandra of their predicament.

"They don't like fire, either," Gideon said. "They're vulnerable to it."

"So he uses the veil of false night to block sunlight *and* red mana," she mused.

"And that same sorcery winds up blocking *all* mana, except black," Gideon said.

Falia said, "Yes, my grandmother says there once used to be other mana here. Other colors in the æther. Other kinds of magic." She gave them both an assessing gaze. "You are not from Diraden, are you?"

They both went still.

After a moment, Gideon said, "No."

"Where did you come from?"

"Someplace very far away," Gideon said. "And we can't go back there while Velrav's power holds."

"And you would *like* to go back there? Together?"

"Yes," said Gideon. "We would."

Falia said with certainty, "The prince will not help you or give you permission to go."

"No, I didn't think so," Gideon said. "Tell me about this veil of night, Falia, this shroud. It blocks mana and light, but it also keeps things alive, doesn't it?"

"Yes," she said. "Just enough that many things aren't really alive here anymore, yet they don't really die."

"That's a tremendous amount of power. Can he do that all alone?"

LAURA RESNICK

"No," the girl said, "his companions work with him to maintain the veil."

"His companions?" Gideon asked.

"They are the blood demons who helped him develop the power."

"And blood is what feeds their power?" Chandra asked.

"Yes," Falia said. "When they feel the hunger, they seek more blood to sustain them. To empower their dark work."

"How often do they get hungry?" Chandra asked.

"Often."

"And then people are taken." Gideon said.

"People. Goblins. Creatures. Animals." Falia paused. "They like people best. But any blood will feed the hunger. People, though . . . those thrill them."

Gideon studied her. "Do people with power thrill them in particular?"

Falia nodded.

"People with power," Chandra said, "such as a monarch?"

She lowered her eyes. "Yes."

"You're in danger?" Gideon asked quietly.

"Always," Falia said.

CHAPTER TWELVE

Falia offered them water to wash their skin and damp cloths to wipe away the worst of the grime and dirt from their garments. She loaned them a comb and got one of the village men to lend Gideon his razor. After they were clean and tidy, she suggested they all get some rest.

She was willing to share her hut with them . . . but not with Jurl.

"Goblins are treacherous," she said. "Even with his hands bound, I wouldn't feel safe sleeping in the same dwelling with him. We should put him in a secure place."

Chandra thought that made perfect sense, so they woke Jurl, who was cranky about being disturbed, but became more so at the prospect of being locked up while the rest of them slept in relative comfort.

One of the huts in the village had originally been built to protect livestock at night. However, most of the livestock on Diraden had long since died and now the building was empty. There was also a large, sturdy cage in the hut, which Falia said had formerly been used to keep wild boars being fattened for the annual harvest feast. There had been no harvests since Prince Velrav came to power, obviously, and it had been some time since the villagers had even seen a wild boar.

They locked Jurl in the cage. He was hotly opposed to the idea, and it took Gideon some effort to get the goblin into the thing. Afterwards, Falia took Gideon back to her hut to clean the scratches that Jurl's claws had left on his skin.

Chandra remained behind in the livestock hut and said to the goblin, "Stop that snarling! We can't let you go, and that's your own fault."

"Bad," said Jurl.

"Nonsense. You'll be perfectly comfortable in here."

"Village eat goblin," he said ominously.

"What?" She realized Jurl must have heard her dinner conversation with Gideon. "Don't be silly. We were joking. They won't roast you."

"Stranger," Jurl said bitterly. "Stupid."

"I consider the source," Chandra said, "and feel unmoved by the insult."

She left him sulking and made her way back to Falia's hut.

Predictably, perhaps, the girl had convinced Gideon to remove his tunic, and she was making a lengthy and intimate task out of tending what were only a few negligible goblin scratches on his chest. Chandra gave the two of them a dismissive glance, then went over to the bedroll that had been provided for her, smoothed it out on the floor, and lay down. While doing so, she noticed in passing that Gideon had a broad, hard, mostly hairless chest, and his arms were well muscled. There were several scars on his left arm, and another on his stomach.

At length, Falia ministered to his wounds. Then she offered to comb his hair for him, which was still rather tousled.

Chandra snorted.

Giving no sign that he had noticed Chandra's derision, Gideon smiled kindly at Falia and assured her he was accustomed to doing it himself. "But thank you for the offer."

Rosy-cheeked and glowing from within now, Falia looked quite different from the pale, hollow-eyed girl whom they had first met. "Please make yourself comfortable in the other bedroll," she said to Gideon. "I must go and get another."

"Am I taking yours?" he said. "I don't want to deprive you of your bed, Falia."

"Please, you're my guest. It's my pleasure that you should sleep in my bed!"

I'll *bet* it is, Chandra thought.

"I'll get another bedroll for myself from my aunt's hut," the girl said. "I'll be back shortly."

As soon as she left, Chandra said reprovingly to Gideon, "She's a *child*."

"Actually, she's probably older than either of us, Chandra."

"You think?" She propped herself up on her elbows and looked at him in perplexity.

"One of the typical effects of blood magic is that it slows or even halts the normal aging process."

"But surely she's not a blood drinker?" Chandra said.

"No, I think she's exactly what she says she is: the village menarch. You heard what she said. The wise woman passes her wisdom to her successor through a blood ritual."

"Yes, I did hear that." Chandra lay down again and stared at the flickering light from the candles as it bounced off the ceiling. "The wise woman passes along knowledge and wisdom through her blood, and maybe some power. And part of the power involves ensuring that the next wise woman remains the exact same age she is at the time of initiation . . . until it's time for her to turn the duty over to her successor?"

"It seems necessary," Gideon said. "She remains young so that she can marry and bear children, but that could take a long time considering how few people are in the village. I imagine mortality rates among infants is high in this kind of environment."

"I think she sees you as a potential mate." Chandra thought it over. "How old do you think she is?"

"We'd probably be able to make a better guess if we met the aunt who was the wise woman before her."

"Well," Chandra said, "no wonder Falia seems so, er, ready for marriage."

"That's a surprisingly tactful way for you to put it. You must be tired." He stepped over her prone body and started laying his bedroll in the narrow space between hers and the wall.

"What are you doing?" she demanded. "You're *not* sleeping this close to me."

"Yes, I am. I want you lying between me and her," he said firmly. "You're my protection."

Chandra snorted again. "Oh. All right. Fine."

She rolled over on her side, with her back to him, and closed her eyes. She assumed Falia wouldn't be pleased with this arrangement when she returned to the hut, but Chandra was much too tired to care.

* * * * *

She dreamed of fire.

Not the hot power that had mingled with her fear and fury when she killed the Enervants. And not the wild flames that had scalded her in the Blind Eternities as she made her escape from the Prelate's dungeon.

The fire in her dreams wasn't the seduction of a boom spell, or the fragile sparks of a new enchantment. No, this was the fire of sorrow and grief, of shame and regret.

"I don't want to kill any innocents," Gideon said in that calm, impassive voice he often used. White flames danced around him as he said it. Pure white.

And in those flames, she could hear their screams clearly. Their bodies writhed in the fire, and the stench of their burning flesh made her want to vomit, as it always did. Her throat burned with sobs that wouldn't come out.

But the sobs *must* be coming out, because she could hear them. Choked, desperate, tearful gasps.

"Chandra," he whispered, his voice cool against the heat of the agonized screams of the innocents dying in the fire.

She tried to move, but her limbs were immobile. She wanted to scream, but only a helpless moan emerged from her throat.

"Chandra."

And when the blade of a sword swept down to her throat, she awoke with a strangled gasp of horror.

It was dark. No candles were burning. And Chandra had no fire to call upon here.

"Shhh, it's a dream, just a dream," Gideon whispered. His arms came around her. "Shhh."

She struggled against the imprisoning arms.

"It's me," he whispered. "You had a nightmare."

Her heart was pounding. Her temples throbbed. She was sweating. A strangled sob escaped her throat, humiliating her.

His body was pressed up against her side as she lay on her back. One hard arm encircled her shoulders, the other curled around to cradle her face. "Shhh. You're fine. It was just a dream."

Chandra raised her hand to the hand that cupped her cheek. She intended to reject that intrusive, offending caress. To fling off his hand . . . But somehow, instead, she found herself grasping it. He returned her grip and squeezed gently.

"Just a dream," he said again.

She focused on her breathing, trying to steady it.

"Maybe going to bed on a belly full of grub worms wasn't such a good idea," he whispered.

A choke of surprised laughter escaped her.

Then she felt queasy. "You had to mention that," she murmured. "I'd actually forgotten."

"Sorry," he breathed against her ear.

She took a deep breath, then let it out slowly. She could still hear her heart thudding with terror and guilt.

Gideon said, "Do you want to tell me what you dreamed?"

"No."

He accepted this, and they lay quietly together. After a while, he lifted his head. Then he whispered, "It's too dark to see, but I think she's still asleep."

Chandra was glad she hadn't disturbed the girl. Having woken Gideon was embarrassing enough.

He lowered his head again, letting it rest close to hers. "I can't tell how long we've been asleep. The light's always exactly the same here."

"The moonlight, you mean."

"Mmm."

She tried to get her mind off the shadows of her past. It was better to think about the present—even *this* present. "Now that we know more about Velrav and this place . . . I don't feel we're any closer to knowing what to do about it. How to get out of here, I mean." She kept her voice soft, so as not to wake Falia.

"Widespread rebellion would be handy," Gideon said, "but I doubt it'll happen."

"Because it hasn't happened yet?" she whispered. "In all these years of suffering?"

"And also because this whole plane is steeped in dark magic."

"Including our hostess?" Chandra guessed.

"That blood ritual? Yes." Lying entwined with him like this, she could feel him shake his head slightly. "They won't unite. The different groups here won't help anyone but themselves. And however tormented the situation may be, it's got a sort of consistency and balance that they're used to by now."

"You'd think the food alone would be cause enough to rebel. *Grub soup?*"

She felt his soft puff of laughter against her cheek in the dark.

"If they *would* rebel," Gideon said after a moment, "then the flow of blood to Velrav and his companions might be reduced. Even cut off."

"So that's our plan?" she said doubtfully. "Lead an uprising?"

"No. It would take too long. Years, if it worked at all. Which it probably wouldn't." He added, "Besides, it might also take a while for Velrav to feel the effects of going hungry and start weakening. We need a faster plan."

"Yes. Faster is better."

"I thought you'd think so."

"But in our current condition," she whispered, "how can we attack someone that powerful?"

Gideon sighed and shifted his position a little. "I don't know."

Instead of rolling away from him, she shifted her position, too, getting more comfortable in his arms. The feel of his body was comforting. The whisper of his breath along her cheek, his voice soft in her ear . . . For now, he was a safe place to hide from her nightmares.

"You said blood drinkers are vulnerable to fire," she whispered. "Maybe we should burn down the castle. The normal way, I mean. With torches and that sort of thing."

"We'd have to go see the place to get an idea of what it would take to burn it down without magic. But stone walls added to a damp climate . . ."

The prospect wasn't promising. Chandra tried to think of another plan. "Jurl captures people and delivers them to Velrav. Actually, he probably captures goblins, too. He's obviously not sentimental about his own race."

"You think Jurl may know more about Velrav than we've learned so far?" Gideon guessed.

"But whether what he says will make much sense . . ."

"Well, we can try in the morning." He paused. "Or, uh, when it's time to get up, I mean."

The night was so still and silent, the villagers must all still be sleeping.

His hand brushed her hair as he whispered, "Try to get some more sleep."

Chandra's lids felt heavy, but she was afraid to go back to sleep. Afraid of what her dreams might hold. She'd rather stay here, with him. "I'm not sleepy," she lied.

She was sure he heard the fatigue in her voice, but he didn't argue. Instead, he stroked her hair in silence for a while.

Finally he said, "I'm wondering . . ."

"Hmm?" She didn't move or open her eyes.

"Will you . . ." He hesitated and again, then said quietly, "What happened to your mother?"

Chandra drew in a sharp breath and went tense all over. She knew he felt it. The stroking hand on her hair became still.

"What?" Her voice was cold.

"You cried out for her. In your dream—your nightmare. It seemed like . . . What happened to her?"

She sat up, tearing herself out of his embrace. When she felt his hand on her arm, she flung it off.

He sat up, too, but he didn't try to touch her again. "Chandra . . ."

She started to speak, then changed her mind. Anything she might say now would reveal too much—even if only how forbidden the subject was.

"I apologize." His voice was calm. Trying to make *her* calm. "I shouldn't have asked."

Chandra inhaled deeply. *In, two, three.* Then exhaled. *Out, two, three.*

She could feel him peering at her, and was glad the darkness hid her face, as it hid his.

When she thought she had control of her voice—of her words, and thoughts—she said, "You're right, we should get some more sleep. I'm still tired."

There was a pause. "Of course."

His voice had that impassive tone he often used.

Chandra lay down on her bedroll with her back to him. She felt him move away from her, returning to his own bedroll, where he should have stayed in the first place.

She lay awake for a long time in the dark, with her eyes wide open, forbidding herself to think about anything. *Anything.*

✳ ✳ ✳ ✳ ✳

Although she didn't expect it to happen, Chandra drifted off eventually, and she slept soundly. When she awoke, Gideon had already risen and gone back out into the night. Falia said some of the men had taken him to speak to someone who could tell him more about the Fog Riders that they had seen earlier.

"The rest of the villagers are all doing their work." Falia said to her, "There is no one to guide you to where he is. You must remain here."

The girl's manner toward her now was noticeably cool. It was all too easy to guess why, given where Gideon had chosen to place his bedroll when they all went to sleep. Chandra might have told Falia that she had no interest in Gideon, let alone in competing for his affections. But that seemed like too absurd a conversation to have with someone who looked so young.

Not wanting to stay on Diraden—or in Gideon's company—one moment longer than she had to, Chandra decided to tackle a task that she and Gideon had talked about: questioning Jurl. So she went into the livestock hut to see him.

The cage was empty. The goblin was gone.

Chandra turned around, intending to go alert the villagers. She found Falia in the doorway behind her. The girl had followed her here.

"He's escaped!" Chandra said.

"No," Falia said.

"Then were is he?"

"Being skinned and roasted."

"*What?*"

"Goblins make good eating." Falia gave Chandra's horrified reaction a look of cool amusement.

"You've *killed* him?"

"We've butchered him."

"You're going to *eat* him?" Chandra couldn't believe this was happening.

"Of course."

"Oh, *no.*" Chandra covered her face with her hands, swamped with guilt. "No wonder he was so angry at me! He *knew* you might do this! And Gideon and I locked him in here! We made him helpless!"

"He was a *goblin*." The girl's voice was contemptuous.

"But he was my . . ."

Actually, friend would be wildly inaccurate. Jurl had tried to kill her and Gideon; and they had taken him prisoner and brutalized him when he resisted their questions or orders.

Such behavior, on either side, wasn't exactly the basis of friendship.

Chandra knew full well the goblin was treacherous, amoral, and vicious. She had no doubt that, given a chance, he'd have fed her to Velrav without the slightest hesitation or pang of regret. She had also known that a situation might arise where she or Gideon would have to kill Jurl.

But she had never intended to turn him into a helpless, caged victim that the villagers could skin and skewer at their leisure.

But that was exactly what she had done.

Chandra stared at the smirking girl in the doorway. "How can you eat someone you've *talked* to? Someone you've given food to?"

"I fed him because his skin looked a little too loose when you got here. A well-fed goblin is juicier."

Chandra was aghast that she had slept in the same small hut with this revolting, sneering, deceitful child! "I think I'm going to be sick."

She was so angry she felt dizzy. She also thought she felt a sudden headache coming on. There was a pounding in her ears, a harsh, uneven drumming that echoed around her . . .

Chandra frowned, realizing the sound wasn't inside her head. And it was, she realized with a creeping chill, familiar.

"If you plan to vomit, get it over with." The girl's voice was hard. Her eyes were narrow and her lips tight with loathing. "The riders are coming for you."

"What?" Chandra breathed.

"The Fog Riders are coming to take you to Prince Velrav." Falia's tone dripped with dark satisfaction.

Chandra heard the echoing beat of approaching horses, their hooves thundering against the ground. "Me?" Chandra felt the hut closing in on her. "But . . . why? I mean, how do they know I'm here?"

"Because I summoned them."

"You?"

"I told you, people thrill him. Power thrills him. Why do you suppose he has not fed on *me*?"

"Power," Chandra murmured. "*Power.*" She tried to call on mana. Any amount. Any feeble flow that she could use to power her fire.

"Because I trade with him for my life." Falia looked much older than she had before. Perhaps even older than her true age. In that moment, she looked hard, ruthless, and casually cruel. "I find special things for him. A fire mage, such as you . . . Oh, my. *Very* exotic, Chandra."

She looked at the girl sharply. "Did you drag that out of Jurl with your skinning and roasting tools?" She knew Falia hadn't heard it from her or Gideon.

"He traded the information for his life. But goblins are stupid. He was still caged when he gave up your secret, you see. He didn't even realize there was no reason not to kill him once he'd told us. If only more goblins were merchants."

"So you're one of the takers," Chandra said, calling on her fury, calling on fire . . . and scarcely even able to feel her chilled blood warm a little bit.

"This is Diraden." The girl's voice was flat. "*Everyone* is a taker. Some of us are just better at it than others."

Chandra decided they had chatted long enough. Fire magic wouldn't work. Velrav had seen to that. She'd have to evade those Fog Riders the old-fashioned way—by running, hiding, and finding a means to fight them even without her power. And the first step was to get out of this hut and away from this smirking *brat*.

Chandra ran, straight into Falia, driving the flat of her palm against the girl's face and striking upward. Falia shrieked in pain and fell backward. Chandra dashed past her . . . and found herself running straight into about a dozen spears.

She barely managed to stop her headlong rush into the ambush without skewering herself on the sharp metal points. She stood, frozen on the spot, looking down at the spear blades pressed against the vulnerable flesh of her throat, her breasts, and her belly.

The hoof beats were getting closer. The riders would be here in moments.

Falia arose from her sprawled position on the ground. Her nose was gushing blood. It flowed down her face and into her mouth, coating her teeth with red as she snarled at Chandra. Her dark eyes blazing with fury, the girl walked over, spat in Chandra's face, and then slapped her, hard.

Chandra gave very serious though to retaliating . . . but she didn't favor dying of a dozen spear wounds in exchange for the pleasure of hitting the brat. Instead, she demanded, "What have you done with Gideon, you warped little bitch?"

"Gideon is where I told you he was."

"Is he alive?"

"Of course!"

Chandra studied her. "Ah, I see. You got him out of the way so you could have me carried off without his interference."

"When he returns, I'll tell him you disappeared. I'll be very convincing." Falia wiped her bloody face with her sleeve, but this only succeeded in smearing the blood all over her skin. "He'll never know what happened to you. And he'll forget about leaving here. Once you're gone, he'll stop thinking about going back to wherever you came from."

"And, of course, you'll comfort him tenderly while he grieves for me?" Chandra said.

"He will forget you," the girl said with malicious satisfaction. "You are *nothing*."

"I thought I was special enough to be a life-saving treat for your dark prince?" Chandra shrugged. "Listen, you sickly, demented, venomous *child*, if you think Gideon will *ever* notice you, then you're even sillier than I thought you were."

"He has already noticed me. I have more at my disposal than you may think. He will be mine," the girl said furiously, her blood-smeared, sallow face going an unbecoming shade of puce. "If I am ever to be allowed to live, and better, to die, I need to produce a healthy successor. Gideon will help me do that."

In that moment Chandra understood. Falia was as trapped as she was, perhaps even more so.

The noise of galloping hooves became too loud for further conversation, which was something of a relief.

The first thing Chandra saw was that fast-moving cloud of white fog traveling across the ground, glowing in the moonlight. Then she was able to see the riders, their looming black shapes rising out of the fog as they raced toward her.

They looked so terrifying that, for a moment, she couldn't move. It was like being trapped in one of her nightmares. She wanted to scream, to flee, to weep, and she couldn't do any of these things.

Then her wits came back to her in a welcome rush.

Spears! she thought. That ought to be an effective weapon against a rider.

And *fire*. Gideon had said that blood drinkers didn't like it.

The four riders entered this part of the village and cantered around Chandra and her captors, circling them like a pack of predators. The thick mist swirled around the villagers and amongst them. Chandra felt as if icy snakes were twining around her knees when the fog reached her.

Perpetual nighttime worked in her favor on this occasion. Several of the men surrounding her were carrying torches.

She simulated terrified hysteria—which wasn't that big of a leap—and staggered to her right, feigning confusion and panic as she shrieked. The men broke position, some of them falling back, others stepping to one side. She found her opening and seized a torch from one of them. She swung it around like a club, using the fire to keep her captors away.

"Seize her!" Falia shouted.

Chandra shoved the torch into the face of one of the men. He staggered backwards, lost his footing, and dropped his spear. Chandra caught it with her foot and kicked it up to her other hand. Warding off her captors with the spear, she used the torch to set fire to thatched roofs of two nearby huts. With the light wind, there as a good chance the fire would spread to more huts. Meanwhile, it was already distracting the villagers and sparking some panic among them. She hoped that, beneath the dark pall that covered Diraden, a big enough fire would be visible from far away. It would alert Gideon, if he saw it.

She had never used a spear before, but she assumed that sticking the pointy end into soft flesh would be effective.

Turning suddenly, she dashed toward one of the riders and shoved the spear into his guts.

The force of her blow almost unseated him, but he was a skilled rider and clung to his mount. She could see the rider's face as he moved away, the spear lodged in his belly. It was a bony and ghastly white visage, with black eyes, and lips so dark they looked black, too.

The villagers had backed off to the edge of the fray, but Falia was screaming for them to seize her. They apparently thought it was a challenge best left to the Fog Riders. They were more concerned about their burning village.

Chandra turned with her torch to attack another of the four riders. As he came toward her, she shoved the torch into the dark horse's face. The animal whinnied, reared up, and danced sideways. She was about to follow up her attack and go after the rider when instinct warned her to look behind her.

The rider she had stabbed had withdrawn the spear from his guts and was swinging the long wooden handle straight toward her head.

In the moment before it hit her, Chandra thought irritably that Gideon hadn't warned her that blades wouldn't kill blood drinkers.

CHAPTER THIRTEEN

Chandra gradually became aware of a weight on her head. So heavy it hurt. Hurt *terribly*.

It felt as if an enormous rock was pounding *into* her skull, over and over. It hurt to move, it even hurt to groan. She lay there in dazed silence, wishing the pain would go away.

She heard unfamiliar voices, echoing noises, laughter, growls. Sometimes she heard sighs or sobbing and felt wetness on her face.

"There, there," said a deep, melodious voice.

For some reason, the voice frightened her. She hoped it would go away and never come back.

But it did come back.

"You look better, my dear."

There was a groan. Chandra thought she had made the noise. To test this theory, she deliberately tried to repeat the sound.

Yes! She heard it again. *She* was groaning.

But the effort was exhausting, and she sank back into oblivion.

"Yes, I think you may surprise us and survive," said the voice, some unknown time later. "I love surprises. Are you waking up?" the voice asked, dripping with amusement. "That's it. Open those eyes wide. Surely it's time for us to meet?"

Chandra squinted even in the dim light of the room. She heard a feeble moan and was embarrassed that *she* had made that pathetic sound.

Her vision adjusted and she gradually recognized that she was lying in a bed, with a red, silken canopy overhead. The opulent room was large and lighted with candles.

The pain in her head gave her a dazed feeling that she at first attributed to her unfamiliar surroundings.

"Ah, she lives," said the deep, melodious voice that had become so familiar to her recently.

Chandra didn't like the sound of it any more now than when she had been out of her senses. Moving carefully, she turned her head in the direction the voice had come from.

A young man stood next to a dormant fireplace on the far side of the room. He was tall, slim, and fair-skinned, with black hair that gleamed as if it had been polished, and red-rimmed dark eyes. His lips were so dark, they looked almost purple.

Chandra did not find him an attractive example of manhood.

"I've won," he said.

"Won?" she tried to say.

Her tongue wasn't quite working yet, but the man seemed to understand what she meant.

"The wager," he said. "Some bet you would die shortly after you were brought here. Others gambled that you'd linger for a bit, then quietly expire. I, however, knew that you would make a full recovery."

"Recover?"

"Do you remember what happened?"

"I . . ." Chandra had a feeling, despite the relative comfort of her bed, that this was not a good place to be.

She started wading through the debris in her mind. Abruptly, the details of her capture came back to her.

Where is Gideon?

She groaned.

"Oh, dear," said the young man. "That tragic?"

"Price Velrav," she croaked with certainty.

"At your service!" He swooped down in an elaborate genuflection. "May I call you Chandra?" He added, "Since you've been lying in my bed for so long, I feel like conventional formalities would be absurd."

She ignored the throbbing in her head, and looked under the sheet that covered her. "Where are my clothes?"

Her throat was so dry, she choked a little from the effort of speaking.

"I had them taken away to be cleaned. They were filthy." He crossed the room to sit on the bed beside her prone body. "I didn't want them soiling my sheets."

She glared at him. "This is *your* bed?"

"Well, *all* the beds here are mine, but for now it's yours," he said, leaning forward as he reached out to trail his pale fingers along her naked shoulder.

"Touch me and I'll break your fingers," she snapped, knocking his hand away.

"There's water on the bedside table, it sounds as though you need it. Please," he gestured to a pitcher, his movements light, almost feline. "Drink, you will feel better."

Chandra jerked her chin at him. "Off the bed."

"As you wish, my dear." He rose with an amused look on his face.

She held the sheet in place as she laboriously pushed herself into a sitting position, always aware of the prince's red-rimmed gaze. She turned and poured herself a cup of water; she drank and felt better, pouring another glass as soon as she'd finished. Only after drinking a third glass did she look at him again.

"I like a woman who's that concentrated on fulfilling her needs," Velrav purred.

"I don't care what you like." Her voice sounded more normal now. She must have been unconscious for quite some time.

He grinned. Chandra steeled herself so as not to react to the eerily white teeth that were filed to sharp points revealed by his broad smile.

"The story the riders told me is easier to believe now." Velrav shrugged. "Lying there unconscious, you looked lovely, despite the bruises, and certainly very, er, *healthy*." His lascivious gaze traced her body up and down. "Even, one might say, robust."

"I attribute my good health to a steady diet of grub soup," she said sourly.

"That's a very nasty scratch on your thigh, though it's healing well. What did that to you?"

"A goblin," she said.

"Ugh. Nasty creatures," Velrav said fastidiously.

"And yet you eat them."

"*I* don't, my dear." He sounded appalled. "That's peasant food! Goblins are brought here only to feed some of my, er, less refined companions. What about that cut on your arm? It was festering nicely when you arrived."

She said nothing; it took her a moment to realize he was referring to the incision made by the Enervant to remove the burrowing snake.

"Hmmm, the red hair is exotic. Just as I hoped." Velrav tilted his head, studying her. "And now that your eyes are open, I find their color intriguing. Almost amber . . . fiery . . .

"When they brought you to me I was unimpressed. Despite your unusual coloring, you seemed like any other woman offered as a tithe."

He grinned again. "Now that you're awake, however . . . Yes, *now* I see the woman they told me about!"

"Get my clothes," she said coldly. "I want to get dressed."

"A lone woman who fought off a dozen villagers and four Fog Riders? It sounded too improbable! I thought perhaps the riders were trying to save their own lives by inventing the tale."

She frowned, distracted. "How would telling you I fought them save their lives?"

"Ah, it would satisfactorily explain the messy condition you were in when you arrived! Unconscious. Pulse faint. Breath shallow. Face bruised. Your head split open and bleeding," he said. "Of course, I had the servants clean you up."

Chandra ran a hand over her head and found a gash on her temple. She explored it delicately with her fingers. It was tender and swollen, but healing.

"The spear handle," she murmured, remembering. Evidently the rider had come close to killing her with that blow.

"Mortal bodies are so fragile," Velrav said sadly. "Yours is obviously stronger than most—remarkably strong, I would say. But nonetheless vulnerable."

"Yes, well, why did you care what condition I arrived in? Does blood taste better to you when the victim is awake and screaming?" she said scathingly.

"My dear! Vitality is of the utmost importance! I was positively enthralled by the description of such a healthy and vivacious young woman when the Fog Riders were summoned." He sighed. "I rarely get such a special treat.

Life is so . . . *dispirited* here. Naturally, I wanted you in perfect condition. And I gave orders to that effect." He folded his arms and smiled pleasantly at her. "The Fog Riders know how dangerous it is to disobey my orders."

"Well, sunlight can do a lot for morale," she said, not really interested. "You should look into it."

"Yes . . . Sunlight . . . You do say the most interesting things. Wherever did you get such an idea? I can't help but wonder. And wonder, I like to say, is the first of all passions."

"Listen here, Prince," Chandra said. "If you think I'm going to kindle anything but your funeral pyre, you are sadly mistaken."

"I can't tell you how happy that makes me, Chandra," he said with true glee. "Things have been so dull here for the past half-century."

Chandra wasn't sure how to react to that. Velrav just stood there looking at her, smiling, waiting.

"Maybe I could have my clothes now?" Chandra asked after what seemed forever.

The Prince's smile vanished. "How very boring," Velrav said, crestfallen. "The conversation was going so well for a minute . . . Mother always told me to temper my expectations."

"I suppose that's why you cut her head off?"

"Ah . . . Witty *and* well informed. You are a gift, Chandra. What could I have done to deserve this?"

"I'm sure you'll come up with something, but the clothes would be nice while you consider it."

"Yes, in due time. But I am curious about you. A *fire mage*, the girl claimed, although I can't imagine how this could be." Velrav said with evident fascination. "Is it true?"

"No need to ask me. Just release the enchantment you have on this plane, and you'll find out for yourself whether it's true."

"How rare and wonderful!" he said. "A fire mage! I haven't seen anyone who practiced fire magic since . . . Well, since before I murdered my family."

"I'd be happy to show you what I can do," she said.

"Oh, how I would enjoy that!"

"In that case, why don't y—"

"If only it were as easy for you as it is for me, eh?" he said with regret. "But how could I do so in good conscience? I do have to look out for my best interests, after all. And since there has been no fire magic on Diraden for quite some time," he said, "nor anyone of such enchantingly good health here for many years . . . Perhaps you'd like to tell me where you come from?"

"What does it matter? You can't go there."

"What makes you so sure?" he said. "You came here, after all. So why can't I go there?"

"I didn't come here on purpose." Staying somewhat close to the truth, she added, "And I don't know how to go back."

"Then fortune is mine."

"And the past doesn't matter."

"Oh, but it does," he said as he moved to a window to look out. "The past is what created who we are now, after all. But you will tell me in time. And if you don't, then perhaps your lover will."

"My lover?"

"The girl claims the man who came to the village with you is your lover. She saw proof of this." He added, "I, of course, didn't intrude on her delicate feelings by asking what she meant by that."

"He's a bounty hunter. I was his prisoner," she said, hoping that Gideon was not in Velrav's custody.

"And now you're mine . . . The menarch was quite upset when we took her prize."

"Her prize?"

"Yes, your *bounty hunter*," said Velrav, still looking down at something from his position at the window. "And she objected. So forcefully that the riders considered killing her." He glanced over his shoulder at Chandra. "But they knew they couldn't do that without asking me first. And I certainly would have said no."

He returned his gaze to something outside, beyond the window. "If the menarch is going to die, then *I'll* be the one to kill her. But, in truth, I have no wish for that. She finds such interesting treats for me, after all."

"Treats." The word was flat. His arrogance was astonishing.

Pulling the sheet with her, Chandra rose slowly from the bed. She was light-headed and her legs felt shaky. She wrapped the sheet around herself.

"Besides," Velrav said, "she's such a puny thing, I don't think she'd satisfy my hunger. No, it's far better to let her live as long as she keeps giving me wonderful gifts."

Walking on bare feet across the cool stone floor, Chandra asked, with a growing feeling of dread, "What about the bounty hunter?"

Velrav met her gaze, then he nodded in the direction of the window. "See for yourself."

Chandra tried to brace herself for whatever was coming, but her heart was pounding and she suspected Velrav could see that she was breathing a little too fast. She approached the window and looked down, trying to see what Velrav had been gazing at.

She found herself looking into a courtyard, which was surrounded by the wings of the castle on three sides. On the fourth side was a huge gate, bordered by a gate house and stables for a dozen or so horses. There were no trees or plants in sight, and the whole area was well-lit by torches that were positioned along the surrounding walls.

The courtyard was empty apart from one man.

Chandra clenched her teeth together as she stared at him in horror, willing herself not to cry out or satisfy Velrav with a shocked reaction.

Gideon stood between two tall, thick wooden posts. His arms were stretched out and securely tied to the posts. His long black hair was tangled and matted, and his head hung down. But since his legs were supporting him—albeit just barely—she knew he wasn't unconscious or dead. Not yet, anyway.

His torso was naked. The wounds that Jurl had left there had reopened and bled anew. The claw marks gaped wide, red, and angry, and rivulets of dried blood stuck to Gideon's fair skin. But Chandra didn't remember there being so *many* wounds, nor that they were that severe . . .

She drew in a sharp breath through her nostrils.

Most of those marks could not have been from Jurl, she realized. Someone had been deliberately cutting him.

Aware of Velrav's amused gaze on her, she kept her expression stony. When she was sure she could control her tone, she said, "The bounty hunter."

"He appeared—out of nowhere, I gather—as the riders were about to carry you out of the village. And he interfered." Velrav made a *tsk tsk* sound. "Most unwise. We would have never known about him if he hadn't."

Chandra ground her teeth together and focused on her breathing. She knew it was too loud, knew that Velrav heard it.

"He had the most remarkable weapon," Velrav continued. "It's mine now, and I adore it! You've seen it, I assume? It's sort of a three-bladed whip. He killed one of the Fog Riders with it."

193

Since running one of them through with a spear hadn't worked, that surprised her. "How?"

Velrav ignored the question. "After we captured him, Falia sent a message asking me to meet her. A very bold thing to do, don't you agree? Naturally, I was curious."

"Did she throw another tantrum?"

"No, evidently she had resigned herself to her loss. Instead, she offered me more treats." When Chandra glanced at him with a frown, he nodded toward Gideon and said, "Information about him."

"Ah." So the girl continued making herself more valuable to Velrav alive than dead. And she also ensured, by telling the cheerfully vindictive prince that Gideon and Chandra were lovers, that their supposed relationship would be remade now into a source of suffering and torment, rather than comfort and satisfaction. "What a nasty little girl."

"This man is, like you, unusually healthy and strong. Also tall." Velrav concluded, "You both come from the same place?"

"He followed me."

"And then he tried to rescue you."

She suspected where this conversation was going. "Rescue? No, I guess he was trying to keep *his* prize." Chandra tore her gaze away from Gideon to look at Velrav. "He's a bounty hunter. No prisoner, no reward."

"What crime did you commit?" the Prince asked with interest.

"It's a long story." She allowed herself a deep breath. "And I am not going to tell it."

"Oh, I hope you will someday," he said. "I suspect it must be a very engaging tale. That man down there—Gideon?"

"Uh-huh."

"Gideon killed a Fog Rider, which no one has ever done before, and he gave the other three riders quite a fight." Velrav sighed voluptuously as he gazed down at his bloody captive. "You must have committed a *very* impressive crime, for a man like that to come after you."

"Has he been tied up there the whole time I've been lying in here?"

"More or less. And I believe he's been looking forward to this moment!" Velrav knocked hard on the window.

"Don't!" she said reflexively. The sound would carry well in the empty courtyard.

"Why ever not?" Velrav knocked harder.

As she had feared, Chandra lost control of her composure as Gideon's head slowly lifted. She pressed her palms against the window and looked down at him, distressed and appalled.

He looked up at the window. The torchlight illuminated his face, which was pale from blood loss and darkened by a thick shadow of hair on his jaws, chin, and upper lip. His left eye was blackened and swollen shut.

Gideon's weary, impassive expression didn't change, but she knew he saw her, silhouetted in the candlelight that shone on her unmistakable red hair.

"You look heartbroken, my dear," Velrav said smoothly. "I thought he was hunting you?"

"He was." She kept her gaze locked with Gideon's, though she doubted he could see her face clearly in this light. "That was just . . . business. What you're doing though . . ." She shook her head. "This is *disgusting.*"

"I suppose it's a little . . . ostentatious," Velrav admitted. "But I assure you it's not our normal custom. We usually have some sport with our captives—"

"Sport?" she repeated with loathing.

"—and then feed on them. On rare occasions, we might

bring someone into the fold. Someone like you, for example. But the rest die soon after arriving."

"So why is he . . . on *display* like this?"

"He killed a Fog Rider." Velrav's tone suggested the reason should be obvious, even to her. "So a certain amount of extraordinary treatment is expected. And I couldn't disappoint my companions and loyal servants, now could I? They deserve this."

She didn't try to continue speaking.

"You know, he's not looking at you like a hunter," Velrav observed, gazing down at Gideon. "No, indeed. The *hunt* is not what's in those lovely blue eyes of his."

"What do *you* know about hunting?" she said contemptuously. "You sit in this castle and have victims brought to you."

"Actually, I do still hunt a little," Velrav said, not sounding at all bothered by her disdain. "But not often, I must admit. Not anymore. Like everything else, I find it so *boring* by now."

"You've been alive for a long time." As she gazed at Gideon, Chandra remembered what he had told her about blood magic.

"Yes," he said. "Yes, I have."

"You've had total power, with no challengers, feeding on the blood of your people to stay young. You've had no purpose except to satisfy your own hunger." Chandra continued staring down at Gideon. "Night never turns to morning. The seasons never change. Even the moonlight never changes."

She could see Gideon's gaze growing more alert and intent as his exhausted, pain-fogged mind started to focus. She doubted he had known until this moment whether she was still alive. Even so, he maintained his control. She envied him that ability.

"What could possibly make your existence worthwhile anymore?" Chandra said to Velrav. "What could make your pointless existence still worth living?"

The prince was silent.

Someone entered the courtyard below. Like Velrav and the Fog Riders, this individual was male, slim, sickly pale, black-haired, with those unnaturally dark lips. He appeared to be in a hurry, going from one wing of the castle to another. As he passed Gideon, he withdrew a dagger from its sheathe on his belt and, with a casualness that shocked Chandra, slashed the blade across Gideon's back. He bent down and licked at the flow of blood.

She gasped and slapped her palms against the window.

Gideon grimaced and closed his eyes for a few moments. He lowered his head, and even from here, Chandra could see his chest heaving with his rapid breaths as he tried to master the pain.

"I've sometimes wondered the same thing myself," Velrav said somberly. "Why go on? Why not just end it? The weight of my boredom sometimes becomes so *unbearable*, I think I'll go mad."

"You *are* mad." She couldn't take her eyes off Gideon.

"I have indeed wondered, from time to time, what could possibly make my life worth living again."

Gideon tilted his head up again and looked for her in the window. She balled her hands into fists against the glass and didn't bother to try hiding how enraged and upset she was. Velrav knew, anyhow. Of course he knew.

"And then you both arrived," Velrav said, "and now I know."

"Know what?" she asked absently as she leaned her throbbing head against the window. Her heart was beating like it wanted to escape her chest.

"Know what would make this existence bearable again," the dark prince said. "Know what can make this tedious life as exciting as it used to be, long ago."

She tore her gaze away from Gideon and turned to frown quizzically at the prince. "Not that I care," she said, "but what are you talking about?"

"Now I know there is more beyond Diraden." he said. "So much more, in fact, that I am eager to explore it. And somehow, you and your bounty hunter will help me."

CHAPTER FOURTEEN

"That's his plan? To become a planeswalker?" Gideon's voice was weary.

"Yes," Chandra said.

"What have you been telling him?"

"He kept pressing me about things and really I just got tired of it. I felt like if I told him the truth he would leave me alone."

"Well, it's really the least of our worries. It'll never happen."

"Well, there's a little more to the plan. He's going to use you to do it. He has some blood ritual that he's preparing with the court magi. He thinks he can transmute your essence, or something."

They were talking through the door of Gideon's dungeon cell. He had been moved from the scene of his public bloodletting in the courtyard once the Prince had come to a decision. That had been some days ago.

From the next cell over, an old man's demented laughter rang out intermittently.

"Has that been going on the whole time?" she asked. Chandra had been given leave to move about the castle unsupervised. Velrav was so confident in his enchantment that he felt he had little to fear. Nevertheless, Chandra's feet and hands were shackled so that every where she went, she did it by taking mincing little steps. She didn't go many places. Still, she had been able to bribe one of the castle guards with a small bit of fire quartz that Brannon had given her on her last night at Keral Keep. That a simple rock was so exotic was a testament to Diraden's charm. She was grateful it had gotten her down here to see Gideon.

"Yes. If our man is to be believed, that's the king."

"Oh, yes indeed! I am the king and my rule would be absolute had my rule had not been absolved," he said, before breaking into uncontrolled laughter.

"That's not even a good play on words," said Chandra.

"It's better than some. Most of the time he doesn't make sense," said Gideon, over the ever-louder howls of laughter. "But the story Falia told us was more or less true. In between his laughing fits, he has told me a little about the prince's power, and his own. It seems that magical power here is based on lineage."

"What do you mean?"

"I'm not sure exactly, but all of this, the pall, the dampening spells, he achieves it all through rituals using the king's blood. It seems the prince's only true power comes from the king. That's why he has kept him alive for all these years.

"Indeed! The whelp knows he's nothing without me. If he ever wants total power, I must give it to him and he knows I never will." The maniacal laughter followed again. "And if I die without passing it to him, another will be born. He will have nothing. So he keeps me here, the next best thing, prolonging my life with blood magic."

Silence followed for a few moments, one of the rare lulls in his laughter.

"If it's your power, why can't you use it against him?" asked Chandra.

"He has cursed me. Imagine that! Cursed me with the help of demons. He thinks he paid with the blood of his family. He thinks he will live forever, but there is more to come, and they will have their payment."

"Lovely," was all Chandra could think to say. The vitriol in the old man's voice made her skin crawl. There was little doubt for her that this was the king.

"All lovely things have an ending . . . *ha!*" Whatever was funny about this was lost on the two of them.

"This is how it goes," said Gideon. "A moment or two of lucidity and then he moves from word to word. If there is a point I don't see it."

"Gideon, things are really looking bad. I mean, I may just be stuck here. He says the two of us will explore the Multiverse together, but he's going to kill you. Why did you have to come after me when the Fog Riders came?" she asked.

"You were slung over their saddle like a sack of grain. There was so much blood pouring from your head, I wasn't sure you'd live." He gaze went to the healing wound on her temple. "It looks a lot better now."

"It is. But why did you fight them for me? You could be on the outside trying to figure something out."

"I guess I didn't think. I thought they were going to kill you. I panicked."

"You weren't thinking?" Chandra asked, despite everything, unable to conceal a hint of enjoyment.

"You don't reserve the right to act irrationally, Chandra. Let's remember I'm the one imprisoned in a dungeon. You're the one sleeping in a nice bed and being offered a life spent trapsing across the planes of the Multiverse."

"I don't think his offer is reliable," she said. "He seems a little . . . cracked."

"It seems to run in the family," Gideon said dryly.

"Look, we made a deal when you got to Diraden, and you've stuck to your part of the bargain, so I'll stick to mine. We'll keep working together to get out of here."

He looked at her through the barred opening in the door, his gaze impassive. She knew that this was the face he offered to people when he wanted to conceal something. It made her feel impatient with him, even angry. He had nothing to conceal from her, not if they were going to escape.

"Why did you risk your life twice to steal the scroll on Kephalai?" he asked.

"You knew the scroll was precious," she said irritably. "You had it in your possession. Are you trying to tell me you didn't even look at it?"

"I looked at it."

"And?"

"And *what*?" He shrugged, then winced a little as his fresh wounds protested. "A spell written in a text I'm guessing you can't read—"

"Can *you*?"

"No, I can't read it. But I know where it is from."

"Don't mess with me Gideon."

"It's old, which explains what it was doing in the Sanctum of Stars. But that doesn't explain why *you* want it so badly."

"What does anyone want with anything? It's old, yeah. But it's unique. There's nothing else like it in the whole Multiverse, is what I've been told. It's a spell, yeah. But the monks back on Regatha think it could lead to something of immense power. Something way bigger than you or me." She paused while the king entered into another round of hysterics. "I don't know, Gideon. I wanted it for the glory. Something to make the Blind Eternities see."

"Never rely on the glory of morning, nor on the smile of a mother-in-law. Ah, ha, ha . . ."

As they waited for this latest laughing jag to subside, Gideon considered what Chandra had said, the passion she'd showed.

"It's from Zendikar," he said. "A plane of some repute. It is said to be host to some of the most powerful mana sources in the Multiverse, but it is also unpredictable, irratic. Violent and pacific in the same moment."

"Have you ever been there?"

"Never, but in my youth I searched."

Chandra stared at Gideon without seeing him, her mind fixed on what the scroll could lead to.

She wrapped her fingers around the bars that separated them. "You're sure the plane exisits?"

"I can't be certain, but, yes, reasonably sure."

"Do you know what this means, Gideon?" A light burned in Chandra's eyes. "If we could get to Zendikar and find this thing that the monks talk about? Think of the things we could do. Think of the power! The adventure!"

"Chandra, you don't even know what it is. It could be anything. It could be the darkest power you've ever known. It could kill you. It could . . ."

"You said it, Gideon. It could be anything. And we'll never know until we find it."

After a moment, Gideon looked into Chandra's eyes. They sparkled with a clarity he had never seen before. There was hope there, to be sure, but there was something more. To say that it was fire would be obvious. To say that it was life would be an understatement.

"We can't do anything until we get out of here," he said in a monotone.

Φ

Chandra hung her head. There was silence in the dungeon.

"If I may say so," said the king in a remarkably clear voice. "I believe I can help."

Chapter Fifteen

The plan was a little crazy. So many things could go wrong, she was sure Gideon would never go for it, preferring instead to sacrifice himself so that she could live, or some ridiculous thing like that. But the king said he could help. He told them he still had some tricks up his sleeve.

This was how he told them they could beat the prince and escape the shroud that held Diraden in darkness and restricted their connection to mana. The king would need some of Gideon's blood. Not much, maybe a spoonful and he would offer a similar amount of his own. He would use a bit of childhood magic he'd learned to confound his parents so many centuries ago. He and his siblings had often traded a bit of their blood in order to assume one another's appearance and so get out of lessons. The king was a bit hard to stop once he started on his reminiscence. Chandra had to be diligent in keeping him focused.

The king said he could make himself look like Gideon and vice versa. The old man had been alive too long, he said. It was time for him to die, especially if his death were vexing to the ungrateful whelp sitting on his throne. He would go in Gideon's place to be killed. When the prince mistakenly killed him, the shroud would be lifted. The prince would be powerless before them.

"But what about this transmutation he hopes to achieve? What if he is able to incorporate your essence?" Gideon asked, still skeptical of the plan.

"If it were possible, he would have tried. Don't you think?" asked Chandra. She had been in the dungeon for some time now. She couldn't rely on the guard to let her stay forever, or even be at the door when she tried to leave.

"The boy knows nothing. It is impossible," said the king. "My time has come and he cannot stop it."

"I am not filled with confidence," said Gideon.

"What else are we going to do?" asked Chandra. "I don't see a lot of options."

"Okay, but how are we going to move the blood between cells?"

"It must be in the woman's mouth!" shouted the king before entering into the first round of laughter in quite some time.

The thought was ridiculous to Chandra. Was this all an old crank's plan to put his tongue in her mouth? For the first time she moved down the hallway to the cell the king occupied and looked inside. What she saw nearly made her faint. Sitting cross-legged on the floor of his cell, the old man looked so pallid as to be translucent. Light blue veins covered his naked body like the veins of some gelid mineral. He was unbearably thin. He laughed with his toothless mouth wide, his tongue dryly avian. His black eyes were as lusterless as the surrounding stone.

"Gideon. We have to do this, but I'm not using my mouth."

⁂ ⁂ ⁂ ⁂ ⁂

In the hours, perhaps days, following her conspiratorial meeting with Gideon and the king, she thanked that shred of humanity that allowed a cup and pail of water in Gideon's cell.

She had ferried the blood back and forth and the the two had both drunk their portion. The king said the effect of the transmogrification would last indefinitely, but once he were killed, the effect would disappear. Putting their faith in the old man was risky, to say the least, but what other choice did they have?

Velrav had decided that he wanted Chandra present for the ritual. She assumed that was for no better reason than to enjoy her reaction to Gideon's death.

She'd been passing the time unwillingly in her room, where she could remain unshackled, waiting. She didn't think she had ever been this anxious. She went over all sorts of scenarios even when she had no idea what to expect. The image of the laughing king burned into her mind so that every time she closed her eyes, she saw him there, like a malevolent idol.

It was a relief when one of the nameless castle guards finally came to escort her to a wing of the castle she had never seen. He led her into an oval room without appointment save a long stone table at one end. The plane of the table slanted toward the middle of the oval at a sharp angle. Four straps were positioned at the corners, presumably to hold something, or somebody, in place. She was placed at the opposite end of the room and made to stand in a slight depression covered with a metal grate.

Her wrists and feet shackled, Chandra stood wondering what she was supposed to do as the guard went around the room lighting sconces. Next Gideon—she hoped it was the king—was escorted into the room by two guards. He was hunched slightly and his hair hung over his face; his naked torso, criss-crossed with wounds and mottled with bruises, was deathly pale. She hadn't noticed some of the wounds before. *Were the bruises new?* The guards picked him up, turned him upside down and strapped him to the table so that he faced up, his head pointing toward the floor. He offered no resistance. When his hair fell away from his face Chandra could see that he wore the stony expression, the impassive look she had come to know from him.

Chandra felt a little relief. At least they had gotten this far. But just then, another set of guards entered the room, carrying the king's body into the room. What was Gideon doing here? Did Velrav know the truth? The guards placed Gideon equidistant between Chandra and the king, at the wall so that the three of them formed a triangle, and left the room. Chandra was worried by this latest development, but there was nothing she could do.

And in walked Velrav. As tense as she felt, Chandra had to keep herself from laughing. He was wearing a lush and obviously expensive cloak, but he also wore a long conical hat with a broad brim and chin strap. The effect, though doubtlessly intended to make him look imposing, made him look like a fool, a sad minstrel imitating the pomp of royalty.

Velrav turned to Chandra. "I believe you know my father, the king? Are you surprised? No, of course not. Could you believe that I wouldn't know about your little clandestine visit? I thought I would let you visit your bounty hunter one last time."

Chandra couldn't respond. Her mind was racing. The whole situation was getting really annoying. Not a single thing had gone right since she got to this forsaken plane, and by now it was really going wrong. She could feel her skin begin to flush, all the familiar feelings of anger and frustration, but there was something missing. The bloom at the base of her skull, that power that she normally felt coursing down her spine and into her limbs wasn't there—but her blood was moving and that, at least, felt good.

"I brought him to bear witness to his only living son's transformation."

The old man began to laugh, that unmistakable laugh. Chandra balled her fists and clenched her jaw. Her mind raced uncontrollably. She tried to calm her mind down, tried to breathe, but she couldn't do it. Everything she knew, everything she'd done, nothing mattered. She felt it all fall away from her as the rage took control.

"I'm sorry, Chandra. He knows," said Gideon, from the table. "He came soon after you left and beat me within an inch of my life. With the body of the old man, I couldn't do a thing to defend myself."

The old man laughed still, rocking back and forth.

"Quiet, you old fool!" shouted Velrav as he pulled Gideon's sural from beneath his cloak and whipped at him clumsily, but it did nothing to stop the laughing. If anything, it only served to make the king laugh harder.

The fire in the sconce burned more brightly as Velrav kept whipping his laughing father, and Chandra felt it. She felt the mountain inside her. She was the volcano.

Everything slowed down when she got this way. She felt like she was moving outside of time as the power bloomed in the base of her skull, as the fierce flower she'd been missing filled her head and her hair became a raging halo of fire. Her fists became torches, her feet lit with alchemical intensity. She spread her arms wide, her shackles a molten puddle on the floor beneath her as she began to levitate.

Velrav turned to look at her, his mouth agape. The king's laugh raised to a fever pitch, his eyes gaining life as he reveled in Chandra's inferno.

Boom! Chandra brought her hands together in a thunderous clap as her feet returned to the floor, and a blade of fire rose from her hands. She turned to her right, spinning and swinging the flaming blade in order to carry through with all her momentum. When she came full circle she struck the prince in the neck, cleaving his head and opposite shoulder from his body. The cauterized flesh smoldered as the body fell to the side and Velrav's right arm and head landed in the laughing king's lap. It did nothing to quiet him.

The king patted the face of his son, and moved the head to the floor. He stood and crossed to Chandra, who was beginning to register what she had just done. Her flaming sword still burning brightly, and the old man only stopped laughing when he grabbed the blade. His flesh sizzled and burned immediately, the hideous hissing sound of the water in his body boiling away. With amazing resolve he impaled himself on the blade, even as Chandra tried to pull it back, but her shock made her too slow. The flames died, but not before the king. His body slumped on top of his son's.

Chandra turned to Gideon, who still lay upside-down on the table, blood coloring his once-pale face.

"Help me off," he said.

She turned and went to him. "Can you feel it? Mana!"

"Yes, I can feel it."

She wanted to revel in the flow of red mana that was suddenly *there*, had been there. She felt giddy, almost light-headed. She undid the straps holding him to the table and helped him off it.

"Let's leave. I'm sure I can planeswalk. Can you?" she asked him.

"I think I can, yes." He was looking at her in astonishment. "Chandra, what was that?"

"It was a blade of fire. I've never done that before."

"But how? I thought you were going to incinerate all of us. I've never seen anything like that."

She thought about it for a moment, then laughed with pleasure. "I feel *strong*." Her gaze wandered over his damaged, haggard appearance. "What about you?"

He looked down at his wounded, blood-streaked body. "I've been better." Gideon's eyes were wary, as though he was witnessing magic for the first time.

"We've got to get out of here, before someone comes, things are sure to be getting different out there," she said.

"You're right." His face resumed the confident calm she knew. "We need to planeswalk."

"Regatha?"

"I'm following you," said Gideon as he went and gathered his weapon.

After several minutes of concentration they left Diraden.

※ ※ ※ ※

They entered Regatha gently, landing on soft grass in a sunlit meadow.

Chandra lay on her back in the grass, looking up into the familiar sky. Gideon was stretched beside her. The sun came peeking through the lush trees at the edge of the meadow at an angle.

She touched his wounded, bloody chest. "Does it hurt very badly?"

His gaze dropped to her mouth. "Does what hurt?"

The trees overhead . . .

Chandra suddenly sat up.

Shoved aside, he lay looking up at her quizzically. "Is something wrong?"

"We're in the Great Western Wood," she said. "I'm, uh, not sure I should be here."

He sat up, too, and looked around. "Ah."

"We should go," Chandra said.

And then she realized she wasn't sure what to do with Gideon. She wanted to take him with her . . . but she thought it likely that the Keralians, though generally tolerant, would object to her bringing a mage with Gideon's particular talent. Especially given how tense things were between Keral Keep and the Order.

Chandra stood up, looked around, and got her bearings . . . and then realized where she could take Gideon.

"A friend of mine lives near here," she said. "We'll go to his home."

Samir would be distressed to see her in the forest, but she was confident he would nonetheless welcome them with sincere warmth and hospitality.

"This way," she said to Gideon, leading him toward Samir's nearby compound in the lush, green woodlands.

"Actually, Chandra, there's something . . ."

His voice trailed off and they both stood still, listening intently.

Chandra heard the rustle of a bush, then the crackling of a twig underfoot.

"Someone's coming," she whispered unnecessarily.

Oufes rarely made that much noise when moving through the forest, but she felt tense until she saw who it was. When a lithe, familiar figure came out of the dense greenery a few moments later, Chandra relaxed.

"Samir!"

"Chandra!" He smiled and waved. "You're *back*?" He looked around, as if fearing a hoard of angry oufes might instantly drop out of the trees and attack. "You shouldn't be here!"

"I know," she said. "And I'm leaving. But first—"

Samir's horrified gasp distracted her, as did the expression of shocked dismay on his face. "What *happened*?"

"What? Oh." She realized he was looking at Gideon. And as she glanced at her wounded, bloody, bearded, unwashed, unkempt, half-naked companion, Chandra realized that Samir's reaction was understandable.

"Chandra!" Samir said sharply, coming closer as he gazed at Gideon with appalled concern. "What did you *do* to him?"

"*I* didn't do anything to him! It was . . . uh, never mind. Listen, Samir, I would appreciate it if—"

"Young man, you're badly injured! You need healing!"

"It looks worse than it is," Gideon said.

Samir blinked. "Wait a moment. Have we . . ." He frowned and studied Gideon's face more closely. "I know you, don't I?"

Chandra said, "No, he's—"

"Yes!" Samir said. "Of course I do! It's Gideon, isn't it?"

Chandra froze.

"We met . . ." Samir's face clouded with dawning realization. "We met at the Temple of Heliud."

There was a tense silence as Chandra turned her stunned, appalled gaze on Gideon.

"Yes, that's right," Gideon said, his voice calm, his expression impassive. "I hope you've been well since then, Samir?"

Ⲫ

CHAPTER SIXTEEN

"You're from Regatha?" Chandra said in blank shock. Gideon's blue eyes met hers. She couldn't read his expression.

"From Regatha?" Samir repeated, sounding puzzled. "Er, where else *would* he be from, Chandra?"

Her gaze flashed to Samir. She blinked stupidly at him, abruptly remembering that he didn't know she was a planeswalker. Indeed, she doubted Samir had ever even *heard* of planeswalkers. And this was no time to start explaining the concept to him.

"I mean, you're from *here?*" she said to Gideon, feeling dumbfounded. Why had he never said so?

"I'm from Zinara." Gideon's voice was clear and firm. There was a flicker of warning in his eyes, reminding her to guard her tongue until they had a chance to talk alone together. Then he turned to Samir and said, by way of explanation for Chandra's puzzling remark, "As you can see, we've been through an ordeal. Chandra's disoriented."

"I am not!" she snapped.

Both men looked at her, then at each other. There was a brief, silent moment of commiseration between them that she found infuriating.

"Chandra . . ." Samir approached her, his expression concerned, and laid a gentle hand on her arm. "You're covered in blood."

"What?" Chandra looked down and realized he was right. Almost every part of herself that she could see was messily splattered with blood—most of it Prince Velrav's, she supposed. Cutting off his head had been messy, though that had not been her concern at the time. Chandra realized how grisly her face must look right now.

"I'm fine, Samir," she said dismissively.

"But your friend is not," said the woodland mage. "He needs—"

"We're not friends," she said, glaring at Gideon.

The truth about her mysterious companion was dawning on her with a deluge of appalling implications.

"You *followed* me," she said accusingly to Gideon.

The two men looked at each other again.

"We should go to my home immediately," Samir said to Gideon. "It's nearby."

"I'm not going anywhere!" Chandra said.

Even after learning he was a planeswalker, she had assumed that his business with her had originated on Kephalai and had something to do with the scroll. He'd been following her all along.

She said to him, "You lying, treacherous, *cowardly*—"

"Chandra!" Samir shook her shoulders. "We must go to my home. We can't stay here."

"I'm *not* staying here!" she said, contradicting her earlier assertion that she wasn't going anywhere. "Not with *him*. I'm going to Keral Keep."

"You can't," said Samir. "Not by day."

"Of course I can!"

"No, it's not safe."

Gideon looked sharply at Samir. "What do you mean?"

LAURA RESNICK

Samir said to Chandra, "A great deal has happened while you've been away. Come home with me, and I'll explain, while you wash and I look after Gideon."

"He doesn't need looking after!"

"He can't go all the way to Zinara like this," Samir said reasonably. "Those wounds should be cleaned and tended immediately." Samir glanced at Gideon's pale, haggard face. "He obviously needs food and drink, too."

"You're going to *feed* him?" she said. "You're going to feed this scheming . . ."

"I'm going to feed you, too," Samir said. "Perhaps then you'll make more sense."

"Samir," Gideon said, "what changes are you talking about?"

"Not here." Samir looked around nervously. "If Chandra is seen here now, I fear she may not live until sundown."

She said dismissively, "I can handle a few angry oufes."

"The problem has grown much bigger than that, Chandra," Samir said. "Much more serious."

"How serious?" asked Gideon.

"Two days ago," said Samir, "the inter-tribal council of the Great Western Wood agreed to capture Chandra and turn her over to the Order."

She stared at him in shock. She'd expected the situation would blow over, not worsen.

✷ ✷ ✷ ✷ ✷

With mingled reluctance and resentment, Chandra agreed to accompany the two men to Samir's family compound. As soon as they reached it, Samir showed her and Gideon into a small, fragrant hut that was primarily used for drying herbs.

"Wait here," he instructed them. "I'll get you some water for washing and some balm for those wounds. And I'll ask my wife to prepare some food."

Φ

"Oh, don't fuss over *him*, Samir," Chandra said. "He doesn't deserve your kindness."

"He's my guest," the village chief said.

And that, Chandra knew, settled the matter as far as Samir was concerned. She shrugged and folded her arms, knowing it was her anger that was letting her say things that risked letting Samir know their secrets, but not caring enough to stop herself. "Fine. Suit yourself. I just hope he doesn't give you cause to regret it."

Gideon's expression was so blank, it was as if he didn't even hear her speaking.

"I'll be back shortly," Samir said as he left the hut.

They stood alone together in the shadowy interior, staring at each other.

"You followed me to Kephalai!" she said as soon as Samir was out of earshot.

"Yes."

"From here!"

"Yes."

"Why?"

"Maybe we should sit down," Gideon suggested.

"Answer me!"

"Well, *I'm* sitting down," he said. "I think half my blood is lying on the pavement of Velrav's courtyard."

"How did you know I was going after the Scroll?" she demanded, watching him ease himself onto a wooden stool.

Gideon looked light-headed, probably because he had indeed lost a lot of blood and was certainly in need of food and water. He also looked as if the pain of his wounds had returned now that the excitement of escape had worn off.

It served him right.

"I *didn't* know," he said. "I'd never heard of the scroll. I'd never heard of Kephalai, either. I was just following you."

"*Why?*"

"Like I told you on Kephalai, you'd made yourself conspicuous."

"Yes, but that was on K—"

"Actually, I meant you'd made yourself conspicuous *here*," he said. "You misunderstood, of course, because you had just made yourself even *more* conspicuous on Kephalai."

"Did you follow me there so you could lecture me about my behavior?" she snapped.

"I followed you there," he said patiently, "to take you into custody."

"*Custody?* For who? Walbert?" When he nodded, she said, "So you *are* a bounty hunter."

"No, I'm more like a . . ." he shrugged. "A soldier."

"A soldier," she repeated.

"Yes."

"For the Order?"

He nodded again.

"Are you from Regatha?" she asked. "Originally, I mean?"

"No. I've only been here a short time." He added, "Even less time than you've been here."

She frowned. "How do you know how long I've been here?"

"Because not long ago, someone started practicing extreme fire magic in the mountains."

"How do you know about that?" she asked in surprise.

"You're not exactly discreet, Chandra," he said with a touch of exasperation. "And no one on Regatha had ever seen anything like that before. Except for *one* person, Walbert said. A planeswalker who was here long ago, according to legend, and whose power and, uh, personality inspired the establishment of Keral Keep."

"Walbert knows about planeswalkers?"

"Yes. Doesn't the mother mage of the monastery know? I mean, if it was founded because of a—"

"Yes, she knows. It's her monastery. But how does Walbert know about Jaya Ballard?"

"That's the name of the planeswalker who was here?" Gideon said with a shrug, "Walbert knows a lot of things. He's well educated, well informed, and well organized."

"He's also arrogant, interfering, overbearing—"

"When he became aware of the spells being practiced," Gideon said, speaking as if he hadn't heard her at all, "he suspected that another planeswalker had come to Mount Keralia after all these years. So he kept an eye on the situation. He soon learned that there was a brand new resident at the monastery, a woman who had arrived right before all that big magic started being let loose in the mountains." After a pause, he added, "And no one seemed to know anything about this woman, except the she was unusually powerful. She had simply . . . arrived one day, and she never talked about her past or where she came from."

"How did he learn this?"

"I told you. Walbert's well informed and well organized." Gideon added, "Besides, gossip travels faster than galloping horses. Even if it wasn't malicious, there was bound to be talk, Chandra."

"Hmph. So why did *you* come to Regatha? To sit at Walbert's feet in admiration?"

"I came for the Purifying Fire," he said.

"Ah. I've heard of it." She tilted her head and studied him. "You came to Regatha to increase your power."

"Yes." He'd evidently decided, once Samir blew his cover, not to hold anything back, and she was distantly pleased that she was going to, finally, get some honest answers from him, but more than that, she was still enraged at what he'd done.

Chandra thought it over and said skeptically, "So did Walbert simply give you free access to this mysterious source of white mana that people say is what has made the Order *so* powerful here?"

"He wanted something in exchange," Gideon said.

"You mean, he wanted you to go after the planeswalker that he suspected had come to the Keralian Monastery."

"Yes."

"And do what?" she said, feeling her blood heat. "Kill me?"

"Just take you into custody."

"What does *that* mean?"

Silence.

"Gideon?" she prodded. "What did Walbert plan to do once he had me in custody?"

"I don't know." There was a pause. "I didn't ask. At the time, I didn't particularly care."

"Of course not," she said. "You just wanted access to the Purifying Fire."

"Yes," he agreed. "But then you chased down a ghost warden and killed it for no reason—"

"No *reason*?" She couldn't believe her ears.

"It was harmless," he said. "It had minimal defenses, and it only used them when directly threatened."

"It was a *spy* for the Order!"

"You also *burned down* part of the Western Wood—"

"Which is not your concern! Or Walbert's!"

"—and you attacked four peacekeepers without provocation."

"Peacekeepers? Without provocation?" Now she was truly enraged; she could feel the fire igniting in her blood. "I chased away four *invading soldiers* who had no business being here! And Walbert has no right to try to impose his will on the woodlanders!"

"You imposed *yours* there when you set fire to their lands," Gideon pointed out. "I'd say that turned out a lot worse for them than Walbert trying to govern some of their excesses."

"What *excesses*?"

"Summoning dangerous creatures, engaging in deadly tribal feuds—"

"How is any of that Walbert's concern? Or yours?" Chandra challenged.

He said tersely, "It became Walbert's concern when some of those creatures—which, hard as this may be to imagine, Chandra, aren't always well supervised after they're summoned—started terrorizing farmers and villagers on the plains."

"If their farms and villages border the woodlands, then they've got to expect—"

"*What* do they have to expect, Chandra? To see their children stolen? Their crops destroyed? Their livestock eaten? Their villages rampaged?"

"Problems like that don't give the Order a right to interfere in the forest!"

"Of course it does! But what gave *you* the right to interfere here?"

"*I* was protecting the woodlanders!"

"*That's* your idea of protecting them?" Gideon unleashed his anger. "Killing a harmless creature that was summoned here for their own good, and setting fire to their forest?"

"*For their own good?*" she shouted.

"If the excesses practiced in the forest don't cease, what do you suppose the farmers and townspeople will do, Chandra?" He didn't give her a chance to respond. "It will be a bloodbath!"

"And you think that gives Walbert a right to try to dictate how people live in the woodlands? And in the mountains?"

"Yes." Gideon looked tired again. His voice was calmer when he said, "Look, do you think you're the only person that the woodland oufes have decided to kill lately because they got angry about something? You're not." He added irritably, "You just happen to *deserve* it. But it goes on all the time now, Chandra."

"So?"

"You must have noticed how often innocent people wind up in harm's way when the local oufes decide someone has to die?" he said. "It's too dangerous."

Chandra thought of Mother Luti, Brannon, and the others at the monastery who'd been endangered by the attempts on her life. But she just glared silently at Gideon.

"Things have to change on Regatha," he said. "Walbert's trying to bring peace and order to this plane. Life has become dangerously chaotic here. It can't go on any longer."

"Things were *fine* here until Walbert started interfering in lands where he has no right to intrude!"

He sighed. "So after the mysterious pyromancer that Walbert was concerned about incinerated a ghost warden, burned down part of the forest, incited a call for assassination from a tribe of hysterical oufes, and attacked four peacekeepers, I agreed with Walbert when he said you had to be contained.

"After that, this wasn't just about the Purifying Fire for me," Gideon said. "Not anymore. Because I realized you were too dangerous to leave on the loose here."

"So Walbert sent a letter to Mother Luti demanding she turn me over to him? Did he really think that would work?" Chandra said contemptuously.

"No," Gideon said. "He thought it might determine for certain whether you were a planeswalker."

"What?"

"All things considered, he thought his demand might be the final push that the mother mage needed to decide that you should disappear for a while."

For a moment, Chandra felt as if she couldn't breathe. "It was a *trick*? To get me to planeswalk?"

"Yes," he said. "It was the only way I could be sure you were exactly what Walbert feared you were."

A red blaze of fury burned through her. "You manipulated me!"

"Chandra." His gaze followed the glow of flames moving along her skin as rage coursed through her, turning her blood into fire. "Don't."

"Don't *what*?"

"Don't make me fight you."

"Whyever *not*?" she snarled.

"Because I don't want to," he said wearily. "A lot has happened since we each left Regatha."

His gaze locked with hers.

She remembered that he had turned her over to the Prelate's soldiers, to be violated by the Enervants and probed by mind mages. She should kill him for that alone!

And then she remembered that he had hidden the scroll from them, to buy her time to escape . . .

"Please stop," he said quietly, remaining motionless while fire raced down to her hands and through the tendrils of her hair.

She remembered that, without his power to protect him, he had fought the Fog Riders for her.

"All so you could bring me back to Regatha?" she breathed.

"No." He thought it over. "Well . . . On Kephalai, yes," he admitted. "Walbert seemed certain you'd come back here. I was supposed to make sure you came back to *him*, incapacitated, instead of returning to the monastery to cause more trouble."

That renewed her rage. "If Walbert wanted me to stop causing *trouble*, then why didn't you just let me die on Kephalai?"

"If it had been strictly up to me," Gideon said, "I would have."

His honesty disarmed her. She was still furious . . . but she felt the flames of uncontrolled rage subsiding.

And in truth, looking at him, she knew she couldn't bring herself to kill Gideon. Not after everything that had passed.

"I don't know why," Gideon said, "but Walbert *wanted* you back on Regatha. In his custody, rather than roaming free."

"So that's why you created circumstances for me to escape from the Prelate's prison?"

He nodded. "That's why I followed you to Diraden, too."

"And then?"

They looked at each other for a long, silent moment.

"Things changed," he said at last.

Yes. Things had changed.

Chandra shifted her gaze away from him. "And then, when we escaped, I said I wanted to come back here." Her tone was sullen. "That certainly made things easier for you."

"I wasn't thinking about that," he said. "I was thinking about being alive and together and getting away."

She glanced at him.

A slight smile curved his mouth. "I never mentioned it, but I thought all along that the chances of getting out of there alive were pretty remote."

Φ

Feeling suddenly exhausted, Chandra sat down on the other wooden stool in this humble hut. "So we're alive and both back on Regatha. Now what?"

"Now . . . I don't know."

They were silent again.

Chandra heard footsteps approaching and she stiffened with tension for a moment, but relaxed when Samir came bustling into the hut.

He set down a pitcher of water, a basin, two small clay pots, and some soft cloths. "My wife has taken the children to stay with another family while you're here, so that there won't be any risk of them seeing Chandra. They're good children, but they're too young for me to be sure they'll remember not to say anything to anyone."

"It's risky for you to have me here," Chandra realized. "I'm sorry."

"*I'm* sorry, Chandra," Samir said, pouring water into the basin. "I spoke against Walbert and the Order . . . Er, no offense intended," he said to Gideon.

"None taken."

"But I failed to persuade the other members of the council. Most voted in favor of cooperating with Walbert."

Gideon asked, "What's been happening here?"

Samir picked up one of the two small pots he had brought with him and poured some pale yellow powder into the basin of water. While stirring it around to dissolve it, he said, "Shortly after Chandra left on her journey, the Order's intrusion on the woodlands increased. More soldiers, more patrolling, more spies."

With the powder dissolved, Samir soaked a cloth in the water, then began cleaning the savage cuts on Gideon's chest and arms. "This will sting," Samir warned, "but it will fight infection."

Gideon made no sound as the liquid soaked into his open

cuts. But Chandra could tell from his focused expression that it was painful.

Samir continued with his story as he worked. "Most of the woodlanders blamed the escalation of these impositions on Chandra's, er, encounter with the Ghost Warden and the soldiers. They felt we were suffering for her rash act."

Chandra was incensed by this . . . but since she knew Gideon condemned what she had done, and since Samir had endured a great deal of trouble because of it, she kept her mouth shut.

"Then Walbert made his proposal to the inter-tribal council." Samir explained, "The council has one representative from every tribe or clan in the forest. It only meets when there is a problem or decision to be discussed that affects all the inhabitants of the Great Western Wood."

Chandra realized there was a gash on her left hand that she didn't remember getting. She picked up one of the cloths Samir had brought into the hut, dipped it into the basin of water, and applied it to her hand.

She drew in a sharp breath through her nostrils. It *did* sting.

"What was his proposal?" Gideon asked.

"You don't know?" Samir said in surprise. "When I met you at the temple, I had the impression you were in Walbert's confidence."

"I've been away. With Chandra. Whatever the proposal is, Walbert must have decided on it after I left."

"He has offered the races of the Western Wood a treaty," Samir said. "If we cooperate with the Order on certain matters, then all Ghost Wardens, all soldiers, and all forms of intrusion or interference will be completely withdrawn from the forest. And they will remain outside our land so long as we continue abiding by the terms of the treaty."

"What are the terms?" Chandra asked.

"There are some restrictions on summoning creatures. There will be penalties if our way of life affects the people of the plains. And there's a requirement that all grievances that have formerly led to violent reprisals hereafter are presented to an arbiter of the Order for judgment."

"And the council agreed to this?" she said in surprise.

"Well, it remains to be seen how sincere some of the council members are in their agreement," Samir admitted. "And some other members, of course, don't habitually think long-term."

"You mean," Chandra guessed, "that some woodlanders think they can bend the new rules once they're not being watched by ghost wardens and pestered by soldiers in their own territory. And the oufes are focused on getting the Order out of the forest *now*, rather than on what will happen next time they send assassins after someone who lives beyond the woods."

"Indeed." Samir finished cleaning Gideon's wounds and now picked up the second small pot he had brought with him, which contained some green balm. "This will be soothing, and it will help prevent further bleeding until you return to the Temple—where I imagine the mages can heal you better than my humble efforts."

"Thank you for your help," Gideon said. "It would have been hard to make it back to Zinara without any treatment."

While applying the balm, Samir said, "So the members of the council see a way to make all the trouble here stop . . . if they also agree to the final term. Which is to turn you over to the Order, Chandra."

"I suppose that after the fire I started here, it's not surprising that they agreed."

"Not everyone agreed," he assured her. "But, alas, enough of them did. And that's why you're not safe in the

Western Wood anymore. You're too easy to recognize, and such interesting news travels fast. So you must stay hidden here until nightfall. Then we'll cover your hair and make our way out of the forest."

"But why did Walbert make my capture a condition in his treaty with the inter-tribal council of the forest?" she asked in puzzlement. "I live with the Keralians, not with the woodlanders."

"The Keralians have received the same offer," Samir said. "Mother Luti rejected it. Rather emphatically."

Chandra nodded. She would have expected that.

"And now that the woodlanders have decided to accept the proposal . . ." Samir sighed. "It has put us on a different path."

"Walbert probably knew the Keralians would refuse," Gideon said pensively. "By getting your people to agree to his terms, he eliminates any alliance against the Order that might have existed between the woodlanders and the Keralians."

"Yes," said Samir sadly.

"He also gains partners in trying to secure Chandra's capture, and he reduces the places where she can hide—"

"Hide?" she repeated, affronted.

"—or roam freely." Gideon paused before continuing, "And since he knows the woodlanders have long been friendly with the monastery, he also counts on Samir's people to urge the monastery to accept the same treaty and surrender Chandra to the Order."

"The Keralians will never cooperate," Samir said with certainty. "They despise the Order, and they place a very high value on independence and freedom. If Walbert is determined to capture Chandra, he'll only succeed one way."

"By destroying the Keralians," Gideon said.

"Will he really go that far?" Samir asked.

The woodland mage and Chandra both looked at Gideon, awaiting his answer.

"Yes," he said, finally.

"You seem certain," Samir noted.

Gideon nodded. "Walbert will do whatever is necessary to achieve his goals. Including destroying Keral Keep."

CHAPTER SEVENTEEN

I don't understand," Chandra said to Gideon after Samir had left them alone in the hut again. "Walbert knows I planeswalked, doesn't he?"

"He must. I followed you, and he knew I planned to do that." Gideon added, "I didn't exactly say goodbye, but he knows."

"Then why is he trying to get others to capture me?" she said. "Why doesn't he just wait for you to bring me back?"

"Because we've been gone a lot longer than he expected. A lot longer than *I* expected."

"Oh. Right." She hadn't expected to be gone this long, either.

"He thinks I failed." Gideon said, "He probably thinks I'm dead."

"And that I killed you?" she said.

"Yes."

"But all this effort to capture me . . . He was *that* certain that I would return to Regatha?"

Gideon nodded. "Yes, he seemed sure you'd come back. And he wanted your return to be under his control."

"But *why* was he sure I'd come back?"

"I don't know." Gideon's expression was impossible to read as he met her gaze in the shadows of the hut. "But you did come back, didn't you? And he knew you would."

"If Walbert thinks I killed you, then he must also think I'm very dangerous."

"You *are* very dangerous," Gideon said. He didn't sound like he was joking.

"And yet he's encouraging woodlanders like Samir to try to capture me." She said disdainfully, "He doesn't seem to have a problem with risking other people's lives, does he?"

"Neither do you," Gideon pointed out. "How many people died in the Sanctum of Stars because of you?"

"I didn't plan on that," she snapped.

"How many were inside when it collapsed, Chandra?" he persisted. "Ten? Twenty?"

"I don't know," she said tersely. "I was fleeing for my life, at the time."

"And the people you were fleeing from died because it was their duty to protect the Prelate's property from you," he said.

She was about to reply when she heard Samir's footsteps again. He entered the hut carrying a basket that held food, as well as a fresh pitcher of water for them.

"I hope you'll enjoy this," Samir said to them. "My wife is a wonderful cook!"

In truth, Chandra had never enjoyed anything she'd eaten at Samir's home, always finding the food bland and overcooked. But given how revolting the food on Diraden had been, this meal today tasted like one of the finest feasts of her life. Gideon evidently felt the same way. They both ate voraciously and spoke very little.

After the meal, Samir gave Gideon a threadbare tunic to wear, saying, "It's old and much-mended, but it will

LAURA RESNICK

hold together until you reach Zinara."

"Thank you." Gideon pulled it over his head. "For *all* your hospitality."

"A guest brings good luck," Samir said with a smile.

"Not necessarily," Chandra said gloomily.

Samir asked Gideon, "Are you returning to the Temple?"

"Yes."

"I'm *not* coming with you," Chandra warned him.

"No." He assured Samir, "Walbert will never know anything about today."

Samir glanced at Chandra, then smiled at Gideon. "I don't understand you, but I do believe you."

"I hope we meet again," Gideon said politely to him.

Samir glanced between them. "You two probably have a few things to say before you part. I'll wait outside, Gideon. When you're ready, I'll guide you to a path that leads east out of the forest. You can find the road to Zinara easily from there. And with so many of the Order's soldiers patrolling here now, you may encounter, er, colleagues on horseback soon after you leave here. Perhaps they'll help you get back to the Temple."

"Thank you, Samir." When he was alone again with Chandra, Gideon said to her, "You have to leave Regatha immediately."

"I just got back," she pointed out.

"No one is safe while you're here."

"Given how certain Walbert is that I'll come back, I don't think anyone will be safe after I *leave*, either," she said. "He'll just keep looking for me."

"This will only end if you go and never come back."

"I won't run away," she said. "Not while the Keralians have to deal with Walbert's obsession with capturing me."

"I'm letting you go free now," Gideon said, "but—"

"*Letting* me?" she repeated. "Do you imagine you could possibly—"

"—this is as far as I'll go for you," he said. "You've committed wrongs, Chandra."

"So has Walbert!"

"You'll only make it worse if you stay," Gideon said. "If you leave Regatha *now*, I'll lie to Walbert. I'll say you never came back here, that you died on another plane. But I won't do more than that for you."

"You don't even have to do *that* much."

"If you stay, I won't help you," he warned.

"I don't want your help!"

"I won't betray the Order." He took her by the shoulders, "Do you understand me?"

"Take your hands off me," she said through gritted teeth.

His grip on her tightened. "I won't turn away from my duty."

"What duty?" She frowned. "What does any of this have to do with you? You're not from here. You've been here even less time that I have!"

"The Order of Heliud isn't limited to just one plane, Chandra," he said. "Walbert's Order is . . . a local unit, you might say, of something much bigger. Something that extends across other planes of the Multiverse."

She drew in a long breath, her head spinning as she realized what he was saying. "So that's how Walbert knows about planeswalkers? He would have to know, wouldn't he, if he's part of something that exists on multiple planes?"

"Yes. Walbert knows. So does his designated successor. No one else, though."

"And if you're part of this thing, too, then that must be how you knew about the Purifying Fire before you ever came here. Because . . ." She gave him a quizzical look. "How did you put it? Gossip travels faster than galloping horses. Even across planes, it seems."

"And to places only a planeswalker can travel."

And as a planeswalker, she realized, Gideon would be highly important in a movement that existed on more than one plane. She asked, "So what *is* your duty?"

"I serve the Order. My duty is whatever is needed of me."

"And what purpose does the Order have?" she said. "Pestering people in every dimension until they behave the way you want them to?"

"Its purpose is to bring harmony, protection, and law to the Multiverse."

That statement awoke old ghosts. She smothered them and said nastily, "Oh, then it's a good thing you ate a hardy meal to keep your strength up."

He let go of her. "Well, it's not easy to keep up with a fire mage who thinks nothing of murder, pillage, and destruction."

"How *dare*—"

"I have to return to Zinara," he said. "Will you leave Regatha now?"

"No."

He looked momentarily sad. "Then I can't help you."

"I told you, I don't *want* your help."

"I won't let your choice become my weakness," he said firmly.

Chandra folded her arms and glared at him. "As long as you keep your word not to implicate Samir in anything, then what you do when you leave here is no concern of mine."

He looked at her for a long moment, saying nothing. Then he raised his hand to touch her cheek.

She intended to pull away and tell him again not to touch her . . . but as their eyes met, she found that she couldn't.

"Chandra . . ."

He didn't say more. What was there to left to say, after all?

She remembered wanting to kill him back on Kephalai when she was imprisoned in the Prelate's dungeon. She longed to feel that kind of rage toward him again. Chandra missed the clarity of that hot, simple hatred. She missed the familiarity and sharp-edged certainty of those old feelings so much, she almost wanted to weep for their loss.

And now, instead of killing Gideon, or fighting him, or telling him not to touch her . . . she listened in sorrowful silence to her erratic breathing and felt her aching heart beat too fast while they stood close together, their gazes locked, his fingers brushing her cheek so lightly that his touch almost tickled.

Then Gideon let out his breath and turned away. In the doorway of the hut, with his back to her and his hand resting on the coiled sural that hung from his belt, he said quietly over his shoulder, "You saved my life on Diraden."

Feeling a weight on her chest, she admitted, "I may only be alive now because you were there with me."

"Goodbye, Chandra." He left.

❊ ❊ ❊ ❊ ❊

With a cloak covering her red hair and with Samir as her guide, Chandra escaped the green wood that night by the silvery light of the waxing moon.

The branches of trees and bushes clawed at her as she walked, she could scarcely see where she was going, and she knew that all manner of mundane and mystical creatures roamed the forest after dark; Chandra nonetheless found the Great Western Wood by night so much more pleasant and healthy a place than Diraden had been. There was life here, in all its robust and changing variety. And even in the current situation, at least not *everything* in the forest wanted to kill her, eat her, torment her, or betray her. So after recently surviving Diraden, sneaking out of the forest on Regatha by night just didn't provoke that much anxiety in her breast.

Samir, on the other hand, was *extremely* anxious. While Chandra was in his lands, he felt responsible for her safety. And once they reached the edge of the dense woodlands and arrived at the rocky path that led up to Keral Keep, Samir's anxiety didn't ease.

"You must push hard to reach safety before sunrise," he advised her. "The forces of the Order are patrolling the lower slopes of Mount Keralia now, too. If they see you, they may attack."

"Then they'll be sorry," she said grimly.

"With the Order tightening its noose around the monastery," Samir said, "trade and communications are both becoming difficult for the Keralians." He handed her a small scroll. "Please give this message to Mother Luti. I will not endanger my people by openly violating the decision of the inter-tribal council, but I am Luti's friend—and yours—and so I will do what I can to help you, if my help is needed."

"Thank you, Samir." She clasped his hand warmly after taking the scroll from him.

"What would be best for everyone," he said, "is for all the factions of Regatha to re-establish balance and once again live in tolerance of one another."

Actually, Chandra thought that Walbert's death in a raging bonfire would be best for everyone, but she said only, "Yes, you're right."

"Now go quickly," he said. "You need to be inside the monastery's walls before dawn."

Despite recent hardships, Chandra was energized by rest, a decent meal, and the return to a plane that wasn't warped and twisted by Velrav's dark curse, so she was able to travel quickly as she ascended Mount Keralia.

Unfortunately, though, her speed wasn't enough to save her from discovery. The moon's position in the sky had scarcely changed since her parting from Samir when a sharp male voice in the dark said, "Halt! Who goes there?"

Chandra froze in her tracks, wondering whether the stranger could see her.

Another voice said, "Identify yourself!"

She remained silent and motionless in the dark, waiting to see what would happen.

A moment later, her course of action became clear. A small white orb appeared in the shadowy darkness of her rocky surroundings. It grew quickly in size. As it floated up into the air and began circling the immediate area, she saw it briefly illuminate the figures of two men. If she moved again on the rocky path, they would hear her. And in another moment, that floating orb, which was coming her way, would shed light on her, and they'd see her.

Filled with the rich red mana that permeated the mountains of Regatha, Chandra called forth fire and sent a bolt of flame flying straight at the orb, to destroy it. It exploded in a pleasing shower of mingled white and golden light, then scattered itself on the mountain breeze. The two men were shouting.

"Did you see who that is? Is it her?"

"I'm not sure!"

Another glowing orb appeared. This one came straight toward Chandra, followed by the two armed mages as they quickly advanced on her with swords drawn, ready for combat.

She moved, scrambling off the path and through a gap in some boulders nearby, praying she wasn't about to disturb a sleeping snake or bad-tempered fox. The fabric of Samir's cloak caught on something, and pebbles rumbled noisily as Chandra yanked it free.

"What's that? There!" cried one of the soldiers. "Just off the path. Do you see?"

Her hood fell off as Chandra whirled around. She was bathed in the white light of the floating orb as she called flames into her hands again. She felt her hair catch fire.

"It *is* her! Seize her!"

One of the men fell back, screaming in agony as a huge fireball hit him in the chest and ignited his clothing. He staggered backward and fell from the path, down the steep slopes in the dark, his body consumed by flames. The screaming ceased when Chandra heard his body bouncing off rocks far below this steep path.

"Wait! No! Don't!" the other soldier shouted at Chandra. "I'm not going to kill you!"

"Damn *right* you're not going to kill me," she said, forming another fireball.

"Our orders are to take you into custody!"

Chandra heard the fear in his voice at the same moment she realized he was backing away from her. That was when she noticed, in the light cast by the glowing orb, how young this soldier was. He looked barely eighteen. And scared.

She realized she didn't want to kill a frightened boy.

Holding the fireball poised for deadly action, she said, "If you don't want the same fate as your companion, then go. Go *now*. And don't come back."

He licked his lips, looking uncertain. "I have orders," he said breathlessly. "You have to come with me."

"Do you really want to die tonight?"

The young man slowly shook his head.

"Then go. Right now. Before I change my mind."

Looking devastated by his failure, he turned around, moving awkwardly, and began heading down the mountain.

Chandra threw her fireball at the slowly sinking white orb he had left behind, destroying it.

Then she heard more shouts and the voices of other soldiers. They had heard the commotion here. They were heading to this spot and would scour the mountainside in search of her.

She realized with frustration that she'd have to abandon the path she was on. They'd be looking for her there and would chase her all the way up to the monastery.

Fortunately, she knew of a seldom-used, older trail that was not too far from here. But getting to it, in the dark and trying not to be heard by her pursuers, would be a laborious scramble over rough terrain.

With an exasperated sigh, Chandra turned and started making her way carefully in that direction. Samir was right. She must push hard to reach the monastery before daybreak.

❅ ❅ ❅ ❅ ❅

Within days of Chandra's nighttime encounter on Mount Keralia, Walbert's forces laid siege to the monastery.

Soldiers swarmed up the mountain and established base camps nearby, just beyond the range of the aggressive fire magic that the Keralians attempted to use on the intruders in their land.

The mages of the Order surrounded the monastery with an insubstantial but efficient white barrier. No one could sneak into the monastery or escape from it without passing through this mystical ward, which would capture the individual and instantly alert the hieromancers. It effectively cut off the Keralians from all access to the world beyond their red stone walls.

To preserve their supplies for as long as possible, Mother Luti organized a system of rationing for the monastery's food, ale, wine, and medicine. Fortunately, the deep well within the monastery walls could supply them with plentiful water for as long as the siege lasted. But, even with rationing, all other essential supplies would run out before long. The monastery had been built as a sheltered place for study and learning; it had never been intended to withstand a long siege by determined enemies.

Chandra knew this stalemate must be resolved. And soon. She just didn't know how.

"I've had another message from Walbert," Mother Luti told her one evening, after Chandra responded to her request to come to Luti's workshop. "It arrived, rather dramatically, wrapped around an arrow that was shot into the south tower."

"Did it hurt anyone?" Chandra asked with concern.

"Fortunately, no." Mother Luti took a seat and gestured for Chandra to do the same. "And I suppose we'll have to expect similarly unconventional means of communication hereafter."

Their eyes met, and Chandra nodded. An angry pyromancer had killed a courier from the Order who had come to the monastery two days earlier. Obviously, Walbert wasn't going to risk sending another one.

Luti said, "Brannon has claimed the arrow as a war prize. The boy has become interested in archery since you were nearly killed by that bowman the oufe tribe sent after you. He's been practicing while you were away, and I must say, he's become rather good at it."

Chandra asked, "Is there anything new in Walbert's latest message?"

"No, it's the same as the previous one. You were seen ascending the mountain by night, Walbert knows you're here, he demands that we surrender you to him. He doesn't wish to destroy the monastery, but he will do it unless we deliver you. If we cooperate, we'll be left in peace, so long as we abide by certain terms. And so on and so forth." Luti sounded bored and disgruntled. "The terms he proposes are similar to the ones that Samir told you the woodlanders had accepted."

Chandra rubbed her hands over her face and wondered what to do. The Keralians were united in their absolute, unconditional, unanimous rejection of Walbert's demands. Mother Luti had held two meetings at which the matter was discussed and voted on; one immediately after Chandra's recent return, and another last night, by which time it was clear how devastating the siege was going to be.

Not one single Keralian was willing to turn Chandra over to the Order.

It wasn't personal. Well . . . maybe in a few instances, it was; several of the Keralians, including Mother Luti herself, as well as the boy Brannon, were fond of Chandra. But, mostly, the refusal was based in the Keralians' way of life.

Being who and what they were, they would not bow down to anyone, give in to any ultimatum, surrender to any threat, or back down in the face of any challenge. They would not secure the safety of their monastery at the cost of Chandra's individual freedom. And nothing could induce them to abide by rules or conditions set by the Order—or by anyone else.

"What I still find puzzling," Luti said, "is Walbert's obsession with you."

"I'm puzzled, too," Chandra said.

"I've been thinking about it. It has to be because you're a planeswalker," Luti said. "Walbert's reasons for pursuing you—and planning to execute you, I suppose—are presumably the fire in the Western Wood, the attack on the ghost warden, and your encounters with his men. But none of that really explains all *this*." Luti waved a hand toward the window, indicating the siege that lay beyond the monastery's sheltering walls. "And since this man you've described to me, Gideon, is also a planeswalker . . ." The mother mage shook her head. "Well, it's obviously not as if Walbert believes you're the only planeswalker on Regatha. So whatever it is that Walbert fears or wants from you, it must be due to something about *you* in particular."

"But he doesn't *know* anything about me in particular."

"Well, he knows one thing," Luti said. "So I deduce that it must be the *crucial* thing: Unlike Gideon, *you* wield fire magic."

"So what?" Chandra said. "I still don't understand what he wants with a planeswalking fire mage or why he's doing all this."

"I don't it understand, either. Is his obsession with you a symptom of madness? In which case, can we hope he'll be assassinated soon and replaced by someone who'll end the siege and go home?"

"Gideon knows him, and Samir has met him," Chandra said, "and neither of them seems to think he's mad."

"Oh, well. Wishful thinking on my part." Luti added, "You *could* just planeswalk out of this problem, you know."

"No," said Chandra firmly. "I won't flee to safety and abandon you to deal with the consequences of my having been here. Besides, what will that accomplish? Will Walbert be merciful to you because you let me escape rather than surrendering me to him?"

"It's very interesting," Luti said pensively.

"*What's* interesting?"

"Walbert was convinced you would come back, and you did," the mother mage mused. "Now he's evidently convinced you won't leave . . . and, indeed, you won't."

That gave Chandra a chill. Did Walbert know more about her than she realized? Gideon hadn't seemed to think so . . . but that might only mean that Walbert hadn't confided fully in him.

For the first time, Chandra wondered if she *should* leave Regatha.

But then she thought of the Keralians, who'd be left in the middle of this mess, and of Samir, who had risked so much to protect her . . . and she couldn't believe that abandoning them all was the right course of action. Even though her being here didn't really seem to be right for them, either.

"I don't know what to do," she said to Mother Luti.

"Neither do I," Luti admitted. "Not about this, anyhow. But I have come to a decision about something else."

"Oh?"

"I have decided not to tell Brother Sergil what you've told me about the scroll."

"Why not, Mother?"

"Because I don't want the monks to pursue this any further."

"You don't?" Chandra said in surprise.

"No. It's much too dangerous." Luti frowned thoughtfully as she continued, "An ancient scroll that was *that* fiercely protected? A mysterious plane—which may or may not exist—where mana works differently than anywhere else in the Multiverse? And an artifact of such immense power that it will certainly be sought, coveted, and fought over by people far more ruthless than any Keralian . . ." Luti shook her head. "If there is such a place as Zendikar, and if the artifact described in the scroll really can be found there . . . No," she said with finality. "I *don't* want it brought back here. I don't want anyone ever coming here to look for it. And I don't want Keral Keep to be involved with an object as dangerous as I believe that artifact must be." She gave a brief sigh and shrugged. "So I will tell the brothers that you couldn't find the original scroll and believe it has been destroyed. They'll study the copied text a little while longer . . . and then get frustrated or bored, set it aside, and move on."

They'd only move on if they survived this siege, Chandra thought. But she didn't say it. "As you wish, Mother."

Luti studied her. "But *you're* still interested in the artifact, aren't you?"

"Yes," Chandra admitted.

"I thought so." Luti nodded. "Fair enough. Individuals must pursue their own choices and destinies. My decision is made only with regard to what's best for this monastery."

"And if I someday find the artifact," Chandra said, "you're sure you don't want me to bring it here?"

"Chandra, if you ever find that artifact, I don't even want to *know* about it," Luti said with certainty. "Nor would I encourage you to tell my successor, whoever that may be."

And Chandra thought again that they were talking about the future as if the monastery definitely had one. Which wasn't at all certain at the moment.

⁂ ⁂ ⁂ ⁂ ⁂

Chandra awoke from her nightmares sweating and breathing hard, with a scream on her lips.

The death of innocents was on her head. Because of her rash acts, her impulsive nature, and her reckless deeds.

She looked around her darkened bedchamber in Keral Keep and understood, for the first time in all the years she had been having this dream, why she had had it *tonight*.

The Keralians had welcomed her as one of their own kind when she first arrived here, and they had shared their home, their humble comforts, and their teachings and knowledge with her ever since then.

Now, as a result of that, soldiers and white mages were massed outside their walls, laying siege to their home, intent on destroying their way of life, and threatening to kill them.

All because of her.

Chandra swung her legs over the side of her narrow bed and, feeling nauseated, rested her head between her knees and concentrated on taking slow, steady breaths.

It's happening again. Because of *me*.

She must prevent it this time. She *must*.

Chandra knew she couldn't live with something like that happening twice. Indeed, she couldn't even live with what *had* happened—she was always running away from it.

I can't outrun two memories like that. I can't.

And suddenly, sitting here in the dark, breathing hard, sweating, shaking, hunched over her knees and trying not to be sick . . . She knew exactly what she must do.

She had been confused and uncertain ever since returning to Keral Keep. Ever since things here had instantly spiraled into this crisis upon her return. She had floundered and vacillated. She had guiltily avoided eye contact with her fellow mages. She had expressed outrage when she mostly felt consuming guilt. She had considered fleeing and rejected it, and she had resolved to stay and then wondered if that was a mistake.

And all to avoid *this*, she now realized.

All to avoid the decision she knew she must make now—the one thing she could do to prevent the Keralians from meeting the fate that others had met because of her.

For a moment, she felt terribly sad as she thought about what would happen shortly. She was still young. There was still so much she hadn't seen or experienced. And now she never would.

Then a kind of peaceful resignation settled over her. Perhaps this was her fate. Perhaps she had been heading toward this choice ever since the nightmares began.

She stood up, walked over to the simple table and chair that were in the corner, and sat down there to write a brief message on a short sheet of parchment. Then she got dressed and left her chamber, heading for Brannon's bedroom. When she got there, she shook the boy awake.

Chandra indicated the parchment in her hand. "I have to send a message. I need your help."

He blinked sleepily. "Huh?"

"Bring your bow and arrow." She pulled back his covers and hauled him out of his bed.

He stumbled after her, following her out of his room and along the corridors of the monastery. By the time they reached the south tower, he seemed to be awake.

"We're sending a message to them?" he asked, looking down at the mountainside with her. The moon was full tonight, casting a glow over the landscape. "The way they sent one to us?"

"Yes." She rolled the piece of parchment tightly around the arrow Brannon had brought, then tied it with a thin piece of twine she had brought from her room. "Here."

He looked at her handiwork and nodded. "Yes, this will fly."

"If they shot an arrow into the south tower . . ." She looked down at the rugged landscape below the tower. She could see the white glow of illumination from a base camp. "Yes, there they are. Can you shoot that far?"

"What am I aiming at?"

"That white glow. It's probably there to help a sentry keep watch in the night. If the arrow goes that far, they'll find it."

Brannon took a deep breath and nodded. "Yes, I can do that. I've been practicing."

"Mother Luti told me. And to make sure they see it . . ." She filled her breath with fiery heat, then blew gently on the head of the arrow. It caught fire. "Here. Quickly now."

He took the arrow with a nod, his talented young fingers comfortably handling the burning head as he prepared to shoot. Brannon raised the bow, drew back his arm, and aimed. After several steady breaths, he drew back a little further on the bow, his whole body taut with the strain, his gaze focused intently on his target. When he loosed the arrow, Chandra heard it sing through the air as it left the quivering bow behind. The small flame sailed through the night, landing at the edge of the base camp.

There wasn't enough light for her to see any figures in the distant camp. But she was able to see that the flaming arrow was lifted off the ground and its fire doused.

"They've got it!" Brannon said. "Now what?"

"Now we wait for a reply."

✻ ✻ ✻ ✻ ✻

Chandra waited anxiously all the next day for a response to her message, but it didn't arrive until the day after that. And then she understood why it had taken so long.

She was playing with Brannon, trying to help relieve the natural restlessness of an adventurous boy now forbidden to go beyond the walls of the monastery. Brother Sergil came looking for her, to tell her she was wanted in Mother Luti's workshop. Brannon followed her there, but waited outside the door, as instructed.

When she entered the workshop, Mother Luti said to her, "Chandra, you have a visitor."

Her stunned gaze was already fixed on him. *"Gideon?"*

He nodded to her in silent greeting.

Gideon looked considerably better than he had the last time she'd seen him. His thick black hair was neatly braided down his back, and his face was clean-shaven and free of bruises. His pale brown tunic and leggings were clean and tidy, and he looked healthy and alert. The healing magic of the Order was obviously effective.

He did not have his sural with him; as a member of the Order, he would not have been admitted to the monastery while carrying a weapon.

And Chandra, though surprised to see him, specifically, wasn't at all surprised that he had agreed to come here alone and unarmed, even after a pyromancer had killed one of his colleagues at the gate the other day. She knew by now that Gideon did what others wouldn't or couldn't do.

"What are you doing here?" she asked.

"Walbert accepts your terms," he said. "I've come to take you into custody."

"Terms?" Luti repeated, looking quizzically at Chandra.

"He accepts?" When Gideon nodded, Chandra took a deep breath. "Good. I'm glad."

"*What* terms?" Luti asked.

"I'm turning myself in," Chandra told her. "Once I am in custody, Walbert will withdraw his forces from the mountain." She looked at Gideon. "Will he keep his word?"

"Yes."

She nodded, believing him—his promise confirmed what she expected of Walbert from what others had said of the man. Then she said to Mother Luti, "There are no other conditions. The Keralians will not be expected to abide by any terms or rules."

"Chandra," Luti said with concern, "are you sure this is what you want to do?"

"I'm sure." She looked at Gideon. "And I'm ready to leave."

"No!" Brannon burst into the workshop. "You can't go!"

Chandra turned around to look at the boy. She should have realized he would eavesdrop. "I have to go," she said to him. "Mother Luti will explain it to you."

"Something bad will happen to you there," Brannon said with certainty.

"Maybe," she said, "but I have to go."

"I'm coming with you!"

"No." She shook her head.

"But you promised! You said that the next time you left, I could come with you."

"I did *not* promise," she said firmly. "Anyway, I feel certain that you'd be very unhappy in the Temple."

"Why?"

"It doesn't suit people like us," Chandra said.

The boy looked to Mother Luti for a second opinion, but it was Gideon who spoke. "Chandra's right. You wouldn't like it there."

"*You* won't like it there, either," Brannon said to Chandra.

"No, but that doesn't matter anymore," Chandra said. "This is my choice, Brannon."

He looked angry and sad. "When are you coming back?"

She didn't answer, not knowing what to say.

"Soon?" he prodded.

"No," she said truthfully. "I don't think I'll be coming back soon."

CHAPTER EIGHTEEN

Chandra walked through the large front gate and beyond the monastery walls with Gideon at her side. When the gate closed behind them, she let out her breath in a rush.

Her decision was made, accepted, and enacted. She had committed herself to her fate, however unpleasant—and perhaps *short*—it might be. The Keralians wouldn't suffer or die the way others had indeed suffered and died because of her. She had prevented it from happening again.

Mother Luti had dealt with Walbert at a distance for years, and she knew his reputation was good, though she disliked what he intended to see in the world. She would not have let Chandra leave if she suspected Walbert of treachery or dishonesty in this matter. And Gideon had said Walbert would keep his word, and Chandra believed him.

Now she stood between the walls of the monastery and the mystical white barrier that had surrounded it for days. Beyond the barrier, a dozen armed soldiers awaited her.

Not quite knowing how to proceed, she glanced at Gideon.

He was looking straight ahead, wearing the impassive

253

expression he relied on when he wanted to conceal things from others.

"Gideon?" she prodded, wondering what to do.

"Walbert asked me to come," he said quietly, without looking at her, "because he wanted to send someone you couldn't ambush. In case your offer wasn't sincere."

"It *is* sincere," she said.

"I know." Now he looked her at her. "Why?"

She wasn't going to answer. But then she glimpsed some of the concern that his cool expression masked, and she shrugged. "Ghosts, you might say."

"Ghosts?"

"I can't carry any more of them."

"I don't understand," he said.

"No, I don't suppose you do."

Gideon looked ahead again, his gaze on the translucent white barrier that separated them from the soldiers. "I didn't come to help you get out of this."

"I didn't think you had," she said.

"If you were counting on—"

"I'm not."

"You've made your choice," Gideon said firmly.

"Yes. And now that I have . . ." She gestured to the white barrier that separated her and the monastery from the world. "I think it might create the wrong impression if I blasted a fiery hole in this thing. So how do I get through it?"

"Just walk through it," he said.

"Just . . ."

"You'll be fine."

She shrugged again and walked forward. As soon as she entered the shimmering wall of white, she felt the binding weight of ice surrounding her. She took a breath, trying not to panic or let fire start glowing along her skin in defensive reaction . . . until the white barrier began collapsing and contracting, moving in on her from all directions with alarming rapidity.

Startled, she called forth fire and tried to blow her way out of the smothering blanket of white that was enfolding her.

"Don't," Gideon said calmly, approaching her as she struggled within the shrinking wall of light and power. "It won't hurt you."

White magic was surrounding her, moving in on her, and covering her. It doused her fire as soon as she called flames to life. She tried again, and it happened again. Her hands, her hair, her arms all were smoking with her futile efforts to defend herself.

A trap!

The barrier was shrinking into a cloak that draped over every bit of Chandra's body. She struggled against it in horror, trying to tear it off or punch a hole through it, but it just kept folding in on her and shrinking. Then it started molding itself to her, following the contours of her body, the curve of her breast, the line of her thigh, and even the tapered shape of each individual finger.

"Gideon?" She heard how breathless her voice was and realized she was panting.

"It won't hurt you," he repeated. "It's just to prevent . . . accidents."

The thing settled all over her body and finally stopped moving. It didn't affect her vision, but she could see that it covered her entirely, like a second skin. It even covered her hair. The enchanted sheath didn't hurt, tingle, or sting, and it didn't impede her physical movement in any way. But another failed attempt to create fire revealed to her exactly what it was.

"My very own portable prison," she said grimly. Her

power was trapped inside this close-fitting shell of magic, just as she was.

"They thought it was for the best." Gideon nodded toward a place further down the hill, where the white mages who had created and maintained the barrier around the monastery were still camped. "They were a little concerned about what you might do in Zinara."

"You didn't do this to me?" she asked with a frown. "They did?"

"Yes," he said. "They're afraid of you."

"And you're not?" she challenged.

He gave her a bland look.

"But you *knew* about this," she said with certainty. And he had told her to step into it.

"Yes." His eyes held hers. "I told you to leave Regatha. You should have listened."

⁂ ⁂ ⁂ ⁂ ⁂

Under other circumstances, Chandra would have found her entrance into Zinara interesting. It was an attractive city of tidy, pale stone buildings, spiraling towers, neatly-paved streets, and red-tiled roofs.

However, as she rode through the city gates with her armed escort, she was uncomfortable with the attention that she immediately attracted. She seemed to be entering the city via a major commercial street, and it was a busy afternoon. As Chandra, Gideon, and the soldiers of the Order rode slowly through the crowded area, people stopped what they were doing to stare openly at her, point her out to others, and exchange speculations about her.

She could tell from their puzzled expressions, as well as from the bits of conversation that she overheard, that nothing had been said about her beyond the walls of the temple. The common people staring and pointing at her seemed only to wonder who she was, and whether she was a dangerous prisoner or, instead, an important visitor. Either circumstance could have accounted for her impressive escort.

Above all, people were curious about the way she glowed white all over. Because of this effect, she noticed, many of the people she was passing seemed to conclude that she was an important hieromancer. Some of them even bowed respectfully as she rode past them.

It was amusing, but Chandra wasn't in a mood to laugh about it.

The soldiers and mages of the Order had begun packing up and preparing to withdraw from the mountain as soon as Chandra had been taken into custody. She saw them making preparations even as she left the monastery behind her and followed Gideon down the mountain. The long ride across the plains to Zinara had happened in silence. She wasn't feeling talkative, and Gideon seemed preoccupied.

It was late in the day now. Chandra was tense as she rode through the city and approached the Temple of Heliud, but it was a relief to get here at last. She was ready to find out what fate awaited her, and to get on with it. She had never been any good at waiting, and she'd been wondering what the outcome would be ever since making her decision two nights ago.

Chandra assumed Walbert was going to execute her. Since he knew she was a planeswalker, he knew how easily she could escape imprisonment, after all. She couldn't planeswalk at the moment, of course, not with this shimmering white shell entrapping her. But it would make no sense for Walbert to keep her power ensnared for many years to come, rather than simply eliminating her altogether. Even if he kept her imprisoned and guarded, the threat of mayhem or escape would always exist while she remained alive. Executing her was Walbert's only sensible choice.

In any event, she had achieved her goal. The Keralians were out of danger now and free of Walbert's demands and interference. Chandra had gotten what she wanted, and she would pay the price for that, as she had promised in the message that she had sent flying through the night on a burning arrow.

Her docile horse followed the mounted soldiers to the end of this busy street, around a corner, and into a large square. On the far side of the square sat a massive palace of marble with tall, thick, white pillars. Broad steps led up to a large set of carved doors. About twenty soldiers stood guard outside the building.

"The Temple of Heliud," she said. It was as impressive as the descriptions she had heard.

"Yes." It was the first time Gideon had spoken since they'd left Mount Keralia.

"Oh, so you still have a tongue?" Chandra said. "I was beginning to wonder."

He didn't react or respond.

When they reached the other side of the broad plaza, they dismounted. Chandra stood at the foot of the broad steps and, for a long moment, gazed up at the massive white edifice where she was going to die.

"Walbert is waiting," Gideon said.

She nodded and started ascending the steps. He made no attempt to take her elbow or touch her.

When she reached the top of the steps and started crossing the wide marble landing, two soldiers moved to open one of the massive doors so she could enter the palace.

She walked into an enormous hall of polished white marble with pale blue veins running through it. Beautiful tapestries hung on the walls, and elegantly carved stone benches sat along the outskirts of the hall at regular intervals. Two long staircases curved together to the balcony overhead. She looked up at it and saw a man looking down at her.

"Walbert," she said with certainty.

He was exactly as Samir had described him: tall, slim, well-groomed, gray-haired, and about Luti's age. His blue eyes were bright with interest, but chilly.

His lean face broke into a sudden smile. Samir had said that even his smile was cold; but evidently something filled Walbert with unprecedented pleasure now, because his smile looked surprisingly warm.

"Hello, Chandra. Welcome to the Temple of Heliud."

He gazed down at her for another moment.

Then Walbert said pleasantly to Gideon, who stood beside her, "Let her refresh herself from the journey, then bring her to my study."

※ ※ ※ ※ ※

Walbert's study was grander than Mother Luti's workshop, which Chandra had expected, but it was nonetheless a workmanlike room, rather than a showplace. He had a large desk that was covered in parchments, scrolls, inkpots, and books. The walls were also lined with books. All of the furnishings in here were obviously chosen for durability and comfort, rather than just to look elegant.

Chandra entered the room, followed by Gideon. Four soldiers, who had shown her to a private chamber where she had "refreshed" herself, remained in the corridor now, just outside Walbert's door. The high priest of the Temple was sitting at his desk, signing a parchment that he handed to a young man, who nodded and left the room without speaking.

As soon as the door closed behind the young man, leaving the three of them in privacy, Chandra said to Walbert,

"Gideon says you'll keep your word to withdraw your forces completely from Mount Keralia and leave the monastery alone from now on. Will you?"

Walbert looked amused. "No wasting time, I see! I like that, Chandra."

"I don't care what you like," she said. "I want to know—"

"Yes, I will keep my word." His amusement vanished, and he looked serious and intent. "As long as you remain in my custody, then I will leave the Keralians alone to destroy themselves however they please."

She ignored the provocative comment. "Then I won't try to escape execution."

"Execution?" He lifted his brows. "Oh, I'm not going to execute you, Chandra."

"What do you plan to do, then? Keep me like *this* the rest of my life?" She made a gesture that indicated the glowing second skin that imprisoned her.

"No," he said, "that's just a temporary measure. After tonight, there'll be no need for it."

She frowned. "Why? What's going to happen tonight?"

"Tonight, my visions will be fulfilled at long last."

"Visions?" Chandra repeated.

"The visions I have had for years," Walbert said, "when meditating in communion with the Purifying Fire."

Gideon's head moved. It was a very small motion, but he had been so still until now, it caught Chandra's attention. She glanced at him and saw that, although nothing showed in his expression, he was staring intently at Walbert now.

Evidently Walbert had never mentioned the visions to him.

"What are your visions about?" Chandra asked.

"Mostly, Chandra, they're about you."

"*Me?*" she blurted.

Walbert smiled again, and his expression was warm and serene as he gazed at her, his enemy and prisoner. "For years I have believed you would come during my lifetime. For years, I have awaited you."

She glanced at Gideon. He kept his face under control, but she could tell from the redoubled intensity of the gaze still focused on Walbert that he was as stunned as she was.

"You are the herald of the chaos that's on the verge of overwhelming this plane," Walbert said. "Your arrival on Regatha threatens to usher in an era of ungoverned madness here."

"I just came here to study and learn," Chandra said. "Not to, er, herald and usher."

"I knew you would come, and you did," Walbert said. "I knew you would return, with or without Gideon, and you did. I knew you wouldn't leave again, even though you could have left—and, indeed, should have." He nodded. "You are the one whom I have seen in my visions, and it's your destiny to change everything here."

"No, it's not," she said firmly. "We each make our own destiny, and the only destiny *I* ever intended to have here—"

"Intended? You aren't in control of your destiny," Walbert said contemptuously. "You flow with your impulses and bounce erratically off your own emotions. I have seen you in the Purifying Fire, and I know who you are."

"Fine," she said in exasperation, "so your visions told you a fire-wielding planeswalker would come to Regatha and cause trouble."

"No, an earthquake is *trouble*, Chandra," Walbert said. "You are a cataclysm."

"A cataclysm? Oh, for—"

"I have known ever since I first bonded with the power of the Purifying Fire that this day must come. I have seen in my visions how dangerous you are, what a deadly threat you are to the Order and our goals."

"Goals like ruling the forests and the mountains?" she said sharply. "Dominating all the mages of Regatha with your own rules, your own—"

"You came to Regatha to destroy everything I have built," Walbert said darkly. "You came here to prevent me from bringing peace and harmony to this plane."

"I told you why I came here," she snapped.

"You are the kindling of the cataclysm that I have foreseen," he said with solemn certainty, "and I must stop you."

"Your notion of a cataclysm sounds like other people's idea of restoring balance to Regatha," she said. "Or being left alone to pursue their *own* goals instead of submitting to yours."

"I have prepared for this day for many years," Walbert said, "and tonight I will begin a new era on Regatha. One that is free of the destruction that threatens us here."

Gideon asked, "What are you going to do?"

He had been silent for so long, they both reacted as if one of the chairs had spoken.

Then Walbert recovered his composure and said, "I will give her to the Purifying Fire."

CHAPTER NINETEEN

F ire won't kill her." Gideon's voice was quiet and without expression.

"As I said, I don't intend to kill her," said Walbert.

"What will happen in the Purifying Fire?" Gideon asked.

"It will cleanse her."

"Cleanse me of *what*?" said Chandra.

"Of your power. It will purify you," Walbert said with evident devotion. "The Purifying Fire will eliminate the destructive poison of fire magic from your existence. It will forever sever your bond with the corrupting force of red mana."

"You're taking away my power?" Chandra said, appalled. "I don't understand. Why don't you just kill me?"

"Because once you're stripped of your power, you'll be an example for others."

"An *example*?" she repeated.

"You are the most powerful fire mage on this plane," Walbert said. "And *I* will take away your power."

"She'll be bound to this plane," Gideon said.

"Yes," said Walbert, holding Chandra's gaze. "No more planeswalking. You'll spend the rest of your life on Regatha. Powerless. Defeated. Subject to my will."

263

"*No*," Chandra said, a sick dread washing through her. She had anticipated death, not being stranded for life on just one plane, robbed of her power and with no reason to live.

He ignored her outburst. "I won't have to challenge the Keralians or invade the mountains again. They will *see* you stripped of all power and utterly impotent, and they will realize what they risk by continuing to oppose me. And so they will submit to the rule of the Order."

"No, they won't!"

"They *will*. I have foreseen it," he said with cold satisfaction. "The woodlanders will see you, too, vanquished and humbled, and they will understand that the Order must not be thwarted or disobeyed any longer."

"I thought I was coming here to die!" Chandra said angrily. "I agreed to be *executed*, not . . . violated, humiliated, and put on display!"

"Your message didn't mention execution as a condition of our agreement," Walbert said. "As far as your part of our bargain goes, you said you would surrender to my custody. And that was *all* you said."

"I *didn't* say that I'd allow you to feed me to the Purifying Fire!"

"The ceremony will take place tonight," Walbert said. "I have a great deal to do before then, so this conversation is over."

"I won't let you do this me, Walbert!"

He ignored her again as he shouted, "Guards!"

"*No!*" As the door behind her opened, Chandra leaped forward and threw herself across the desk at the old mage.

Alarmed, Walbert tried to evade her, but the speed and force of her attack shoved him back into his chair as he started to rise from it. She punched him in the face as footsteps thundered into the room. Chandra got her fingers on his throat and began squeezing just as several pairs of hands seized her. She kicked, bit, punched, and screamed threats as the soldiers pulled her off the high priest and subdued her.

Walbert tried to speak. He choked, coughed, and tried again, successfully. "Bring her hands together," he instructed the soldiers.

They did—with some difficulty, since Chandra continued struggling violently.

Walbert covered her wrists with his hands and closed his eyes, breathing deeply. Chandra felt something cool encircling her flesh, and she looked down to see a thick, shining white coil binding her wrists together, in addition to the shimmering sheath that already covered her flesh.

With her wrists bound together and four men holding her back, she tried to attack Walbert again. It was futile, but she was too enraged to give up.

Walbert turned to Gideon, who still hadn't moved, and said angrily, "Were you just going to stand there and watch her kill me?"

Gideon shrugged. "You've got guards."

Chandra was still kicking, struggling, and shouting when they dragged her from the room.

※ ※ ※ ※ ※

She was alone in a locked chamber, with her wrists still bound, when he came to her.

Chandra's stomach clenched when the door to the chamber opened. Were they coming to get her for Walbert's ceremony? There was one small window in this room, high up on the wall, so she knew that night had fallen some time ago.

When he entered the darkened room and closed the door behind him, she asked, "Is it time?"

"Not yet," Gideon said. "Soon, though."

"If you've come to tell me you didn't know what he would do," Chandra said coldly, "I'm not in—"

"That's not why I came."

"Then why *are* you here?"

"To tell you there may be a way out," he said.

She blinked. "You'll help me escape?"

"No," he said. "That's not possible."

"Of course it's possible," she snapped. "All we have to do is—"

"It's not possible without killing a lot of people," he said. "So the answer is *no*, Chandra."

She looked at the faintly glinting metal of the sural that was coiled at his belt. "Then kill me now."

In the dim light, she could see him shake his head.

"*Please*, Gideon." She heard the pleading in her voice and hated it, so she didn't say more.

He shook his head again.

She looked away.

"I'm sorry," he said. "I just . . . can't."

Chandra shrugged, gazing at the floor. "Maybe someone else will." And she would do her best to encourage them.

"There may be another way," he said.

When he didn't continue, she looked at him again. "Well?"

"I'd have come sooner, but I've been with the Keepers. And since I didn't want to arouse their suspicion, it took time. I had to be . . . circumspect about my questions."

"The Keepers?"

"Of the Purifying Fire," Gideon said. "It's never left unguarded."

She sat down on the narrow cot, which was the only item of furniture in the room, and looked at him in silence.

He said, "There may be a way to enter the Fire but keep your power."

"*May* be? You're not certain?"

"No one is certain," he said. "No one has tried it in this lifetime."

"Why not?"

"They're afraid of being cleansed of their power if they enter the flames." He added, "That's why no one in the Order has ever entered the Purifying Fire. Not Walbert, not the Keepers, not anyone."

Gideon crossed the room and sat beside her on the cot. "The Fire is very ancient, much older than the Order. Before the Temple was built, there was another temple that existed on this spot. Smaller, humbler. This place has been a holy site as far back as Heliud. The priests and priestesses of the old faith here, long ago, worshipped the Purifying Fire, and people came from all over Regatha to give themselves to it."

She frowned. "Give themselves? As sacrifices?"

"No. To prove they were worthy," he said. "Some died. Others survived. And if you survived the Purifying Fire, then you could become a priest or priestess of the faith. Because you had proved your soul was clean."

"Clean," she repeated flatly.

"That's how they survived the flames," Gideon said. "Not with magic, not with special protection. They entered the flames with a . . . a clean soul. And they didn't die."

She shook her head. "But I'm not going to die in the flames."

"Yes, you are."

Their eyes met in the shadowy room, illuminated now only by the glow emanating from her shimmering white body sheathe and the bright white coils that bound her wrists.

Ɵ

And she knew he was right. What would happen to her in the Purifying Fire would be, for her, the same as dying.

No, it would be worse than dying. Much worse.

"I can't bear it." Her voice broke.

"I know." He put his hand over both of hers, which were clenched together on her lap. "So we need to prevent it."

"But how does someone clean their soul?"

"You face the things you've done," he said, "and accept the weight of your responsibility for your deeds, without lies or excuses."

"That's it?" she said skeptically.

"That's what the Keepers said."

"And if I do that, then I won't . . . *my power* won't die in the Purifying Fire?"

He didn't answer, and she knew it was because he couldn't guarantee it. He had searched for a solution, for a way to save her. This was what he had been able to find. It wasn't perfect, but it was all that he could offer.

You face the things you've done . . .

"But I've done so *many* things," she said pensively.

"What did you do that gives you nightmares?"

She drew in a sharp breath and stared at him, her heart thudding with sudden fierceness.

He asked, "What did you do that left you with ghosts to carry?"

She tilted her head back and closed her eyes. "I don't talk about that. I *can't* talk about that." After a moment, she said, "I can't even think about it."

"But you dream about it." It wasn't a question.

She was silent.

His voice was kind when he said, "If you need some time alone now—"

"No," she said.

He waited patiently, not moving at all. His hand remained resting on both of hers. His breathing was steady.

"I . . ." She stopped, feeling sick. Her heart was racing. She forced herself to tell him. "I caused the deaths of my family and my whole village."

Gideon didn't move or speak.

Her breath came out in a rush. "I've never told anyone that. No one alive knows."

"That's what happened to your mother? You . . . caused her death?"

She nodded. He had asked her about it on Diraden, after she had cried out for her mother in her sleep. In the burning stench of her nightmares. Now she could give him an answer.

"I was raised in a traditional mountain village," she said, "on a plane I'll never go back to. My family were ordinary people. Decent people. My father was gentle. My mother was strict. I had two younger sisters who irritated me, and an older brother who I adored. He taught me to ride, and to fight, and . . . well, a lot of things. He was killed in the war. By then I had already discovered . . ."

"That you had power?"

"Yes. I played with fire in secret, going off alone into the hills to practice, even though it was forbidden."

"By whom?"

"By everyone. My parents forbade it, because they didn't understand it and were afraid. The elders of our village told me I had to stop, because it was against the law. And the law forbidding fire magic had been passed by the new ruler, when our lands were occupied at the end of the war."

She paused for a moment, then said, "But I didn't stop. I couldn't. It was like . . . Well, *you* know what it's like to discover you have that much power. That kind of talent. It's not something you can quit or give up."

"No."

"The more my parents and the village elders tried to get me to stop practicing and experimenting, the more suffocated I felt. Even though I was too young for it, they started talking about marrying me off, thinking that maybe that a husband and children would solve the problem." She shook her head. "But, of course, the problem was who I was. I didn't yet have any idea *what* I was, but I knew for certain I was never going to settle down to village life. I wasn't ever going to be one of them. With every passing day, I felt more and more . . . different. Separate."

She looked down at his hand, resting on hers, and remembered how alien she had felt in her own birthplace.

"Finally, my parents, under pressure from the village elders, talked seriously to another family about getting me married to their son. When I found out, I was *furious*. I wanted to run away. To leave home. But . . ." She shrugged. "I'd never been anywhere. I had no idea where I would go. And the whole realm was under martial law. I knew I wouldn't get far from our village before I'd be stopped by soldiers. I felt trapped there. Imprisoned in that narrow, smothering life."

Chandra paused again. Gideon waited.

"I had been manifesting greater and greater power. Getting careless. Not hiding what I was doing, even though I knew I should. And now that I was so *angry* . . ." She started breathing harder. "I set off a huge explosion of fire on the outskirts of our village. I . . . yes, I wanted to frighten the village elders. And my parents. And the family who had just agreed to have their son marry me—I wanted them to change their minds, to refuse! I wanted *him* to refuse. I wanted to be set free."

When she stopped again, Gideon asked, "What happened?"

"The explosion attracted soldiers. They didn't know that one stupid, angry adolescent had done this. They thought the people in my village had to be rebels. They assumed the men had been practicing fire magic, in violation of the law, and were planning to use this secret power to attack the occupying forces." Her voice was breathless and uneven as she continued, "So they rounded up everyone in the village, forced them into the cottages that were closest to the fire—which was spreading—and barricaded the doors." Tears started welling up in her eyes. "The fire spread to those cottages . . . and everyone inside . . . burned."

The tears spilled over and rolled down her cheeks.

Gideon asked, "Where were you?"

"I had gone off to be by myself after starting the fire. I came running back to the village when I heard the soldiers attacking. When I saw what was happening, I fought them." She took shaky a breath and wiped her eyes. "It was the first time I'd ever used my power that way. For fighting. It was the first . . ." Tears fell again. "First time I ever killed." She tried to steady her breathing.

"And your family?"

"They burned alive inside our home. I heard their screams. I saw my mother at the window, begging the soldiers to let my little sisters out of the burning building." Her voice broke. "I smelled their burning flesh . . ." She closed her eyes and wiped her face. "They all died because of me. My parents, my sisters, and everyone in the village. Because of *me*. Because I played with fire."

Gideon's gentle clasp on her hands became a firm grip. With his other hand, he stroked her hair.

"No one was left alive," she said. "No one. And it's my fault. I brought that fate down on them."

"And that's what haunts your dreams."

"Yes." She took a deep breath. "Those are my ghosts."

"How did you live through it?"

"When everyone was dead inside the burning buildings and the screams stopped, I didn't have the will to keep fighting. So the soldiers captured me easily then. They made me get down on my knees, so they could behead me on the spot. And when I saw the blade of that sword coming down to my neck . . . suddenly I wanted to live. I was *terrified*. And then . . ." She shrugged. "My spark was ignited. I planeswalked. One moment, I was kneeling in the dirt of my village with the smell of burning flesh in my nostrils and my head about to be cut off. And the next moment . . . I was in the Blind Eternities—with no idea where I was or what was happening." She gave a watery sigh. "And that's when my next life began. My life as a planeswalker."

She took a few steadying breaths. "Sometimes since then, I've wanted to burn down the whole Multiverse."

"And you never went back?"

"No. I never wanted to."

Chandra felt his silent acceptance of everything she had told him. She supposed, from that, he understood the full weight of what she had done, but he didn't withdraw from her or condemn her. It was a surprise to find that he might not.

"I came to the Temple because I couldn't live with something like that happening again," she said. "I couldn't live with causing suffering and death at the monastery, to the people who had taken me in and treated me as one of their own."

"You did the right thing." His voice was very soft.

"And have I done the right thing now?" she wondered. "Telling you this?"

"Are they as heavy to carry as they were before?" he asked. "Your ghosts?"

She closed her eyes, feeling the load she carried. She felt the tears on her cheek and the hand that clasped hers. "No," she said at last, a little surprised. "No, not as heavy as before." The sorrow was as deep as ever, but the burden was lighter now that she had admitted what she had done.

They sat quietly together for a while.

Finally he said, "I have to go. Walbert is busy, but he's going to start wondering where I am. Especially since . . ."

"Since it's almost time?"

"Soon," he said.

She squared her shoulders. "I think I'm ready."

"How do you feel?"

She searched her soul. "I don't know if this is what it's like to feel clean," she said, "but I feel *better*. I feel I can face what will happen tonight."

CHAPTER TWENTY

C handra remained alone in her dark chamber for longer than she had expected. Nothing in her life matched the sorrow of what had happened to her family and village because of her, but there were certainly other things she regretted, other things she had done that weighed on her. Indeed, there were enough such memories to keep her thoughts occupied until someone opened the door of her chamber and ordered her to come out. And then she wondered if she had remembered everything and taken responsibility for it.

She blinked as she entered the well-lit hallway where candles burned brightly in sconces that were spaced at regular intervals along the walls.

The four soldiers who were escorting her led her from this corridor on the upper level of the Temple down various flights of stairs until she finally thought they must be below ground level by now. There were no windows anywhere along this corridor, and the ceiling here was so low that the tallest soldier in her escort had to duck his head in a few places.

As they approached the end of the corridor, she saw Gideon waiting for her. He was holding a torch and

THE PURIFYING FIRE

275

standing beside an open doorway. He gave a brief nod to the soldiers as they turned her over to him. Then they stood guard at the door.

Chandra paused in the doorway, looked down, and said without enthusiasm, "*More* stairs?"

"We're going to the caverns beneath the palace. Beneath Zinara," Gideon said.

Samir had told her that the Purifying Fire was said to burn in ancient caverns under the city, arising out of a powerful source of white mana that ran deep beneath the plains.

"They're waiting," he said quietly.

She nodded. With Gideon at her side, she began descending the steep marble stairs that led down into the belly of Regatha, below the bustling streets of Zinara and the imposing pillars of the Temple of Heliud.

The passage was narrow, barely wide enough for Gideon to descend beside her as her held her elbow to steady her. The stairs were ancient and uneven, and the flickering torch in Gideon's other hand created deceptive shadows. A misstep would be easy, and with her hands bound, she probably couldn't save herself from a headlong tumble. The ceiling of the tunnel was so low in places that Gideon had to lower the torch, holding it out in front of them while their heads brushed the stone ceiling. Chandra focused on her footsteps and her breath as she fought the feeling of being closed in, oppressed and smothered by stone.

After what must have been two hundred steps, they reached a broad, rough-hewn landing. It was made of the same marble as the stairs, but this surface was uneven and unpolished. The low ceiling of the steep tunnel gave way here to a spacious cavern. Chandra took a deep breath, glad to be out of the dark, stony embrace of the tunnel. Gideon released her elbow and turned to set his torch in a niche carved into the stone wall. There were other torches there already, no doubt set there by those who awaited Chandra's arrival.

The landing overlooked the chamber of the Purifying Fire. The high-domed cavern was immense, probably as big as the temple that sat above it.

Hundreds of white, crystal-encrusted stalactites hung down from the ceiling. Some were as slender as a wand, others as thick as the trunks of young trees. Some were so long they nearly reached the floor of the cave. Stalagmites rose up from the rough white-marble floor of the cavern, reaching skyward like the spiraling towers of some fabled city. In several instances, they met and embraced the massive icicles of stone that dripped down toward them from the ceiling, twining together like lovers—or like enemies frozen together in the writhing throes of mortal combat. All of the vaguely menacing shapes glowed from within with mystical light, illuminating the cavern so brightly that Chandra found herself squinting.

At the very center of this extraordinary underground world was a pure white bonfire rising out of a deep cauldron of jagged white rock that was speckled with thousands of shiny crystal shards. Many members of the Order surrounded it—at least forty of them—dressed in plain tunics and leggings. They encircled the Fire, facing it, with their hands held up, palms turned toward their faces. They were still and silent as they . . . communed with the Purifying Fire? Drew strength from it? Probably both, Chandra guessed.

The Purifying Fire was twice as tall as a man, and so big around that Chandra estimated it would take eight people, with their arms spread wide, to fully surround it. Its white flames licked and flickered like those of a regular fire, but it created no smoke and it made no sound. It was utterly silent.

And even from here, halfway across this vast space, Chandra could feel its cool power undulating in silent waves throughout the cavern. It quivered now, as if sensing her presence in the chamber, and seemed to lean toward her. Chandra felt sure its dancing white coolness responded to the red heat that was trapped within her by the shimmering second-skin that still covered her.

"The Purifying Fire," Gideon said.

"Impressive," she admitted.

"Come." He took her elbow and led her to the left edge of the landing.

"And still *more* stairs," she grumbled. Roughly chiseled into the bedrock, these steps looked lumpy, primitive, and dangerously uneven. "Did you people carve these stairs with a spoon?"

"They're old," Gideon said mildly.

With a firm hand on her elbow, he helped her down the rough, ancient steps to the main floor of the cavern. As their bodies touched, she could feel his tension and realized he was anxious about what would happen here tonight.

Chandra was surprised to realize that she was *not* anxious.

Not any longer.

Tonight, she had already faced the thing she feared most. After all these years of running from it, after the sickening nightmares, the chills and sweats in the dark, the refusal to think about it, the evasions and denials . . . tonight she had faced the one thing in the Multiverse that she had long thought she could *never* face. She had stopped running at last from her ghosts, had turned around and accepted them. She had looked directly into the face of what she had done to her loved ones and admitted it—to herself, and to another.

She had confronted that, and it was something she had feared more than she feared the Purifying Fire.

If she could survive that rending of her soul tonight, then she could survive this. Whatever was going to happen inside the Purifying Fire, Chandra was ready for it.

When they reached the circle of white mages, priests, and Keepers standing around the silent flames with their eyes closed, Gideon came to a halt and waited respectfully for them to finish their . . . prayers? Meditation? Whatever.

Chandra saw no reason to emulate his courtesy. "Can we get on with it?" she said loudly. "It's been a long day for me."

Gideon closed his eyes and his lips twitched briefly. She couldn't tell if he was annoyed or amused.

Walbert flinched, glared at Chandra over his shoulder . . . then relaxed and offered her a smile.

Samir was right. It was *cold*.

"By all means, Chandra," the high priest of the Order of Heliud said. "I've waited a long time for this. Let's not wait any longer."

At a signal from Walbert, the circle of worshippers around the Purifying Fire shifted position, creating an opening for Chandra to walk through so that she could approach the dancing white flames. Then six of the men stepped forward, looking directly at her. Chandra saw that they were well armed.

Walbert said to her, "I would rather perform the ceremony in a way that lends itself to your dignity, as well as mine. But if necessary, I will have you forcibly thrown into the Fire."

Out of the corner of her eye, she saw Gideon's chest start rising and falling faster.

"No," Chandra said. "It's not necessary. I have no

desire to lose my dignity as well as . . . whatever else I'm about to lose."

Walbert smiled again. "I'm glad to hear that, Chandra. I don't want this to be needlessly unpleasant. For *any* of us."

"If you really want me to have a pleasant night," she said, "then let me go. Now."

Walbert's smiled broadened as he shook his head. "Alas, I'm afraid I can't do that."

"Oh, right," Chandra said. "*Destiny.*"

"Yes," he said seriously.

"Whatever."

"Shall we begin?" Walbert said to her.

"All right." Chandra took a step forward, then felt a hand on her shoulder.

"Wait," Gideon said, his voice subdued.

She turned her head to meet his gaze. What she saw there almost weakened her resolve. She said suddenly, "Don't stay."

He frowned a little. "Chandra . . ."

"Please don't stay to watch this," she said urgently. "*Please*, Gideon. Go now."

He came to a decision and nodded. His hand tightened briefly on her shoulder before he turned away. Chandra watched as he ascended the rough steps leading up to the landing, reclaimed the torch he had left perched in a sconce there, and disappeared into the tunnel that led back up to the palace.

Then Chandra turned back to Walbert. She saw that he was gazing at her with speculative interest, but ignored it and said only, "I'm ready now."

Walbert nodded, and turned to the gathered mages, priests, and Keepers. "Let's begin."

Except for Walbert and Chandra, everyone present started chanting, and it sounded as if they had practiced well for this occasion. The chant was harmonious and their voices were clear and blended well. But as the sound echoed around the cavern and bounced off the walls and high ceiling, it was so loud that Chandra had to shout at Walbert to be heard.

"What now?" she asked.

Bizarrely, the old mage took Chandra by the shoulders and kissed her forehead. He did it so quickly, she didn't even have time to flinch away from the touch of his thin, dry lips, which she could feel even through the magical barrier that covered her skin.

Walbert did not shout the reply. He merely said, mouthing the words clearly, "Walk into the Fire."

"That's it?"

She hadn't shouted this question, and she was sure he couldn't have heard her words over the head-spinning echo of all those chanting voices. But he obviously understood her meaning. He gave a firm nod and gestured for her to enter the bonfire.

Chandra turned toward the Purifying Fire and started walking forward. The chanting grew even louder, as if her approach to the pure white flames gave strength to the voices of those watching her. When she was close enough to touch the blaze, she started shivering, covered with a piercing chill. She wasn't sure if this came only from the Purifying Fire, or if her own fear contributed to it.

She stretched out a hand and touched the Fire. The flames didn't burn, of course. Not with heat, not even with cold. They were chilly to the touch, but bearable. And they curled delicately around her wrist and seemed to tug gently, as if encouraging her to enter the silent, shimmering flames and prove herself there.

As Chandra stepped into the Fire, she felt the coiled magical binding around her wrists liquefy and melt away.

Then the sheath that had covered her skin peeled away, too, freeing her. She didn't know if Walbert was releasing the spells, confident that the Purifying Fire would make her powerless now, or if the Fire itself was commencing its work of eliminating the magic that had entered its flames with her.

Chandra raised her arms and turned in a circle, whirling slowly inside the head-clearing chill of the white blaze, discovering the experience was not at all what she had expected. Rather than frightened, she felt empowered. Rather than defeated, she felt energized.

She tilted her head back, looking up through the translucent, undulating light embracing her and she surrendered—to her deeds, her past, her guilt, her sorrow. She felt the weight of the things she had done and the things she had failed to do. She accepted the burden . . . and then let it go. She abandoned her heavy load to the Fire, accepting whatever it might do with the regrets and the ghosts that she had brought with her into its purifying chill.

The blaze that surrounded her increased in its cold intensity, closing in on her, embracing and engulfing her. It grew denser and became opaque, blocking Walbert and the other mages from Chandra's view. The Fire stroked along her flesh and seeped inside her body, exploring her inside and out, searching out her secrets, her guilt, the stains on her soul, discovering all that she might have tried to hide from its exploration—all that she had once tried to hide from herself.

The impact of this search was so forceful, Chandra couldn't breathe, couldn't think, couldn't even fear. She couldn't evade the intimate exploration of Purifying Fire, and she didn't try. She spread herself upon the cool white arms of this merciless embrace and gave herself to it without reserve or inhibition.

And when the Fire rewarded her courage by accepting her, she knew. She felt it. The searching intensity of the blaze transformed into a tender flood of welcome. Its piercing chill became a soothing coolness.

As the opacity cleared and the dancing flames again became translucent, Chandra knew that she was free. Golden heat flowed through her blood with rich, reassuring familiarity as she turned toward Walbert.

Her sorrow would always be with her, but there would be no more haunting nightmares. No more screams and acrid smoke pursuing her through her dreams.

Chandra stepped out of the Fire, out of the mysterious flow of white mana that had embraced so many souls for so long. She knew now that Walbert had misinterpreted what he had seen in the flickering white blaze. And if she did indeed have a destiny on Regatha, if there truly was a reason that she had been meant to come to this plane . . . now she knew what it was.

The harsh glow of victory was in Walbert's pale blue eyes as he watched her walk out of the Fire and stand before him.

"Things had to be this way, Chandra," he said confidently. "It's for the best."

She considered this. "Perhaps."

There was no need to prepare further. She had found such focus, such strength, such certainty of intent in the Purifying Fire, all she had to do now was inhale deeply, spread her arms wide, and reach with her will for the rich red mana of Regatha.

Walbert understood an instant before it happened. "No!"

Chandra unleashed a spell that exploded with golden fire and fury throughout the entire cavern.

"You were right," she said to Walbert, raising her voice

283

to be heard about the thundering roar of her spell. "I guess it is my destiny to change everything here, after all. I *am* the cataclysm you foresaw."

"*No!*" Walbert staggered backward, shock and horror contorting his face.

Above them, the ceiling of the cavern started caving in, in response to the power of Chandra's spell as it pushed skyward with boundless fury.

The mages of the Order were screaming and racing toward the steep tunnel that led back up to the palace and a chance of survival. Some of them would make it to safety. Others certainly wouldn't. Too many of them had come down here to watch Chandra be stripped of her power so that their Order could commence an era of unchallenged domination over Regatha.

"Bad decision," she said to their fleeing backsides as they stampeded past her.

"You can't!" Walbert cried, too appalled by the destruction of his dreams and plans to run for his life now.

"I can," she said. "And I'm pretty sure I'm actually *meant* to."

Walbert had gone too far. He had tried to use the Purifying Fire to disrupt the balance on Regatha, to trample on the practices of other mages and other ways of life. He had disrespected and dismissed the value of all mana except that which empowered *him*. And now the white mana flow that ran deep beneath the plains of Regatha had embraced and then freed the fire-wielding planeswalker whom Walbert had brought into these ancient caverns to become the key to his conquest.

Now everything would indeed change.

The madness of sudden, agonizing, unforeseen loss twisted Walbert's face now, and he attacked Chandra, who was off-guard, watching the celebrants run. He was stronger than he looked, and she staggered backward under the weight of his enraged assault.

Overhead, the ceiling of the cavern split open with a terrible crash, and a portion of the Temple, which had sat high overhead, plunged into the far end of the cavern. Moonlight pierced the big, ragged hole that was growing above the chamber, and dust, rocks, and boulders flew recklessly across the cavern at deadly speed. The walls and floor shook, and the hysterical screams coming from the world above were scarcely loud enough to carry through the thundering roar down here of crashing stone and groaning rock face.

A raging burst of red-and-orange heat roared across the chamber. It flowed over Chandra, mingling with the fire that sparked along her skin and the flames that raged in her hair.

Walbert screamed as the fire that engulfed the two of them consumed him. He tried to fight it off with his power, but Chandra could see that none came to him now when he called on it. The white mana that had spared her had also, it seemed, abandoned the high priest of the Temple. Chandra watched dispassionately as Walbert died like any common man.

⚹ ⚹ ⚹ ⚹ ⚹

"Chandra? *Chandra?*"

The sound of her named brought Chandra to her senses. She opened her eyes and wondered why she was lying on the hard stone ground.

The blood that trickled down her face when she sat up, as well as the sharp, blood-smeared rock lying nearby, answered her question. Now she remembered something falling onto her head—*hard*—only moments after she watched Walbert die.

She looked up and saw Gideon stepping through rubble and rock fragments as he approached her. Moonlight shone down on the far end of the cavern, but this portion still relied mainly on the glowing spires of rock for illumination. Chandra looked around and noticed that some of those spires had been destroyed in the cataclysm.

The Purifying Fire, however, glowed white and strong, enduring, as it always had.

"What happened?" Gideon's voice was hoarse.

Chandra touched her bloody forehead. "Falling rocks from overhead. I got knocked out."

"No, I meant . . ." He leaned down, seized her shoulders, hauled her roughly to her feet, and gave her a hard shake. Her neck snapped back and her aching head protested as he shouted into her face, *"What did you do?"*

When she didn't say anything, he shook her again. *"Chandra!* What did you *do* here?"

"You can see what I did," she said, feeling worn out now. "It was a boom spell."

He shoved her away so violently that she bounced off the wall behind her and nearly fell back down.

"I didn't tell you how to save yourself so that you could do *this!*" His face was white with anger, pale and stark against the coal black of his hair.

Chandra looked around at the devastation she had wrought. The fire had been so hot, it had turned bodies to ashes, so it was hard to tell how many members of the Order had died here. She knew it must be at least a dozen. Perhaps more. There might also have been people in the portion of the Temple that had caved in and fallen when part of the cavern ceiling collapsed.

"The temple is ruined," she guessed. "And the Order . . ." She took a breath and thought it over. "Well, in disarray, certainly. Destroyed?" She shrugged. "I don't know. The mana flow is still strong here. They'll regroup in time. But perhaps they'll remember what happened here when their reach exceeded their grasp."

Gideon grabbed her again, and he looked so enraged, she thought he was going to strike her. She didn't resist or try to stop him. She knew he felt betrayed. In his position, she'd want to lash out, too.

But he let her go and turned away, breathing hard. "How could you do it?" he asked in a low voice.

"In a way, I think Walbert was right," she said. "I was meant to come here."

He gave her an incredulous look. When he saw that she was serious, he said, "You don't believe in destiny. Neither do I."

"I don't really believe in visions, either, and yet Walbert had them, and I was in them." She shrugged. "And even if none of that is true . . . it *is* true that someone had to stop him, and I was the one who could."

"I shouldn't have helped you." Gideon wasn't looking at her. He almost seemed to be talking to himself.

"Why *did* you help?"

For a moment, she didn't think he would answer. Then he said wearily, "Because I learned on Diraden what it was like to be without my power, and to think I might be stuck on one plane for the rest of my life." He met her gaze. "And because I saw there what that was like for *you*." He looked away again. "I couldn't see you like that permanently. I . . . couldn't."

"What Walbert wanted to do was wrong, Gideon," she said.

"No." He shook his head. "What you've done is wrong. And I . . ." He sighed and closed his eyes. "I helped you." After a moment, he said heavily, "You planned this. It's why you asked me to leave." It wasn't a question.

"I knew what I would do if I came out of the Fire with my power intact," she said. "And I didn't want to kill you."

He was silent for a long moment. Then he said, "I almost wish you had."

"No," she said. "I . . . can't."

He let out a long, slow, shaky breath. "You'd better go. No one else was willing to come down here so soon after the . . . after *that*. But they'll come soon. They'll attack if you're still here. And I don't want any more deaths here tonight."

She looked in the direction of the steep tunnel of stairs that led out of here, knowing that soldiers would probably be waiting at the top. "I can't leave that way."

And it was the only exit—unless she grew wings and flew out of the gaping hole in the ceiling, high over the far end of the cavern.

"Were you planning to stay on Regatha?" he asked skeptically. "After *this*?"

"No," she realized, "I suppose not. If the remnants of the Order think I'm alive and at the monastery, there'll just be more trouble."

It would be better if everyone on Regatha thought she had died in the incinerating blaze that had swept through the cavern.

"You should leave now," Gideon said.

"You mean planeswalk?" she guessed.

"Start preparing," he corrected. "After you're gone, I'll convince them you died here and your body is ashes."

Chandra hadn't thought this far ahead and, for a moment, she had no idea where to go.

Then she realized which plane she most wanted to find now. And, despite her weary, bloody, head-spinning, thirsty condition, she suddenly looked forward to the journey.

"Gideon . . ."

"I know where you're going," he said. "I know what you want." He shook his head. "You won't find it. But that won't stop you from trying, will it?" He gazed at her without warmth. "You're a fool."

Anger flashed through her. She welcomed its simple, familiar heat. "There's something I didn't tell you about the night my family were burned alive in front of me."

"I'm not interested." He turned away from her.

She grabbed his arm. "The soldiers who killed them belonged to an order of mages that vowed to bring harmony, protection, and law to the land."

He froze.

"Does that sound familiar, Gideon?" she prodded in a venomous voice.

He turned his head to look at her. His expression was a mixture of suspicion, shock, and revelation.

"I have faced what I did," Chandra said, "and laid my ghosts to rest. But I will never forgive those men for what *they* did that night. And anyone who believes in the things they believed in is my enemy. Now and forever."

His breathing was faster as he stared at her, taking in what she was telling him.

"I acted on that here, and I will act on it wherever I go. Do you understand me?" she said through gritted teeth.

"I understand," he said at last, "what you're telling me."

"Then don't get in my way." She let go of his arm and turned away, eager to leave this place. Eager to leave him.

"Chandra."

"What?" she snapped over her shoulder, afraid she would weaken if she looked at him again.

"We will meet again."

She couldn't tell if it was a threat or a promise. Either way, and against her will, she held it to her heart.

Chandra heard Gideon's footsteps behind her, echoing softly in the ruined, charred cavern as he walked away.

She didn't turn around or look back. And when the echo of his footsteps ascending the stairs that led back up to the devastated Temple faded away into silence, she prepared to planeswalk again.

The threat of domination by the Order was ended on Regatha, and balance was restored. There would still be some friction among the hieromancers of the city, the fire mages of the mountains, and the green mages of the woodlands. But there would be no more threat of one group dominating the others. Not in this lifetime.

Now, as she sat down on the charred stone floor of the chamber of the Purifying Fire, Chandra turned her thoughts to the future. She closed her eyes, concentrating on her breathing as she prepared to planeswalk, and she imagined the rich and mysterious plane of Zendikar . . . which in her heart, she *knew* must surely exist somewhere in the vast and wondrous Multiverse.

READ ON
FOR A PREVIEW OF ANOTHER PLANESWALKER ADVENTURE,

AVAILABLE NOW THROUGH YOUR
FAVORITE BOOKSELLER.

MAGIC
The Gathering®

A PLANESWALKER™ NOVEL

AGENTS OF ARTIFICE

ari marmell

Wizards
OF THE COAST®

CHAPTER ONE

As it turned out, the district of Avaric wasn't any more appealing when one was drunk than when one was sober. The fog of irrimberry wine didn't make the filthy cobblestones, the half-decayed roofs, or the sludge coating the roadways any more attractive; and the sweet aroma of that libation didn't remain in the nose long enough to muffle the stagnant rot and the eye-watering miasma that passed for air. The rows of squat houses and shops leaned over the road like tottering old men, and the wide spaces between them resembled gaps left by missing teeth. Perhaps the only redeeming quality of the entire evening was the surprising lack of mosquitoes. Normally the rains brought plague-like swarms up from the swamps and sewers that were Avaric's unsteady foundation, but apparently even they were taking the night off for the Thralldom's End celebration.

Kallist Rhoka, who had spent a considerable amount of coin on the journey to his current state of moderate inebriation, glared bitterly at his surroundings and felt that the world's refusal to reshape itself into a passingly tolerable form was the height of discourtesy.

Then again, the Avaric District wasn't alone in its refusal to change its nature to suit Kallist's desires or his drunken perceptions—and between the stubbornness of a whole neighborhood, and that of a certain raven-haired mage, he was pretty certain that the district would break first.

At the thought of the woman he'd left at the Bitter End Tavern and Restaurant, Kallist's stomach knotted so painfully it doubled him over. For long moments he crouched, waiting as the knot worked its way up to become a lump in his throat. With shaking hands—a shake that he attributed to the multiple glasses of wine, and not to any deeper emotions—he wiped the pained expression from his face.

Not for the first time, Kallist spat curses at the man who'd driven him to such a sorry state. Less than a year gone by, he'd dwelt in the shadows of Ravnica's highest spires. And now? Now the structures around him were barely high enough to cast shadows at all. Now he'd have had to actually live down in the sewers or the under-cities of the larger districts to sink any lower.

It was enough to make even a forgiving man as bitter as fresh wormwood, and Kallist had never been all that forgiving.

Still, it would all have been worth it, if she'd just said yes. . .

Kallist, his wine-besotted mind swiftly running out of curses, stared down at his feet. He couldn't even see the normal color of his basilisk-skin boots, one of the few luxuries he still owned, so coated were they in the swamp sludge that always oozed up from between the cobblestones after the rain. The boots kept swimming in and out of focus, too. He wondered if he might vomit, and was angered that he might waste the expensive irrimberry wine he'd drunk. The notion of falling to hands and knees on the roadway was enough to steady him, however. He could still hear, ever so faintly, the singing and dancing of the Thralldom's End festival, back in the direction of the Bitter End, and he'd be damned thrice over if he'd let anyone from the tavern find him pasting a dinner collage all over the road. With a rigid, yet swaying gait that made him appear sober to nobody but himself, he resumed his trek.

Avaric wasn't really that large a place; none of the local neighborhoods were. It was a backwater district, surrounded by other backwater districts save for those few spots where the underground swamps pooled to the surface, ugly and malodorous cysts on Ravnica's aging face. Those who dwelt here did so only because anyplace else they could afford to move was even worse, and a few small fungus gardens were more than enough to feed the lot of them. Thus, even though the Bitter End was at the far end of Avaric from the house Kallist shared with the woman on whom he currently blamed his inebriated state, it should normally have taken only about twenty minutes to walk from one to the other.

"Normally," of course, allowed neither for Kallist's current shuffling gate nor the fact that he'd already taken the same wrong turn twice. It had now been well over half an hour, he could still hear the faint strains of singing off in the distance; his eyes were beginning to water and to sting . . .

And he really, really had to find somewhere private to release some of that wine back into the wild. Kallist looked down at his feet, looked over at the nearest alley—filled almost ankle deep with a juicy mixture of swamp-water and refuse—muttered a brief "Hell with it," and strode off the avenue.

He shuddered at the soft squishing beneath his boots, but tonight, the urging of a bladder growing fuller by the moment outweighed Kallist's concerns for his footwear. Had he been either a little more sober, or a little more drunk, he might've worried about encountering sewer goblins, or even Golgari fungus-creatures leftover from the struggles that ended guild rule, but as he wasn't, he didn't.

With a deep sigh, Kallist relieved himself against the stained wall that was also the back wall of somebody's house, and staggered back to the road just in time to all but run into a fellow striding the other way.

"Gariel," he greeted the newcomer, trying to straighten himself into a semblance of sobriety.

"Who . . . Kallist? What're you doing in the alleys this late at night? You're not worried about gobbers?"

Kallist spun, expecting in his drunken haze to see a gang of the foul creatures behind him. When none appeared, he sank slowly to the muddy road, waiting for yet another surge of nausea to pass.

Irritably, he looked at his friend, who failed to suppress a smirk. Physically, Gariel was everything Kallist wasn't: dark-skinned to Kallist's natural pallor; heavily muscled where Kallist was wiry; exceptionally tall where Kallist could have been the standard by which average was measured; and with earthen-colored eyes to contrast with Kallist's own oceanic blue. Gariel even wore a well trimmed beard, not out of any desire to follow current trends—the styles of Ravnica's affluent meant little here in the backwaters—but simply because the man had an intense dislike of shaving. "Any knife comes near my face," he'd told Kallist once, "it damn well better have a sausage on the end of it." Had their hair not been similar shades of wooden brown, they might as well have been of different species entirely.

Something must have flashed across his face, something Gariel saw even in the feeble moonlight and the glow of the emberstone he held in his left fist. He dropped his

ARI MARMELL

hand and lowered himself to the grimy roadway beside his friend.

"This doesn't look like a celebratory drunk," he observed, leaning back against the nearest building.

Kallist looked up at him, all but trembling with the effort of keeping his face a stony, emotionless mask. He glared at Gariel as though daring him to say something.

Silence for a few moments, broken only by the call of a spire bat flying low over the few pools of exposed swamp between the wide roadways and cheap row houses.

"She said no, didn't she?" said Gariel at last.

Kallist's shoulders slumped. "She said she'd 'think about it.'"

Gariel forced a grin, though he felt the blood pounding in his ears, furious on his friend's behalf. "Well, at least that's not a 'no,' right?"

"Oh, come on, Gariel!" The smaller fellow punched the mud. "When was the last time you knew Liliana to take her time to think about anything? Everything she does, she does in the moment." He sighed, and tried to swallow the lump that had climbed once again into his throat and appeared bound and determined to stay there. "You know as well as I do that 'I'll think about it' means 'I don't want to hurt you by refusing.'"

Gariel wanted to argue the point, but the words clung to the roof of his mouth like a paste. "Well. . . Look, Kallist. You've been together—what? A few months?"

"Yeah. Ever since . . ." He didn't finish the sentence. In all the time Gariel had known him, Kallist had never finished that sentence.

"All right, a few months. Give it some more time. I mean, she's obviously not ending it, or she wouldn't have bothered to spare you the 'no,' right? Maybe in another year or three . . ."

Kallist couldn't help but laugh, though the sound was poisonous as hemlock. "Right. Because the one thing Liliana does more often than anything else is to change her mind once it's made up."

In fact, in the time Kallist had known her, Liliana had done so precisely once.

And again, Gariel knew them both too well to argue. All that emerged from his mouth, escaping like a fleeing convict before he could think better of it and snap his teeth shut, was, "So maybe you're better off this way.

"I'm sorry," he added immediately. "That didn't come out right."

"Nothing tonight has." Kallist rose and set his bleary eyes toward the southeast. "I'm going home."

"Wait." Gariel rose, too, and placed a hand on his friend's shoulder. "Where is she, anyway?"

"Where else would she be during Thralldom's End?"

Gariel actually saw red. "What?" He'd doubtless have awakened half the street with that squawk, if they hadn't all been out celebrating. "You mean even after your talk . . ."

Kallist shrugged, and couldn't help but smile a bit. "She said there was no reason to ruin a perfectly good dance. Even asked me to stay, but—Gariel? Where are you going?"

The larger man was already several yards down the road. "I'm going," he answered, barely turning his head, "to give your woman a piece of my mind for treating you this way."

"Gariel, don't . . ." But he was already gone around the nearest bend. Were Kallist less exhausted, less depressed, and certainly less drunk, he might have caught Gariel, or at least tried. As Kallist was, he could only drop his chin to his chest and shuffle home, hoping he remembered to get even drunker before he fell asleep.

He did, however, spare a brief thought to hoping that there was still a Bitter End Tavern standing, come tomorrow morning.

❅ ❅ ❅ ❅ ❅

Though the guilds were gone, much of Ravnica still celebrated the Festival of the Guildpact, as if remembering the years of prosperity and order might keep them from fading away in these modern, more tumultuous times. Much of Ravnica—but not all. Some of the plane's districts had suffered rather more than others beneath the guilds, and not a few were just as happy to see them gone.

Some such as Avaric, whose families had long labored in all but serfdom to the usurious patriarchs of the Orzhov. So when the so-called Guild of Deals had fallen, it was the best news the citizens here had received in several thousand years.

The walls, the floor, the tables, and the chairs of the Bitter End shook as though in the midst of an earthquake, as the good folk of Avaric celebrated Thralldom's End. In one corner, a gaggle of performers pounded on drums, plucked the strings on a variety of instruments, blew through various horns, in a veritable frenzy of activity that should have produced nothing but anarchic noise, yet somehow managed to shape itself into actual music. Around the perimeter of the common room, the people not currently caught up in the dance clapped or stomped to the highly charged beat, and the footsteps of the dancers themselves kicked up clouds of sawdust from the floor and brought showers of dust sifting from the rafters. Before the start of business tomorrow, a handful of floorboards, a couple of chairs, and a legion of mugs and plates would need replacing—but the Bitter End was the largest establishment in Avaric to hold a Thralldom's End gala, and if a bit of ruined furniture and broken crockery was the price for such a huge influx of custom, it was a cost Ishri, barkeep and the tavern's owner, cheerfully paid.

Liliana Vess was a whirlwind sweeping through the assembled dancers, leaving footprints not merely in the sawdust, but on the hearts of a score of hopeful men. Her midnight-black hair moved about her head like a dark cloud, or perhaps a tainted halo. Her cream-hued gown, which was cut distractingly low, rose and whirled and fell, promising constantly to reveal more than it should, but, like a teasing courtesan, always managing to renege.

She breathed heavily from the exertion of the rapid dance, spinning and twisting through the arms of a dozen of her fellow celebrants. Her smile lit up her features—high and somewhat sharp, forming a face that few would envision when imagining a classic beauty, yet which all would agree was beautiful once they saw it—but that smile failed to reach her eyes. For all that she tried to lose herself in the festivities, in the adoration of those who watched her, who reached out in hopes of a simple fleeting touch, she could not.

Damn him anyway! Guilt was not an emotion with which Liliana was well acquainted, and she found swiftly that it was not at all to her liking.

The bizarre accumulation of notes and beats and rhythms successfully masquerading as a song came to an end, and so did the last of Liliana's ability to fake any remaining enthusiasm for the celebration. The musicians, bowing to much applause and acclaim, left the stage for a well-earned break, leaving an instrument with enchanted strings to play a slow and lonesome ditty until they returned. Several couples remained in the room's center, swaying to the somber notes, but most returned to their tables to await a more energetic piece.

Liliana watched them go, marveling at these people among whom she'd made her temporary home. They were all clad in their best and fanciest—which here in Avaric meant tunics with long sleeves instead of short, trousers without obvious patches, and vests that actually boasted some faint color, rather than their normal browns and grays. Nobody here could afford the rich dyes or the fancy buttons and clasps of the rich, yet they wore their "finery" with pride; splurged on lean steaks when they normally subsisted on fungi and the occasional fish or reptile hauled from the swampy pools. And they lived it up as though such ridiculous luxuries actually meant something.

Liliana didn't understand any of it. She approved of it, even respected it, but she didn't understand it.

Even as she floated back to her table, hand reaching for a glass of rough beer to quench her thirst, Liliana spotted a figure moving toward her through the crowd. A gruff face, split into what the owner probably thought was a charming smile, leered at her through a thick growth of beard. Two sausage-like thumbs hooked themselves through the pockets of a heavy black vest, perhaps trying to draw attention to the fine garment. The drunkard had been watching her all night, since well before Kallist had ruined the evening and stormed off in a huff. Every night there was always at least one, and she'd wondered how long it would take him to drink enough nerve to approach.

"I couldn't help but notice," he slurred in a voice heavy with beer, "that you finally sent your scrawny friend packing. That mean you interested in spending some time with a real man?"

In a better mood, Liliana might've engaged in some light flirting before telling the drunk to find his own personal hell and stay there. Not tonight.

Liliana lifted her dinner knife, still stained with remnants of her overcooked steak, from the table. "If you don't walk away right now," she said sweetly, "you won't be a 'real man' for very long."

It took a moment, the battle between common sense and belligerent pride that raged across the fellow's face—but finally, aided perhaps by the unnatural gleam in Liliana's eyes, common sense won the field. Grumbling, he turned and shuffled back to his table, where he would tell his friends all about how he'd turned down the woman's advances.

Liliana sighed once as she lowered herself into her chair, and found herself uncharacteristically wishing that Kallist had been here to see that exchange. Damn it, she thought once more, reaching again for her mug. If it's not one thing.

"Hey! Bitch!"

It's another.

Half the tavern turned toward the large, dark-skinned fellow who'd just come stalking through the front door, his boots leaving a trail of castoff mud, but Liliana already knew precisely for whom his call was intended. She rose gracefully and offered her most stunning smile.

"And a joyous Thralldom's End to you, too, Gariel."

"Don't 'joyous Thralldom's End' me, gods damn it!" he growled, pushing his way through a few of the slow-dancing couples to stand before her table. "I want to know what the hell you think you're—"

They were skilled, Liliana thought later, when she actually had a moment to think; you had to give them that. She hadn't noticed them at all, until a blade sped toward her from over Gariel's shoulder.

There was no time even to shout a warning. Liliana brought a knee up sharply into Gariel's gut—she had just enough respect for him as Kallist's friend not to hit him any lower—and caught his shoulders as he doubled over, using his own weight to topple them both backwards over her chair. It wasn't pretty, it wasn't graceful, but it took them out of a sword's sudden arc with half a heartbeat to spare.

The sounds of the chair clattering over, and the pair of them hitting the floor, were just loud enough to penetrate the din. First a couple of faces, and then a handful more, turned away from dinner or dancers to stare at them; a ripple in a still pond, awareness that something was very much not right spread through the Bitter End.

Liliana gasped as the wooden edge of the seat dug painfully into her side, but she didn't let that stop her from rolling. Their bodies tilted across the chair like a fulcrum, her head striking the hardwood floor, but that, too, she ignored as best she could. Twisting her grip on Gariel as they fell, she kept him from landing squarely atop her. She left him gasping on the floor as she scrabbled swiftly to her feet, trying to keep the table between herself and her attacker.

No. Attackers, plural. Damn.

They were strangers here, certainly. Avaric was small, yes, but not quite tiny enough for everyone to know everyone else by sight. From a distance, then, these two blended perfectly, both of roughly average height, both clad as workers gone out to hoist a few after a long day's work, before going home to hoist a few more. But up close, their cold, emotionless eyes marked them as something else entirely.

Well, that and the heavy, cleaver-like blades.

They advanced unhurriedly, even casually, one passing to each side of the table. Clearly, despite the speed of Liliana's evasion, they didn't expect much in the way of resistance.

And in terms of anyone coming to Liliana's aid, they were correct. The folk nearest her had only just begun to run, to scream, or to freeze in shock, as best befit their individual temperaments. From behind the bar, Ishri emerged with a heavy cudgel in hand, but hampered as she was by the bulk of the crowd retreating from the coming bloodshed, there was no way she'd reach the table before it was all over. To his credit, the suitor whom Liliana had just rebuffed was also making his way back across the tavern, fists raised, but he was already so drunk that even if he managed to reach the fray, it was unlikely he could meaningfully contribute.

But then, Liliana didn't require anyone's help.

Crouching slightly, she shifted the dinner knife—hardly an intimidating weapon, but all she had—into an under-hand grip. Beneath her breath, her lips barely moving, she began to utter a low, sonorous chant. Across her neck rose an abstract pattern of tattoos that suggested even more elaborate designs farther down her back, as though burned across her skin from the inside out.

Had they been able to hear it over the ambient noise of a panicking tavern, that sound alone might have given her attackers pause. The tone was surreal, sepulchral, far deeper than Liliana's voice should ever have produced. The syllables formed no words of any known language, yet they carried a terrible meaning that bypassed the mind entirely, to sink directly into the listener's soul.

But they could not hear it, those deluded fools who thought themselves predator rather than prey. And even if they had, it would have been far too late to matter.

As though biting the end off a leather thong, Liliana spat a word of power into the æther, gestured with her blade. Something moved unseen beneath the table, just one more shadow in the flickering lanterns of the Bitter End, summoned from abyssal gulfs beyond the realms of the dead themselves. With impossibly long fingers it stretched out, farther, farther, and brushed the edges of two of the table's legs. Rotting away as though aged a hundred years, in single instant, they folded in on themselves, putrefying into soft mulch. The rest of the heavy wood surface toppled to the side, slamming hard into one of the bandit's calves. He cried out in pain, stumbling and limping away from the unexpected assault, a handful of dishes and a half-eaten loaf of pumpernickel bread clattering around his feet.

At that cry, the second man's attention flickered away from Liliana for less than a heartbeat—but that was enough. Ducking in low, she drew the edge of her knife across his extended arm. Cloth and flesh tore beneath the serrated steel, and the bandit barely muffled a curse of pain behind clenched teeth.

Blood welled up, beading along his wrist in a narrow bracelet. It was a shallow wound, stinging but harmless, and his grimace of pain turned into a savage grin as he realized just how ineffective his target's attack had proved.

But then, Liliana's attack wasn't intended to cause him harm. It was meant only to draw blood—and the attention of the unseen shadowy thing sliding impossibly across the floor. Invisible to all, darkness against darkness, black on black, it stretched forth its talons once more and dipped them into the welling blood. A foul corruption leeched into the seeping wound, intertwined itself around the muscles and vessels of the man's arm.

He screamed, then, an inhuman cry of agony, as gangrenous rot shot through his flesh. The blade fell from limp fingers, lodging itself in the wood by his feet, as the skin turned sickly blue, the blood black and viscous. Flesh grew stiff and cracked, splitting to unleash gouts of yellowed pus. Falling to his knees, the sellsword clutched his dying arm to his chest and bawled like an infant.

Liliana spared him not so much as another glance. His suffering would end soon enough—when the spreading necrotic rot reached his heart.

Growing ever more unnerved, the second bandit had nonetheless recovered from the impact of the table against his leg, swiftly closing to within striking range. Snarling, he raised his chopping blade high and brought it down in a vicious stroke that no parry with the fragile dinner knife could have halted.

Liliana didn't even try to lift her feeble weapon in response. No, lips still moving though she must long since have run out of breath, she raised her left hand and caught the blade as it descended.

The cleaver should have torn through her upraised limb like parchment. Should have, and would have, had it not begun to turn black at the apex of its swing, suddenly cloaked and tugged by wisps of shadow. By the time it should have reached the flesh of Liliana's hand, it was simply gone, drawn away into the nether between the worlds of the living and the dead. The swordsman was left standing, staring at his empty fist.

With a shrug, Liliana bent two fingers into talons and drove them into his staring eyes. Hardly fatal, but more than enough to take him, screaming, out of the fight.

And just like that, the tavern grew calm once more. The eldritch symbols across Liliana's back faded as swiftly as they appeared, leaving her skin pristine. Ignoring the slack faces that gaped silently at her from those partygoers who hadn't already run screaming from the Bitter End, Liliana moved away from the fallen bandit, dismissing the spectral shadow with the merest thought. Only she, of all those present, heard its woeful cry as it spiraled back into the endless dark.

She placed one foot atop the fallen chair and leaned

on her knee to gaze meaningfully down at Gariel—who was, himself, staring up at her as though she'd sprouted feathers.

"What . . . What did . . . What?"

"All good questions," Liliana told him. "Are you all right?"

"I—I'll live."

"Let's not jump to conclusions just yet." She reached down to offer the flustered fellow a hand up—then yanked it away as he began leaning on her, allowing him to fall flat on his face once more. The floorboards shook with the impact. "There's still the little matter," she said with a predatory smile, "of you stalking through that door, yelling at me, calling me all sorts of ugly names."

"I—you. . ." Gariel wiped a hand across his face, smearing rather than removing the blood that now dribbled from his nose. "People are watching, Liliana."

"That didn't bother you when you were shouting obscenities at me."

Gariel could only gape once more, at the gathered audience and at the injured bandits, and wonder exactly how crazy his friend's girl actually was. He'd actually opened his mouth to ask such a question—only to choke on a spray of splinters as a bolt that appeared roughly as thick as a tree trunk slammed into the floor mere inches from his head.

Liliana heard the whir-and-click of a mechanized crossbow even as she jerked away from the sudden impact, glaring at the figures standing in the doorway.

There were three more, all strongly resembling the pair who had attacked her moments ago. Only these three, Liliana realized as she stared at a trio of self-loading identical weapons, were far better equipped.

"The next one," the man in the middle told her gruffly, "goes through his head." His gaze flickered to the two figures on the floor, one breathing his last, one blinded, and his face hardened. "I don't think you're fast enough to stop all three of us, witch."

She scowled in turn. "So shoot him. He means nothing to me, and even with those fancy crossbows, I promise you'll not have time to reload."

"Ah," the man said, voice oily, "but he means something to someone, don't he?"

Liliana's scowl grew deeper still—but her shoulders slumped, and she knew that they saw it. "What do you want?"

"What I want is to put a few shafts through you for what you did to my boys," the bandit told her. "But what's going to happen is this . . ."

MAGIC
The Gathering®

Everything you thought you knew
about MAGIC™ novels is changing…

From the mind of

ARI MARMELL

comes a tour de force of imagination.

AGENTS
OF ARTIFICE

The ascendance of a new age in the planeswalker
mythology: be a part of the book that takes fans
deeper than ever into the lives of the Multiverse's most
powerful beings:

Jace Beleren
A powerful mind-mage whose choices now will forever
determine his path as a planeswalker.

Liliana Vess
A dangerous necromancer whose beauty belies a dark
secret and even darker associations.

Tezzeret
Leader of an inter-planar consortium whose quest for
knowledge may be undone by his lust for power.

Comprehensive and painstakingly detailed...

For an exclusive, insider's guide to MAGIC: THE GATHERING's fall expansion set, *A Planeswalker's Guide to Alara* offers lavish, full-color illustrations from concept art to final cards as well as an in-depth review of each of the shards of this fractured plane. Never before have planeswalkers been given such complete access to the world of MAGIC: THE GATHERING® as creative-team insiders Doug Beyer and Jenna Helland chart a course through unknown reaches of the Shards of Alara.

A PLANESWALKER'S GUIDE TO